D1417629

Seven Wings to Glory

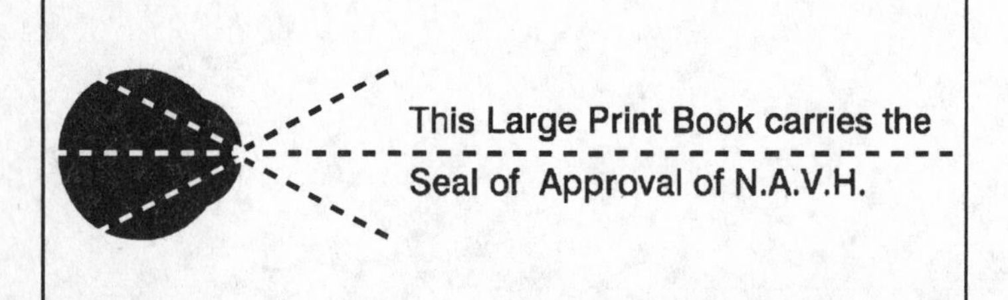
This Large Print Book carries the
Seal of Approval of N.A.V.H.

Seven Wings to Glory

Kathleen M. Rodgers

THORNDIKE PRESS
A part of Gale, a Cengage Company

Farmington Hills, Mich • San Francisco • New York • Waterville, Maine
Meriden, Conn • Mason, Ohio • Chicago

Thorndike Press, a part of Gale, a Cengage Company.

This is a work of fiction. Names, characters, places, brands, media, and incidents are either the product of the author's imagination or are used fictitiously.
Thorndike Press® Large Print Clean Reads.
The text of this Large Print edition is unabridged.
Other aspects of the book may vary from the original edition.
Set in 16 pt. Plantin.

**LIBRARY OF CONGRESS CIP DATA ON FILE.
CATALOGUING IN PUBLICATION FOR THIS BOOK
IS AVAILABLE FROM THE LIBRARY OF CONGRESS**

ISBN-13: 978-1-4328-4480-6 (hardcover)

Published in 2018 by arrangement with Camel Press

Printed in the United States of America
1 2 3 4 5 6 7 22 21 20 19 18

In memory of my little brother,
Larry Lynn Doran.
His tragic death at a tender age
taught me to live.

To my mother, Patricia Lamb Doran,
And my late father,
Richard Leroy Doran,
For giving me the foundation
to explore "the mystery of faith."

And to Denton the Wonder Dog:
You're the one Bubba sent.

ACKNOWLEDGMENTS

A round of applause to my publisher, Catherine Treadgold, and associate publisher, Jennifer McCord, at Camel Press, for offering me a contract for *Seven Wings to Glory,* based on the first hundred pages. Their belief in my ability to deliver a good story on a tight deadline spurred me forward to complete my third novel. Thanks to Sabrina Sun for her superb cover.

A heartfelt thanks to Jeanie Loiacono, President of Loiacono Literary Agency, for brainstorming with me when the novel was nothing more than some scribbled notes and a dream.

I am deeply indebted to Joyce Gilmour of Editing TLC for dropping everything to read each chapter of *Seven Wings to Glory,* knowing I was on a tight deadline. Each time Joyce finished reading a chapter, she'd send me a note asking for more, saying she couldn't wait to see what happened next.

Eternal thanks and blessings to Rhonda Revels and Krystana Walks-Harper, dear friends who've taught me firsthand to pay attention to subtle acts of racism that go unnoticed by so many people in our society.

Author Drema Hall Berkheimer deserves a medal for patiently listening to me read whole chapters over the phone in one sitting. My sisters, Laura Gulliford and Jo Rivera, offered feedback with character motivation and plot issues when I was in a pinch. After spending our childhoods together, they still claim me as kin. Writer Kathryn Brown Ramsperger answered my questions about memory loss based on her family history. Therapist Mary Kathryn Nader gave me hope during one of the most difficult times in my personal life. Because of her compassion and wise counsel, I was able to write through adversity and deliver my book on time.

My deepest respect and thanks to Army Sergeant Douglas Szczepanski Jr, a retired combat veteran who was wounded while on patrol in Iraq. Douglas shared his story with me about getting blown up by a suicide car bomber and undergoing multiple facial reconstructive surgeries. Hand over heart to Gold Star Mother Beth Karlson, whose firstborn son, Army Sergeant Warren S.

Hansen, was killed in action in the early days of the Iraq War. To my amazement, Beth continues to champion my writing efforts, and I count her as a loyal reader and friend.

My heart overflows with thanksgiving for help and advice from military spouses and mothers who shared their journeys with me. In no particular order: Kristen Tsetsi, Aileen Lacsamana, Patti Sweetin-Wolff, Teresa Henderson, Caroline Giammanco, Kit Lambe Bolliger, Lori Hyink, and Lori Bumgardner.

Jewelry designer Starlene DeBord created a talisman bracelet for me to wear while working on the book. Then she refused payment. At my instruction, artist Jenny Zovein painted three watercolors depicting scenes from the book. Each inspired me to keep going. Julie Brinker, Theatre Outreach Director at Campus Theatre in Denton, Texas, gave us a tour of the historic building that plays a role in the novel. We didn't have an appointment.

Thanks to the generous moral support from writer friends Bonnie Latino and Joy Ross Davis. Huge appreciation to Grammy® Award-winning vocalist Leslie Ellis for narrating the audio edition of *Johnnie Come Lately* and giving Johnnie Kitchen a voice. I am grateful to my loyal readers who go the extra mile to write reviews or tell friends and family about my books.

Last but not least, abiding love to my husband Tom, my biggest cheerleader and first reader for thirty-seven years and counting. Lucky me, he's not afraid to offer constructive criticism when needed.

Chapter 1
The Send-off
May 2009, Portion, Texas

Could the ring of Johnnie's doorbell someday have the power to stop her heart? Cade hadn't even deployed yet, but Johnnie Kitchen already dreaded the prospect. She gripped the back of the front porch rocker and watched her uniformed son drop to one knee.

Cade cupped the chocolate Lab's face in his hands. "Brother Dog, your mission is to hold down the fort while I'm gone." He stroked the dog's cheeks with his thumbs and kissed him on the nose.

Brother sat on his haunches and pawed at Cade as if he understood.

Cade lifted his dog tags from beneath his camouflage blouse and jangled them in Brother's face. "Kiss these for good luck, okay, boy?" Brother took one sniff, swiped his tongue over the metal tags, and then licked Cade's face with abandon.

Johnnie closed her eyes, capturing this

moment. She'd had two years to prepare for this day. Two years since that awful night in May when Cade strode through the door and announced to her and her husband Dale that he planned to enlist, and there was nothing they could do to stop him. *Breathe,* she ordered herself. *Look proud. Hold yourself together. Be strong for Callie Ann.*

In yellow running shorts and a tank top, her seventeen-year-old daughter sat motionless in the porch swing, her blonde hair plaited over one shoulder, long tan legs curled up like a pretzel. Callie Ann gazed at Cade, her dove blue eyes giving nothing away. "And what's your job, soldier boy? While you're in Afghanistan?"

Cade rose and flashed a dimpled grin, the grin he'd used to charm others his whole life, all nineteen years and counting. "My job, baby sis, is to kill the terrorists that messed up Tutts' face."

Callie Ann's eyes hardened to iron in an instant, just like Grandpa Grubbs' eyes used to do whenever he got worked up. "And to stay alive, bonehead," she added, jabbing her finger in the air like she wanted to poke his eyes out.

Johnnie took a swig of iced tea, her throat parched at ten in the morning and not even seventy degrees. She emptied the glass, not out of thirst, but out of fear that her throat would close up so she couldn't breathe. Setting the glass down on the wicker plant stand next to the rocker, she wondered if Callie Ann was fighting the same sensation. But today, behind her daughter's high cheekbones and pouty lips, a face that other girls coveted, Johnnie saw anger, not anxiety. She glanced at her oldest son, who'd been quiet since he arrived at the house an hour ago.

D.J. sat on the top step with his back to the others, smoke rising from his cigarette. Gone was the dark ponytail and beard, clipped short now that he'd graduated from college and was employed by a small design firm in Denton, Texas. It startled her how much he resembled her father, the dashing lieutenant with dark hair and deep-set eyes.

"Your job, little brother," D.J. said over his shoulder, "is to take care of your battle buddies and come home safe." D.J. was against the war, but his focus had changed after his best friend from high school and a founding member of their garage band War-4-Money got injured in Iraq. D.J. ground out his cigarette, dropped the butt in an empty Coke can, and stood up. At six two, he towered over Cade by a couple of inches.

Gripping his brother by the shoulder, he said, "By the way, I talked to Tutts the other day. He said to keep your head down."

Cade nodded and put his hands on his hips. "That's cool. How's he doing?"

"He said he has one more surgery, then he'll take a break."

Dual images of Steven "Tutts" Tuttle drilled through Johnnie's mind: the handsome National Guardsman in his black beret and uniform, a week before he deployed to Iraq, and Steven Tuttle now, a wounded warrior who'd undergone facial reconstruction after getting blown up by an IED in 2007.

D.J. turned to Johnnie. "So yeah, Mom. Tutts is moving back to Portion. Says he's going to enroll at the community college. I already warned him that he might end up in a class with you."

Fiddling with her hairclip, Johnnie sidled up next to her sons. "I promise I won't embarrass him if I see him on campus." The truth was, she worried how others would react to his scars. You couldn't hide them. The war had entrenched itself on Tutts' face.

"I'm messing with you." D.J. grinned. "Tutts thinks it's cool you've gone back to college."

Cade winked at Johnnie. "Don't study too hard while I'm gone, mama girl." He scooped her up in his massive arms, a stunt he'd been pulling since he was a kid, trying to prove his strength. His face loomed right in front of her, his breath warm and minty, his square jaw smooth except for a tiny cut on his chin from shaving. His broad chest swelled with his name and rank, the 101st Airborne patch on his left shoulder, his identity no longer wrapped up in a name and number on a team jersey. From Little League slugger to Army man.

Her eyes misted and she glanced away. She'd promised him she wouldn't get weird.

After he set her down, the scent from his aftershave mingled with the stench of D.J.'s recent cigarette. She wanted to grab Cade by his thick neck and pull him back to her. *We can hide you if you go AWOL. Keep you from going to war.* Then she'd turn to D.J., grab his pack of smokes, and grind them into the ground. *Don't you know these stupid things can kill you, son? If they make your breath smell like a chimney, imagine what they're doing to your lungs.*

Taking a deep breath, she glanced toward the front door. "I wonder what's keeping your dad."

Callie Ann slid from the swing and looped

her arms around the waists of both of her brothers. "He's probably stinking up the bathroom, Mom. You know Dad."

The three Kitchen siblings laughed, sharing in some private joke. For a moment Johnnie felt like an outsider, the aging parent not invited into their secret club.

Then Brother got up and wiggled his way into the group, and once again Johnnie felt included. She reached for the top of Brother's head, soft and firm at the same time, and always reassuring. His hot breath brushed against the side of her leg, right below the hem of her khaki shorts. He panted and grinned up at them all, his pink tongue lolling, his warm doggie smell filling up the space between them. It seemed to Johnnie that as the family got older, it became easier to dote on Brother than on each other. They could tell him their secrets without fear of recrimination or judgment.

Dale came out of the house lugging an ice chest, all muscled-up in faded Levis and a plaid cotton shirt open at the collar. "You about ready, hotshot? Got your gear all loaded?"

Johnnie thought her husband looked fitter than men half his age. His job in construction kept him physically active, even into his late forties, but she was always harping on him to wear sun block to protect his fair skin. He was an older version of Cade, only more rugged and a few inches shorter.

Cade checked the front of his uniform, fingering the buttons on his blouse. "Yes, sir. It's in the bed of your truck. D.J. helped me throw some tarps over it in case we hit rain. Got any beer in that cooler, Daddy?"

Dale's blue eyes crinkled in a grin. "Just water and Gatorade, son."

D.J. took the ice chest from his dad and hauled it out to Dale's work truck parked in the bend in the driveway. "It's zero alcohol for you from here on out, little brother. But we'll throw you a party when you get back. You'll almost be legal."

Dale pecked Johnnie on the cheek. "You hanging in there, honey?"

Nodding, Johnnie breathed in his clean masculine scent from his morning shower. Unlike Dale, she had yet to clean up. She'd slapped on some mascara and lip gloss, and even wore her "Proud Army Mom" T-shirt. No sense getting gussied up for the sendoff. She and Callie Ann planned to take Brother for a long walk after Dale and Cade left. Their way of dealing.

Dale caressed the small of Johnnie's back then checked his watch. "You think your mother's going to show? Cade's got to be in place at Fort Campbell."

Dale's comment threw a switch, and Cade started pacing up and down the porch. "Queen Victoria better hurry up and get here or we're taking photos without her." He stopped every few seconds to pat himself down, as if to make sure he wasn't forgetting something. "I swear, y'all, if Granny Opal was still alive, she'd have been on time."

"And she'd of baked one of her famous theme cakes," D.J. groused good-naturedly.

"Complete with G.I. Joes and a battery-powered tank," Callie Ann chuckled.

D.J. twitched his dark eyebrows at the others. "Well, kiddies, if you haven't noticed, our new grand-*maw* isn't exactly Granny Opal, that's for darn sure."

"You can say that again, and if she doesn't show up in five more minutes, she ain't gonna be in the photos either."

Johnnie listened to them banter back and forth. Mama had returned to Portion almost two years ago after a twenty-three-year hiatus. But for Johnnie's children, their maternal grandmother might as well be a stranger. Mama had yet to earn their trust.

"Daddy and I need to hit the road. Kentucky's a whole day's drive from here. My leave is up tomorrow. I got to report in on time or else."

"Or else what?" Callie Ann rubbed Brother's ears as Cade paced back and forth.

Johnnie read the hopeful look on her daughter's face. If Cade didn't report in on time, maybe he wouldn't have to go to Afghanistan.

"He does time in Leavenworth." D.J. shot his brother a wink.

"What's Leavenworth?" Callie Ann asked.

Cade wheeled around and gave his sister one of his *you've got to be shitting me* looks. "Prison, baby sis."

The sound of Velcro ripped through the air. Cade fished for something in a deep pocket of his trousers. "I almost forgot. I stopped by the recruiter's station the other day when I hit town. Y'all remember Sergeant Jackson, the nice black guy I first talked to? He said to give y'all this." Cade handed Johnnie and Dale a banner with a small blue star centered against a white background bordered in red. "It's a Blue Star Service Flag. Hang it in the window while I'm deployed."

Dale slapped Cade on the back. "That's real nice, Son. Your mama will find the perfect spot." He paused, as if collecting his thoughts. "We'll drive your truck now and then; keep it running."

Why couldn't he say what was really on his mind? Johnnie thought. That Cade's leave had gone way too fast, that it seemed like he'd just gotten home.

She reached in her pocket for her cell and tried to call Mama. A woman's scratchy voice came on the line. "If I don't pick up, guess I'm not here."

Johnnie sighed. She was about to put her phone away and tell everyone to gather for photos when a loud BANG startled them.

Johnnie whirled about. "Jeez, what the heck was that?" Cade hadn't even left and she was already jumpy. Brother barked a warning from the top step.

A 1959 turquoise El Camino cruised up next to the curb and backfired twice before it lurched to a stop. Victoria Grubbs stepped out of the cab and peeked over the top of oversized plastic sunglasses.

"Sorry I'm late, y'all. I was working a deal."

Mama sashayed up the walkway in an orange miniskirt, crocheted top, and white, knee-high boots. A fringed rawhide purse swung at her side. "Look what I found in my closet. Ma saved them for me."

D.J. rolled his eyes and thundered loud enough for everyone to hear, "Groovy. It's Granny Go-Go."

Cade let out a wolf whistle. "Granny V! You're stylin'. Nice wheels."

"Yeah, and I'm digging those batwing rear fenders and cat-eye taillights," D.J. added, stepping off the porch to go check it out. "My shop teacher in high school had a '59 El Camino, but it wasn't in this good of shape." He grinned as he passed his grandmother, but he kept walking.

Callie Ann's jaw dropped as her grandmother drew closer. "That's some outfit you've got on." She gestured toward the street. "I like your new car. Or is it a pickup?"

"A little of both, sugar britches. I got it for a steal from an old boy out by the lake."

Mama, with her prominent cheekbones and trim figure, seemed unaffected by time and life's sorrows, despite a rough life. Except for Mama's fading auburn hair, pulled back in a loose ponytail, it was easy to see where Callie Ann got her looks.

Mama smelled of Jergens Lotion and cigarettes, two aromas Johnnie found comforting as a child because it meant her mother had come home. "Hello, Mama. You plan on going anywhere in that getup?"

Mama laughed her smoky laugh, which seemed to bubble up from her soul. Johnnie couldn't remember the last time Mama looked and sounded so happy. Granny Opal had been dead a month, and it seemed to Johnnie that her grandmother had to die in order for her mama to live. Granny Opal's death had somehow set Mama free. This was the second time Mama showed up wearing vintage. Last week she'd arrived in a Chanel suit and pillbox hat, looking like Jackie Kennedy. A grownup woman playing dress-up with her old wardrobe.

"After I leave here, I've got a job interview at the Dooley Mansion. They're looking for a night manager to run the bed and breakfast." She batted her lashes at Dale. "And considering my *son-in-law* served as the general contractor for the renovation. . . ."

Scratching his nose, Dale eyed her a second. "I'll be happy to put in a good word for you. Make a couple of phone calls. But first I need to get on the road." He nodded toward the street, where D.J. was admiring the El Camino's turquoise and white paint job. "That's a nice-looking vehicle, Victoria. But it sounds like it needs a tune-up."

The family posed for pictures, each taking turns using their cellphone cameras. Cade changed out of his uniform, pulled on a T-shirt and jeans, and announced that it was time to go.

After everyone hugged and said their

goodbyes, Dale backed the truck down the curved driveway and laid on the horn. Johnnie closed her eyes, trying to dismiss the image of a bomb going off at Cade's feet.

Come home in one piece or don't come home at all, she started to blurt, but a voice in her head stopped her short. *Let him go.*

Cade stuck his blond head out the open passenger window, above the door panel that read "Dale's House of Restoration." His face lit up like he'd just hit a homerun.

Waving with his whole arm, he hollered, "Y'all be good. I'll see you when I get back."

Johnnie heard Mama suck in her breath. She and Mama had been there before, at a lonely bus station outside an Army post forty years ago. *Be good for your mama. I'll see you when I get back.*

But Johnnie's dad didn't come back. A booby trap took care of that, and pushed Mama over the edge.

Victoria Grubbs crossed her arms, her emerald eyes on fire. "Our family's done given enough for this country. He'll be back, baby girl, don't you worry. Only a mean-spirited God would let the enemy take the life of a bighearted boy like Cade."

Johnnie stopped breathing. She knew Mama meant well, but her words sliced straight through her heart. "What about all the other bighearted boys, Mama? The ones who've already died in this war? What does God have to say about that?"

Mama closed her eyes and put a hand to her forehead. "All I know is we've got to have faith."

When did you suddenly get religion? Johnnie almost snapped but she held her tongue.

Callie Ann locked her arms around Johnnie's waist. "Grandma V's right, Mom. We have to believe Cade will be safe." She paused. "D.J. took Brother around back. Said he needed to have a smoke and clear his head. I think he's back there crying. Maybe I should go check on him."

"That would be nice, Sis. This is hard on him, too." They clung to each other for a moment.

Mama dug around in her purse. "Think I'll go join Francis. Maybe I can bum a cigarette."

Johnnie gaped at her mother in silence.

After a moment, Victoria looked up from rooting around in her purse. "What?"

"Mama, you called D.J. *Francis.*"

Victoria put her hand to her mouth, shocked. "Oh my." She paused for a moment, as the full import sunk in. Finally, she slung her fringed purse over her shoulder and said, "Sorry, baby girl. That boy is a spitting image of your daddy. Right down to his dry wit."

After Mama and Callie Ann left, Johnnie stared at the place in the road where Dale's pickup had gone out of sight. She had finals coming up, a newspaper column to write, and Granny Opal's house to clear out and sell. How the heck was she going to get through the next few days, weeks, and months of Cade's deployment? At forty-five, she was sending her baby son off to war, like thousands of mothers had done since the beginning of time. But this was her son. Her child.

From her spot on the sidewalk, she gazed at the dark red bungalow with the Craftsman-style porch framed by square tapered columns, her home since 1984. The house Dale remodeled with his own hands, a safe haven that came with locks on windows and doors and provided protection from the elements. But now Cade was going to a place where no amount of locks on windows and doors could protect him. No amount of parental love from her or Dale could keep their son from getting blown up.

A bare window to the left of the front door caught Johnnie's attention, a north window that faced the street.

Fingering the blue star banner in her hand, she marched up the steps and headed to the kitchen to hang the banner from the window over the sink. She wanted everybody who drove past her home at 420 Merriweather to know her boy had stepped up, answered the call, decided to serve his country during a time of war and risk his life for theirs.

For D.J. and the rest of the family, the war was no longer philosophical. It was personal.

If she had to cloak herself in Old Glory to survive Cade's deployment . . . well, so be it.

Chapter 2
The Incident

"You know what I hate, Mama?"

Johnnie steered the buttercream Lincoln out of the cemetery and headed south on Dooley Street. They'd stopped by Granny's grave to see if the engraver had been by, but Opal Grubb's death date remained blank.

Mama flicked her ashes out the passenger window and stared straight ahead. "Me smoking in Ma's car. Your granny would have a conniption if she could see me."

Johnnie glanced sideways at her mama. "Maybe she can," Johnnie teased.

For a few seconds she had a reprieve from images of Cade getting shot at or mangled by shrapnel, replaced by the real image of Victoria Grubbs in a pair of white culottes and matching top. It was one of many outfits Granny Opal had mothballed years ago, believing her daughter would return. With Johnnie's Suburban and Mama's El Camino both in the shop, they were driving

Granny's car. Was it Johnnie's imagination, or did Granny's scent of peppermint candy and bakery cake overpower Mama's cigarette?

"Considering the old woman died on April Fool's Day, maybe she's not dead at all. Maybe Ma's just hanging around, waiting to lecture me about one thing or another." Mama's dry laugh crackled between them like brittle leaves.

"I'd like to believe she's in Heaven, reunited with Grandpa and Uncle Johnny."

Uncle Johnny. There, she'd said it. The one name that always caused Mama to flinch no matter how much time had passed since her brother's accidental drowning in 1963.

Mama coughed and a long silence stretched between them.

After a moment, Johnnie curled her fingers around the steering wheel and glanced out the windshield. "What I hate, Mama, is that Cade's only been in country three weeks, but when I tell folks he's in a war zone, they look at me like he's already dead."

Mama sucked in her breath and tossed her cigarette butt out the window. "Jeez, Johnnie girl, don't say that."

"But it's true, Mama." Johnnie could hear the tremor in her own voice, but she talked into the fear because she didn't know what else to do. "Even people at church don't know what to say when I tell them."

Mama played with the flap of cloth that turned her pair of shorts into a faux skirt. "I reckon folks at church mean well." She stared blankly upward, lost in thought. Finally, crossing her arms, she said, "You mind swinging by the war memorial? Being it's Memorial Day and all."

The war memorial was the last place Johnnie wanted to go. But out of respect for her mother, she turned right at Red Bud Lane and headed west toward historic downtown. When they got to Main Street, they headed south past the Palace Theater with its old-fashioned marquee and box office. The theater, City Hall, and the old corner bank building were on their right, the gazebo and Genie's Books with the big bay window on their left.

Trash from the morning parade route littered the flag-lined street.

Up ahead, the afternoon sun shone on the bronze statue, and the old soldier glistened high above the trees as if his sole purpose was to protect the good citizens of Portion.

As Johnnie pulled the Lincoln in front of Soldiers Park, her gaze fell on the "I Voted" sticker stuck to the sun-beaten dashboard, as if this was Granny Opal's final statement after nearly eighty-six years of living. Johnnie smiled at the memory of Granny pushing her walker into the city hall for the last time, shuffling along in her red cowboy boots and threatening to kick any politician that harassed her as she made her way to the polls.

"Isn't that your friend Whit? She always looks like a million bucks." Mama shut the car door and gestured at a woman with caramel-colored skin and a tuft of spiky silver hair. She was stepping off the curb on the opposite side of Main Street, jaywalking toward them. With each stride, the former track star's long creamy skirt swirled around her shapely calves. Prominent cheekbones framed a dazzling smile.

"Like Granny always said, 'With the right accessories, Whit could turn a burlap sack and a belt into a chic outfit.' " Johnnie came around the back of the car and joined Mama on the sidewalk. An "Obama/Biden" bumper sticker and a "Support Our Troops" decal flanked each side of the chrome bumper. In the middle of the back window, faded letters advertising "Opal's Cakery" still had the power to transport Johnnie back to her childhood and the kitchen where she confused food with love.

"Hi there, ladybug," Whit called, scooting

quickly out of the way of a passing motorist. She glanced at the Lincoln as she went to give Johnnie a hug. "How come you're in Granny's car? I thought Callie Ann was driving it now."

"Both our cars are in the shop." Johnnie returned the hug. "Callie Ann took Cade's pickup to work."

Mama pointed with her chin. "So we're stuck driving Ma's *lemon-zine.*"

Whit's bangle bracelets jingled as she went to embrace Mama. "How you doing, Miss Victoria? You sure look snazzy in those culottes. Retro is all the rage."

Mama seemed amused by Whit's comment. "Doing just fine, thank you. Good thing Ma saved all my clothes. I can barely afford new underwear. I'm a little low on cash until I get me a job."

Sometimes Mama sounded so rough around the edges, like she'd forgotten all of her schooling, like she'd never been to college.

Whit studied her manicured nails, painted a brilliant plum to match her lips. "You got any experience working retail?"

"Honey, I've done just about every job imaginable." Mama laughed then started to cough.

I bet you have, Johnnie thought, picturing

her mother in various jobs from scrubbing floors to pole dancing.

Whit cocked her head and eyeballed Mama. "I could use some extra help at the shop next week for the grand opening."

They all gazed across the street at the old-timey storefront with the red, beveled-glass door.

"Whit's Whimsies," Mama pronounced in that slow Southern way of hers that sounded downright flirty. "Looks like a fun place to work."

"How did your interview go at the Dooley Mansion?" Johnnie cut in. She wasn't too keen on the idea of her mama working for her best friend.

Mama scratched at something on her eyebrow. "I'm waiting for a call back. I thought I told you."

Was it Johnnie, or did Mama sound a tad testy?

Whit twirled her key chain around her finger. "Did y'all see the parade this morning?"

Johnnie was grateful for the change of subject.

Mama shook her head and gazed at the soldier perched high on his pedestal. "Naw, Whit, we missed it."

Johnnie stared at the back of her mother's

head. She didn't need to see her face to know that Victoria Grubbs had that faraway look in her eyes, the same look she always got when she stared at the statue.

"It was a good one, too," Whit continued. "The VFW was out in force. Along with the high school band, the twirlers and drill team, *and* those fellas on scooters with the funny hats."

"The Shriners, you mean." Johnnie didn't take her gaze off Mama the whole time she listened to Whit talk about the parade. "They do a lot of good work for kids."

"Lord, I need to sit down." Mama skirted the monument and dropped down on the bench in front of the statue, stretching her legs and fishing for something in her purse. Seconds later her back stiffened and she sat up straighter, craning her neck this way and that. "Do you hear them?"

Whit narrowed her eyes at Mama. "Hear what?"

"The voices," Mama said. "They're coming from every angle."

Johnnie shuddered, remembering the day she'd come here with Brother Dog right after Cade joined the Army. That day she'd heard voices, the voices of young men dying in battle. Brother heard them, too, because he whimpered and wanted to leave.

Johnnie drew closer to the bronze soldier, but her gaze stayed on Mama. "Whose voices do you hear?" *Please don't let it be Cade,* she pleaded silently. She clung to the base of the monument. Even in the heat of the day, the stone felt smooth and cool, like Granny's tombstone back at the cemetery.

A beam of sunlight broke through the leafy canopy of oaks and formed a circle around the bench.

Mama closed her eyes and turned her face to the sun. "I hear the mothers and wives," she whispered, "and the sweethearts like me." Her voice grew jagged and she paused to catch her breath. "All those grieving women and girls. We all lost part of ourselves in war."

Relief and sadness washed over Johnnie. Her vision blurred and she swiped at the unwanted tears. She listened for the voices, too, but all she could hear was the chattering of birds and the traffic going up and down Main.

Then a slow anger built from deep within as she stared at Mama, still in a daze.

Holding a fist against her lips, Johnnie brushed past Whit and muttered, "She forgot about the *daughters.*" Her chest caved under the weight of Mama's omission. "She forgot about me, Whit, and what I lost."

Whit reached out and grasped Johnnie by the shoulder. "Your mama's still struggling with her own grief, ladybug. Don't take it personally."

Then whatever spell Mama had been under broke, and she fished through her purse for a cigarette.

Off in the distance, an engine gunned and Johnnie heard the sound of country music.

Cade!

For a second, she allowed herself to believe that her boy had returned from Afghanistan. He was home, driving around town in his pickup and listening to his favorite tunes.

The music grew louder and louder, and she ran to the curb and glanced up and down Main. A pickup was cruising south toward her, the same gunmetal gray as Cade's. But any similarities stopped at the monster tires and a large Confederate Battle Flag flying on a homemade flagpole behind the cab.

By now Whit had joined her at the curb near the back of the Lincoln.

The truck slowed as it approached the war memorial.

"D.J. calls jacked-up trucks 'manhood

compensators.' " She elbowed Whit, expecting her to chuckle.

But Whit crossed her arms and frowned. "I don't like that flag." Her lips barely moved as she spoke over the blare of the music.

The pickup stopped momentarily right in front of them. Through the open passenger window, they caught sight of a teenage boy wearing a straw cowboy hat and a dirty white T with the sleeves cut off at the shoulders, emphasizing his ropy sun-burnt arms. His eyes were hidden behind sunglasses.

The kid flashed a toothy grin then peeled out down the street.

"He reminds me of Cade," Johnnie joked, "in a country-boy kind of way."

The pickup didn't get far before it whipped a U-turn in the middle of the block, tires squealing, and headed back toward them.

Johnnie heard Whit catch her breath. "I don't hear any music, do you?"

As Johnnie strained to listen, Whit grabbed her by the arm like she was afraid.

The truck veered sharply to the left, crossed the centerline, and barreled straight toward Granny's car.

Clinging to each other, Johnnie and Whit

stumbled back, trying to get out of the way.

At the last second, the driver swerved to the right, barely missing the Lincoln.

He screamed an ugly slur and flung a beer bottle out the window.

As the N-word crackled around them, the bottle torpedoed through the air and exploded at the base of the war memorial, sending brown glass and yeasty foam flying.

Time slowed as Johnnie stared at the kid, his creepy grin reminding her of a jack-o'-lantern. "You stupid jerk!" she bellowed, trying to read the kid's license plate, but the truck sped away too quickly.

Like shock waves, the racial slur reverberated in her ears, and Johnnie went numb when she turned to find Whit standing rigid in the middle of the sidewalk, breathing through her nose. Tears ran down both sides of her cheeks. She sniffed and closed her eyes, as if she couldn't believe what had happened.

"That stupid kid's probably just pissed off because a black man's in the White House. He saw Granny's bumper sticker and —"

"That beer bottle was meant for me," Whit croaked, looking taller and more regal than ever.

"It was meant for all of us." Mama leaned against the war memorial, seeming not to notice her blood-splattered culottes or the blood dripping down one leg.

"Oh my God, Mama, you're bleeding." Johnnie rushed to her side, glass crunching under her shoes.

"It don't matter," Mama said, digging through her purse for what Johnnie thought was a cigarette. Mama pulled out a wad of paper napkins and hobbled over to Whit. "Sorry I don't have any tissues, sugar. These'll have to do."

Whit took the napkins and dabbed at her wet cheeks. "After all this time," she sniffed, her voice choked with tears, "there's still so much hate in this country."

Mama nodded then put her arm around Whit. "And so many ignoramuses like that fool."

Staring up at the bronze soldier, Johnnie vowed to get even. She wanted justice.

"That white kid in his pick 'em up truck isn't the only one in Portion who knows how to turn words into weapons, is he, Mr. Statue Man?"

Chapter 3
Portion Telegraph
"Roundtable with Johnnie Kitchen"

Under a blue Texas sky, on a day set aside to honor our nation's war dead, my mama, my best friend, and I were attacked in front of the war memorial at Soldiers Park. We'd come to pay our respects and to remember a young officer killed in Vietnam. That man was my father, although his identity was kept from me for years. While we visited with the old soldier, the statue that represents thousands of men who've died in battle, we also paid homage to the women and girls whose loved ones were sacrificed at the altar of war.

We were three patriots out on Memorial Day: two white women and one black.

Then it happened. The assault. A white kid driving a big monster pickup and flying a Confederate flag hurled a half-empty beer bottle in our direction while he spewed his verbal sewage of hate. The bottle hit the base of the memorial, desecrating a hallowed monument, and shards of glass flew up and cut my mama on the leg. No amount of bleach will remove the bloodstains in her white outfit, and no amount of hugs and apologies will heal the wound in my friend's heart even though the N-word wasn't directed at *her,* but at *me* for being in her presence. And yet, the racial slur has wounded all three of us.

What I can't figure out is what provoked this attack. Was it the Obama/Biden bumper sticker left over from the last election, still displayed on my late grandmother's car, which we happened to be standing next to at the time of the attack? Or was it simply that a young kid cruising down Main Street couldn't fathom that a white woman and a black woman standing side by side on a public sidewalk might be friends — best friends for that matter.

What the attacker doesn't know is that another kid from Portion is putting his life on the line to defend the freedom of all Americans, even a young racist in a jacked-up truck.

That kid is my son. It's probably a good thing he's over in Afghanistan fighting the Taliban. Because if he was home and heard what happened, I might not be able to stop him from tracking down this racist, home-grown terrorist and teaching him a lesson about real freedom and justice.

~Johnnie Kitchen is a columnist for the *Portion Telegraph.* She was six years old when her father was killed in Vietnam. She is a part-time college student, a mother of three, and a lifelong resident of Portion, Texas. Her youngest son deployed to Afghanistan in early May. You may contact her at: j.kitchen(at)portiontelegraph.com.

CHAPTER 4
COFFEE CAN WAIT

Johnnie stood barefoot at the sink, measuring out water for the coffeemaker.

Dale snuck up behind her, his voice scratchy from sleep. "Morning, Johnnie girl."

Her shoulders hunched on instinct, and she shivered at his unexpected presence. "You scared me."

She was still jittery after the incident at the war memorial. This morning, she'd been lost in thought, staring past the blue star banner in the window to the dew-covered grass, and the vacant lot across the street where Mr. Marvel's cottage once stood. All that remained was the evergreen he'd planted in memory of his little brother Edwin, who'd died when they were boys. Johnnie had kept her promise to her late neighbor that she would look after "Edwin's Tree."

Before Dale startled her, Johnnie had been

remembering the night she'd saved Mr. Marvel's life. How he was lying in a drunken stupor in the middle of the street when Cade returned home in his pickup, almost smashing into both of them seconds before Johnnie rolled the portly man to safety.

"Oh Jeez, Mama! I almost killed you!" The terror in Cade's voice that night still ripped at her heart, but she tried to banish the memory by focusing on Dale.

He wrapped his arms around her and nuzzled her neck, tickling her with his whiskers. "I didn't mean to scare you."

She giggled, squirming under his touch. "You haven't shaved yet." Most mornings, Dale shaved and dressed first, then came into the kitchen to grab a mug of coffee and glance at the newspaper before heading to work.

The sun was just coming up. The kitchen and den were bathed in the pale light of dawn, which filtered through the windows on the east side of the house. On summer mornings, Johnnie preferred natural light to ease into the day.

"I thought we could play first." He nibbled her ear, his voice husky and inviting. He was naked from the waist up, clad only in boxer briefs, his watch, and wedding ring.

Part of her wanted to push him away, her

worry for Cade a constant distraction, along with the memory of a white kid burning with hate somewhere on the streets of Portion. Besides, any minute Callie Ann might stumble in, yawning and groping for her cereal bowl. Or Brother Dog would scratch at the back door, demanding to be let in. "Honey, at least let me get the coffee going."

"Coffee can wait."

She leaned into his warmth, his taut chest and flat stomach and those muscular arms that enveloped her. She was a sucker for those arms — tanned and flecked with golden hair — one of the first things she'd noticed about him the first time they met, besides his big capable hands and soft blue eyes that shone with a quiet strength.

The clock on the mantel chimed six thirty.

The Pyrex measuring cup slipped from her fingers with a thud into the farmhouse sink. She barely noticed.

Dale brushed aside her auburn hair pulled up in a girlish ponytail and kissed the back of her neck. She lolled her head from side to side, savoring the ripples of pleasure pulsing through her body. "We better hurry or you'll be late for work." She started for the bedroom, but Dale stopped her.

"You feel good, Johnnie girl," he murmured.

"But Callie Ann —"

Dale hushed her with his lips. "She's in the shower running up the hot water bill. You know she takes forever. We have time."

Afterward, Johnnie tiptoed across the hardwood floor, past the stone fireplace Dale built with his own hands, and peeked out at Brother to make sure he was okay. From the far end of the room, she listened for Callie Ann, for the water that ran through the old pipes of the house. Satisfied that her daughter was still in the shower, she gazed lovingly back at her hunky husband. He looked up at her and smiled.

You are solid to the soul, Dale Kitchen. Her throat tightened and she pressed her hands together, prayer-like, in front of her lips, recalling the hurt she had hurled upon him when he found out about her affair from long ago.

As if reading her mind, he held out his arms and she banished those dark thoughts by burying her face in his warm chest. He tugged playfully at her ponytail. For a sacred moment, she kept her head bowed and thanked the Lord for such a forgiving husband.

Brother Dog scratched at the back door. They both heard the water shut off in the hall bath and the shower curtain swoosh back on the metal rod.

Before he headed back to shave, they embraced one last time in front of the blue star hanging over the window. Dale kissed her shoulder, and a silent understanding passed between them. It was okay for them to forget for those few blessed moments, in the privacy of their own home, that they had a son half a world away in a war zone. And that any second the blue star could turn to gold.

Chapter 5
The Call

Later that evening, Dale swung through the back door with a platter of pork chops fresh from the grill. "Okay, who's the man?" Grinning, he hoisted the meat high like a trophy, filling the air with the scent of garlic and teriyaki.

Johnnie slid avocado chunks on top of wild field greens and raised her wine glass in a toast. "You are, honey." She smiled at the swagger in Dale's step, knowing she'd put it there that morning.

Brother Dog pranced beside Dale, sniffing his way across the room. No sooner had Dale set the platter on the island and torn off a sheet of tinfoil to cover the chops when his cell phone buzzed from his jean pocket.

Johnnie set her wine down and picked up the salad tongs, gripping them in midair. *If something happened to Cade, we wouldn't get a phone call.* She watched Dale fumble with his phone before he flipped it open.

It could be anybody — one of Dale's men, calling about tomorrow's schedule or a potential client, requesting a bid. Even with the slump in the housing market, the demand for home remodeling was stronger than ever and Dale and his crew stayed busy.

He motioned for Johnnie to cover the chops. "I don't recognize the area code. Could be Cade. He said he'd try to call."

Her hands trembled as she dropped the tongs in the salad bowl and grabbed the foil, trying to keep the crinkling to a minimum while her heart jack hammered in her throat.

Dale scanned the keypad then smashed his thumb against the speaker button.

"Hey, Daddy." Cade's Texas twang blared from the phone, and Johnnie sighed with relief. Brother stopped licking the floor and stared up at Dale's hand.

"Hey, hotshot. I've got you on speaker. Your mom and the dog are here."

"Hi, baby," Johnnie blurted out, leaning toward Dale's phone. "Callie Ann sent you a care package two days ago."

"Hey, Mama. Tell baby sis thanks. Can't talk but a sec. There's a bunch of soldiers in line behind me, waiting to call home. Just want y'all to know I'm okay. How's everybody there?"

"We're all good," Dale said, keeping his

voice even. "Just do your job and stay safe."

"I am, Daddy. We've been setting off some fireworks, if ya know what I mean. Every day's the Fourth of July around here." He sounded hyped up on adrenaline.

Johnnie covered her mouth and closed her eyes, her whole body tuned into the sound of her son's voice broadcasting into the room. She leaned closer, listening intently, as near as you could get to wrapping yourself around a person who wasn't there.

"I'll email when I can," Cade said. "Got to go. Give Labster a kiss for me. I love y'all."

And just like that, they were cut off.

Johnnie glanced up at Dale. His pale blue eyes glistened as he closed the phone and dropped it in his pocket.

She reached down to give Brother a kiss. He was in a perfect sit. Picking up a paring knife, she cut off a sliver of pork chop and slipped it to him.

"This is from Cade," she cooed, breaking Dale's house rule never to feed scraps to the dog.

Brother wolfed it down and waited for more.

Dale placed both hands on the island, his callused fingers splayed out in front of him. "Cade's a good man. Cripes, he's almost twenty."

He cocked an eyebrow at the dog. "What are you looking at?"

Brother smacked his lips and scooched forward on his haunches.

CHAPTER 6
THE WARNING

The next morning, Johnnie clenched her "Proud Army Mom" mug in both hands and waited by the back door for Brother to appear. She took a sip of coffee and pushed back the god-awful dream that woke her with a start right before sunrise: the nightmare where she was running grief-stricken through a tunnel. She'd been about to dump it on Dale when he interrupted her thoughts.

He rustled the newspaper and peeked at Johnnie over his reading glasses. "Looks like you got some blowback from your last column." He sat in his leather chair by the stone fireplace, his steel-toed work boots propped on the matching ottoman.

She blinked over the rim of her mug. "You mean a letter to the editor? How bad is it? My editor tried to warn me."

Dale glanced back at the paper. "It's from an elderly woman named Blanche. She sounds kind of feisty."

Johnnie stared at the brown liquid sloshing in her mug. Breathing in the aroma of freshly brewed coffee, she willed her hands to be still. For a split second, she reached into her memory for her last column. *Oh yes, the assault at the war memorial.* "I guess if I can dish it out, I better learn to take it." She took a deep breath and held the mug to her chest. "Would you read it to me?"

Dale ducked behind the paper, his tone loud and theatrical as he channeled an indignant old lady:

> Dear Sirs:
>
> I'm writing in reference to Mrs. Kitchen's unfortunate encounter with a misguided young man at Soldiers Park. I've lived in Portion my whole life, and I can assure you that nothing like this has ever happened in our community. This town is a peaceful and loving place to raise children. We are not racist. We have always been good to our colored brethren and sisters. Every Christmas, our church takes up a collection of toys and clothes and food, and we personally deliver the goods to the residents of The Pasture. Even in those years following WWII, when rationing and going with-

out were fresh on our minds, we loaded up our pickups and my brand new 1949 Mercury station wagon with donated items and drove to all the shantytowns around Portion, doling out provisions and goodwill.

My message to Mrs. Johnnie Kitchen: Do not let one rotten apple define a community.

We are patriotic, hardworking, and love our boys in uniform.

God Bless America,
Mrs. Blanche Livingood
United Daughters of the Confederacy

About then, Brother barked at the back door.

As he darted past, she got a whiff of his warm puppy smell and huffed, "Granny Opal always said if you have to brag about helping others, you're doing it for the wrong reasons."

Dale sipped his coffee, amused. He crinkled the paper. "Oh, wait. Here's another one."

Johnnie sat down her mug and marched over as Dale handed her the paper. Scanning the newsprint, she found the second letter:

Write on! Johnnie Kitchen. Thanks for shedding light on a subject that nobody wants to talk about, especially in Portion, TX. Racism is alive in this country. I've been living under its oppression for sixty-two years. I could tell you tales that would melt the wax in your ears. When I was a young boy, I witnessed an act of brutality so despicable I've never been able to talk about it. The white press hushed it up. I've seen mean and angry men act worse than animals. Don't even get me started on poll taxes and separate but equal. There ain't nothing equal about segregation.

You're a brave woman for speaking out, Ms. Kitchen. Next time I write, maybe I'll get brave, too, and use my real name.

Until then,
"Jim Crow"

Johnnie stood, unable to move, the black and white newsprint blurring together as she flicked away a tear. Closing her eyes, she welcomed the rush of warmth flowing through her body. When she looked up, Dale's generous mouth slid back in a grin. "You've touched this man's heart, Johnnie girl."

She handed the paper back to Dale. "I wonder who he is. I bet it took a lot of gumption for him to write that letter."

Dale twitched his brow. "Not to mention using that alias."

Brother came up and nudged her on the leg. She stroked his head.

"Sorry, big dog. Did I forget to feed you?" He followed her into the laundry room, his tail thumping against the door as she scooped two cups of kibble into his dish. With each plink, Brother's tail thumped louder. Before setting his dish down, she commanded, "Sit like a gentleman." Brother sat on his haunches, his amber-colored eyes trained on her. All ninety pounds of his chocolate-furred body wriggled with anticipation. When she gave him the signal, he dove in.

Back in the kitchen, she listened to him gobble and crunch his way through his first meal of the day. Across the room, Dale slurped his coffee, the newspaper splayed on his lap. The clock on the mantel chimed seven o'clock.

"This Blanche Livingood lady sounds like a busybody," Johnnie said. "I wonder if Granny Opal knew her. Seems like Granny knew everybody in Portion."

Dale eyed her over his mug. "I think the

old gal means well."

"She sounds a tad snooty, if you ask me." Johnnie hated the tone in her own voice at that moment, harsh and judgmental.

"She's just trying to help people, Johnnie. It's no different than when you worked at the food pantry. Didn't you write about that in one of your first columns?"

"Dammit, Dale, why do you do that? Make me look like the bad guy?" He did that sometimes. Took the side of others. One second he was calling the woman out, the next he was defending her.

Dale cleared his throat. "Look at it this way, honey. Your latest column got a couple of folks thinking. Thinking enough to pen a letter to the editor. Isn't that why you write? To connect with people?"

By now, she was half-listening. The whole time they bantered back and forth, the nightmare loop played over and over in her mind. She had to tell Dale.

He sat his mug down and leaned back, clasping his hands behind his head. "I mean, what's the difference between you doling out charity or some old do-gooder . . ." his voice trailed off.

Tapping her fingers on the countertop, she felt the room begin to close in as her nerves jittered along an invisible thread that yanked from the back of her throat to her bottom.

While Dale's voice receded into the background, Brother Dog crunched on his breakfast and an airliner took off from nearby DFW Airport, the drone of the jet engine reverberating through the house. Her eyes swept over her family room, a cross between country cottage and mountain lodge; the stone fireplace anchored the room.

Above the solid oak mantel, the large photo of Dale's flight-suited dad next to his B-52 shared space with two more photos Johnnie added last week. In the photo to the right, newlyweds Johnnie and Dale smiled for the camera from the front seat of Colonel Kitchen's '57 Thunderbird convertible as Dale wheeled out of the church parking lot, leaving Mama in blue taffeta, waving in the background. In the photo to the left, D.J., Callie Ann, and Cade looked like three peas in a pod, with Callie Ann in the middle, on the porch swing moments before Cade's departure. Cade's toothy grin stood out beneath his dark beret, D.J. dangled a cigarette over the side of the swing — his intense stare challenging the person taking the photo — while Callie Ann held both of her brothers' legs in a possessive grip.

Dale coughed and Johnnie was back in

the moment.

He folded the newspaper, half-watching her. "Johnnie, did you hear me? You zoned out. It's those letters, isn't it? You look so pensive."

Slowly, she shook her head. "I, uh, had a bad dream this morning. It woke me up."

Dale eyed her warily. Johnnie knew what he was thinking. He'd been here before. All those years, when she'd wake thinking she had binged, Dale would reassure her that she hadn't. And still, he asked, "About what?" He stood, tucking his work shirt into his jeans, adjusting his belt.

She took a deep breath, clutching the edge of the granite island. "Cade got killed."

The words torpedoed out of her mouth and slammed him into the chair. One hundred eighty-five pounds of solid muscle dropped by three simple words.

Dale rubbed his chest as if in pain. "Jeez, Johnnie girl. I wished you hadn't said that."

Before he could stop her, Johnnie rushed on. She needed to purge the nightmare from her system, and the only way she knew to do that was to talk about it.

"The doorbell rang. We'd just hung up from talking to Cade. I opened the door and three soldiers stood on the porch, staring at me with hardened eyes. I screamed at them to go away, said we'd just talked to our son twenty minutes before. One of the soldiers started to speak, but I pushed past him and fled. I ran through a wide underground tunnel full of endless glass doors. Each time I threw open a door, another gray section of tunnel swallowed me. I've never felt so tormented in my life. I wanted to die."

She stopped to gulp for air.

Dale strode across the braided rug and gathered her in his massive arms.

"The worst part," she swallowed, her voice dry and thrumming in her ears, "the worst part was when I ran into a tall man in a business suit blocking one of the doors. 'My son got killed in war,' I cried, pounding my fist into his rock-hard chest. The man didn't move. He didn't budge. He just looked at me and said, 'So?' as if he could care less."

She shuddered and hid her face in Dale's familiar warmth, his strong chest reassuring, so different from the stranger in the dream.

After a moment, Dale tucked a loose strand of hair behind her ear and brushed his thumb against her cheek. "So, who's the man in the suit?"

Holding her breath, she peeked out the window one more time, making sure an Army staff car or government vehicle hadn't parked next to the curb, uninvited and unwelcome. A quiet rage burned in her heart. The rage had been building since she first comprehended that wars would come and go, young people would keep getting slaughtered, and those in power, the people who sent them, rarely suffered.

"Who's the man in the suit, you ask?" She took a deep breath and angry words tumbled out. "Why, he's every fat-cat politician and apathetic civilian who could give a crap whether my son lives or dies. They want their freedom like they want McDonald's french fries: cheap and at little cost to themselves. Let somebody else slave over the hot oil."

Dale held her at arm's length. "It was just a dream, honey." Finally, they embraced. Johnnie kept nodding into his chest, and Dale kept patting her on the back, as if they both needed to reassure each other that was really the case.

Then Dale went to grab his lunch pail and large jug of ice water.

At the side door that led out to the portico, where Dale parked his truck, he turned one last time before heading off to work. "Johnnie, I've been thinking. . . ."

She belted her robe and waited. Something in his voice had changed.

"Since Callie Ann likes driving Granny's car — not sure what that's about — I think it might be a good idea if you girls scrape off that bumper sticker. I don't want it to set off another nutcase like what happened downtown, especially if Callie Ann's behind the wheel."

Johnnie cocked her head and frowned. "Granny put *two* bumper stickers on her car. Which one are you talking about?" She knew good and well which one — she just wanted to hear Dale say it.

Dale rolled his eyes. "C'mon, honey, I'm sure as heck not talking about 'Support Our Troops.' "

Johnnie's gaze shifted to a framed photo she'd placed by the computer, one of the many taken at Cade's sendoff. In the photo, Cade knelt to hug Brother one last time. Brother's chin rested on Cade's camouflage shoulder as if he knew his young master was leaving for a faraway land.

She lowered her voice, but her words came out all strangled. "Just whose side are you on, Dale?"

He kissed her on the forehead. "I'm just asking you to think about it. The election's been over for months."

Callie Ann shuffled into the room in lounge pants and a tank top, rubbing sleep from her eyes. "I could hear y'all clear down the hall. And for what it's worth, Dad, the reason I don't like driving Cade's truck while he's gone is I don't wanna be responsible if something happens to it."

Brother pranced up to her, and she bent to give him a rubdown.

Without looking up, she warned them, "Don't mess with Granny's bumper stickers. I was with her the day she stuck them on her car. It was right after Cade joined the Army." She cupped Brother's face in her hands. "Granny Opal should have the final say. Don't you agree?"

Brother snorted and wagged his tail as in approval.

Callie Ann looked over at her dad. "Besides, I'm probably safer in Granny's car than Cade's pickup. That old Lincoln's the size of a tank."

A memory of Granny getting out of her lumbering yellow car two years ago rolled through Johnnie's mind. She and Granny had agreed to meet up at the cemetery by the large monument engraved with a relief of *The Last Supper.*

After Granny shut the door, she said to Johnnie, "Some guy in a Hummer nearly ran me off the road." Granny had flashed her crooked smile, showing off her new set of dentures. "I'd like to have given him the high sign." That sweltering summer day, Granny wore a royal blue sweater and matching sparkly cap. When Johnnie asked her why she was dressed like Old Man Winter had just blown into town, Granny replied, "I can't seem to get warm these days."

As Johnnie went to get ready for class, she wondered if that was the beginning of Granny's decline.

Chapter 7
April Fool's Day
Three Months Earlier

Johnnie sat vigil by Granny Opal's hospital bed. Mama had stepped out for coffee ten minutes ago, and Johnnie was looking forward to her return with the hot liquid. Anything to keep from freezing in this frigid hospital room.

Granny stirred. Johnnie pushed herself out of the chair and went to fuss with the thin blankets draped over her grandmother's shrinking frame. After Granny's stroke in 2007, she'd lost weight but maintained her fierce determination to bake cakes for her family and friends to celebrate every occasion. No amount of cajoling and telling her to slow down could keep Opal Grubbs from her kitchen. The day she got out of the hospital after Mama's return from her twenty-three year hiatus, the first thing Granny did was bake a three-layer spice cake with the squiggly message "Welcome Home, Victoria!" in loopy orange icing.

Then she paid a visit to her lawyer to update her will. Half would go to Victoria, the other half to Johnnie, with Johnnie appointed as executor.

As Johnnie tucked the blanket around her grandmother's increasingly stooped shoulders, an alert beep went off somewhere nearby. Johnnie glanced at the heart monitor. The lines darting up and down appeared more erratic now, like the lettering on the last cake Granny baked five days ago for Johnnie's forty-fifth birthday — her final act of love for the granddaughter she raised. Granny's eyes were shut, her breathing shallow. She had signed a DNR, and she was adamant that her wish not to be resuscitated be honored.

But this didn't mean Johnnie couldn't call for help.

The second Johnnie hit the call button, Granny sat straight up in bed. Her eyes flew open and her saggy, liver-spotted arms flung wide toward the ceiling. "John-neee," she called, her voice raspy but urgent, her face awash in what looked like pure bliss. Her watery eyes glistened with a joy Johnnie had never seen.

"Yes, Granny?" Tears streaked Johnnie's cheeks. She swiped at the salty rivulets with the heel of her hand as a sudden movement caused her to look up.

Mama stood frozen in the doorway, white as the bed sheets that cocooned Granny, a paper cup gripped in each trembling hand. Even from this distance, Johnnie could see coffee burbling out of the tiny drink slits on each plastic lid.

A nurse rushed into the room, sidestepping Mama, her trained eyes assessing the situation.

Time slowed as Johnnie watched the nurse approach the bed.

Granny called out again, "John-neee . . . John-neee . . ." in a voice full of longing and love.

It took Johnnie a second to realize that Granny was not calling to her. She was calling to her lost son who drowned in 1963 at the tender age of eighteen.

They all glanced up at the ceiling, in the direction where Granny's hands were reaching as if welcoming someone. Johnnie knew in her heart that a portal to Heaven had opened. The second Granny's head slumped back against the pillow, Uncle Johnny reached down and pulled Granny right up.

"Ma . . . ?" A little girl's voice filled the room. The sound resembled the bleating of a lamb.

Johnnie swallowed hard. The nurse rushed

to grab the paper cups from Mama's hands before hot coffee scalded down the front of her cotton shift.

Mama stood at the end of Granny's bed, looking lost. "Ma, no April Fool's jokes, okay? This isn't grade school."

Through her blurry vision, Johnnie stroked the soft temples at Granny's forehead. In the blink of an eye, all of Granny's wrinkles had disappeared. As if the second she crossed over, all her worries vanished.

Another nurse and two technicians entered the room, but they stopped short when they realized Granny was gone.

The nurse helping Mama glanced over at Johnnie. "Y'all take all the time you need."

Johnnie nodded and bent to kiss her grandmother for the last time. "I'll miss you, Granny, but I'm so happy you're reunited with your son." She paused a moment to collect herself, unprepared for the ache in her throat and the deep, mournful sob that resounded from the end of the bed.

She closed her eyes against the pitiful image of Mama doubled over, clutching at a wad of blankets bunched up around Granny's feet.

Gazing back at the woman who raised her, she whispered in her ear, "Don't worry about Mama. I'll do my best to take care of her."

A second later, Johnnie could've sworn she heard Granny Opal murmur, "I know you will, my dear."

Chapter 8
The Lady Walks
June 26, 2009

The double blast of the car horn alerted Johnnie that any second Mama would come traipsing up the walkway in some outfit she'd worn forty years ago. Ever since Cade deployed, Mama honked twice before she got out of the car and climbed the front steps.

When the doorbell chimed, Brother charged up the hallway two steps ahead of Johnnie, his bark ricocheting throughout the house. "Calm down, big dog, it's only Mama."

Still, Johnnie held her breath.

Through the beveled glass door, she could see Mama primping out on the porch. Hooking her finger in Brother's collar, she answered the door.

Mama snapped her compact shut and scurried inside, bringing a wave of heat with her. "Hey, baby girl, I'm 'bout to pee my britches." She dropped her slouchy purse on the floor by the entry table and scuttled down the hall, her platform shoes clacking over the hardwood floor. "Glad I caught you at home. Thought you might be in class."

Johnnie released Brother and called after Mama, "Not on Fridays . . . not during summer school."

Closing the front door, Johnnie took a few steps, then stopped, shaking her head at the sight of Brother's rear end sticking halfway out the bathroom door. "Big dog, whaddya think you're doing?" His tail swished back and forth at the sound of her voice. "Did *someone* forget to shut the door?"

Mama's smoky voice echoed up the hall. "Lord, have mercy, sugar pup. That Route 44 went straight through me." Water splashed in the basin and the towel rack squeaked under the light switch as she went to dry her hands.

Johnnie soaked up the atmosphere like a person deprived of sunshine. Every sound meant *Mama is in the house.*

A few seconds later, she came clopping up the hallway, her bellbottoms and psychedelic tunic right out of the seventies. "Dale needs to squirt some WD-40 on that towel rack," Mama said, reaching for her purse.

Brother wiggled between them, clearly wanting attention. Johnnie rubbed his ears.

"You out running errands this morning?"

Mama's face lit up. "That's what I stopped by to tell you. I'm gonna be a working girl again." She squealed like she was sixteen and had just landed her first job.

Brother barked twice, his hackles up.

Johnnie patted him on the head. "It's okay, Brother. Mama's just excited." She hesitated. "Are you going to be working for Whit?" Guilt nipped at her conscience. The last thing a savvy businesswoman like Whit Thomas needed was a gypsy-like Mama showing up for work one day and disappearing the next.

"No, the Dooley Mansion, baby girl. I finally got a call back." Mama grinned and placed one hand on her hip. "*Ahem,* you are lookin' at the new night manager. Starting tomorrow."

The Dooley Mansion! One of the grandest homes in Portion, a two-story prairie-style house with towering chimneys and a generous front porch, built at the turn of the century. The very place where Mama hid out in the attic two years before, chain smoking and gazing out the dormer window, until Dale's work crew showed up and started the renovation. While she was growing up, Johnnie thought it was haunted.

Johnnie clasped her hands together and

smiled. "Wow, Mama, that's great. Wait till I tell Dale. His crew worked so hard on that place."

"And the best part," Mama was giddy as all get out, "I get my old room ba—" All at once she stopped talking and clamped her mouth shut as if she'd developed lockjaw.

Johnnie blinked. *Old room back? What the heck did she mean? Had she lived there in secret all those years ago when no one knew her whereabouts?* Johnnie didn't press her. Too many questions might send Mama running again. Plus, the latest news out of Afghanistan that morning had taken the fight right out of Johnnie. Another soldier had been killed, and every death hammered home the possibility that Cade could be next.

"I'll get free room and board," Mama rushed on, trying to smooth over her blunder. "No more staying at Ma's place. I can't get out of there fast enough."

Mama had lived at Granny's ever since she'd returned to Portion, and Johnnie knew she hated it, especially after helping Johnnie to care for Granny following her stroke. For Victoria Grubbs, the house, the land, and especially the cove, pointed to a crippling sadness and death of her brother she'd been running away from since she was fifteen years old. Johnnie couldn't blame her mother for wanting to move out, especially now that Granny was gone.

Mama pivoted and focused her attention on a painting D.J. created for Johnnie in 2007. *The Lady Walks* hung next to the mirror over the entry table. It depicted the ghostly image of a slender woman walking out of a cemetery, her head turned at an angle that let the viewer know she was looking over her shoulder, spooked by something or someone behind her. That someone, of course, had been Johnnie, along with Brother Dog, as they'd gone for a stroll two years ago and spotted Mama fleeing the cemetery.

Mama fingered the top of her tunic, as if playing with a string of pearls. "This painting gives me the willies, right down to them pearls looped on the fence post." She tilted her head this way and that, transfixed by her grandson's handiwork.

Johnnie breathed through her nose and exhaled without making a sound.

Mama held herself, shaking her head. "I reckon this is me in the painting. It's a little creepy if you ask me."

Johnnie swallowed, her mind scrambling for the proper response. "Why? Because your grandson captured an image of you on canvas after I told him about seeing you for the first time in twenty-three years?"

Mama turned, eyebrows raised. "Maybe. Sometimes I get the feeling Dale Junior hates me."

Johnnie caught her breath. "Hates you? He hardly knows you. How can you hate someone you hardly know?"

"Lots of people hate people they've never met. Take that kid on Main Street. He hated Whit because of the color of her skin. He hated us even more because we were with her." Mama paused and rubbed her midsection. "You got any crackers? My tummy's a little upset."

All discussion about D.J.'s painting stopped as they went into the next room. Mama plopped her purse on the braided rug in the den and Brother sniffed its contents.

Johnnie rooted around the pantry and pulled out a packet of saltines. "Munch a couple of these. Maybe you've got a bug."

Mama took a bite, talking with her mouth full. "Been feeling puny ever since I got out of bed. Sorta reminds me of morning sickness."

Morning sickness. Johnnie stopped twisting the tie on the saltine wrapper and stared at Mama. "Did you get sick a lot when you were pregnant with me?"

Mama nibbled on her cracker, and her high cheekbones seemed to droop momentarily, as if one simple question could rearrange her whole face. "I was so young. Barely fifteen. I didn't know what was happening to my body at first. I woke up one morning thinking I had the flu, but then even the smell of Ma's cooking made me queasy. When my period didn't come, well, you know the rest."

She stopped chomping and looked away, her mind locked in the past. Johnnie knew Mama was dwelling on the day that changed everything. The day that set off a tragic string of events and ended with a pregnant teenager nearly drowned in the lake and her big brother, weighed down by a cast from a broken leg, dead. He'd jumped off the dock where he was fishing, plunging into the water to save his kid sister who pitched herself in then couldn't swim.

After a moment, Mama walked over to the mantel and stared into the empty fireplace. Johnnie wished her mother could dump all her emotional baggage there and burn it.

Mama turned suddenly, her green eyes blazing with that familiar stubborn flame. "I can't change what happened. I told you that when I came back two years ago. All I can do is move forward."

Johnnie wanted to go to her, but too many memories of neglect held her back. She sat down at the farmhouse table and fiddled with the edge of a placemat. "I'm sorry. I was only curious what it was like when you carried me."

Mama went into a full-blown coughing jag. Brother scrambled up from the braided rug and hid under the kitchen table, rubbing against Johnnie's legs.

"You might wanna get that cough checked out," she suggested, reaching one hand under the table to reassure Brother as Mama doubled over, hacking into her fist.

After a few seconds, the cough subsided and she eased herself onto the leather sofa. "Just a smoker's cough, baby girl. Besides, it's not like I have health insurance. I can't *afford* to go to the doctor."

"I can cut you a check from the estate," Johnnie offered, hoping this might ease Mama's worries. Days before her death, Granny had told Johnnie, "I want a responsible person handling my money." That was why she'd made Johnnie executor.

Mama shifted on the couch and batted her lashes at Johnnie. "You been watchin' the news? Kinda spooky how Farrah Fawcett and Michael Jackson died on the same day. One OD'd and the other died of rectal cancer." Mama made a face. "I always loved Farrah. You know she was from Corpus Christie — a Texas girl like us."

Johnnie stood up, walked over, and sat down on the couch next to Mama. "Of course I remember. How could I forget?"

An image of the iconic blonde posing in a red swimsuit in front of a Mexican serape flashed before Johnnie's mind. She remembered watching episodes of *Charlie's Angels* with Mama whenever she was around, but mostly Johnnie recalled that famous poster. Because one day when Johnnie was about twelve, Mama showed up with one from the five and dime, tacked it to the bedroom wall they shared, and declared, "That's it. I'm dying my hair blonde and going on a diet."

Johnnie had been coloring a map for geography. With colored pencils fanned out in front of her, she picked up a red one and studied the tip. It was the same shade as Farrah's revealing swimsuit. Her face got all hot as she looked down at her own flat chest and chunky thighs, then over at Mama's slender but shapely figure in a halter top and cutoffs, her long auburn hair styled in an Audrey Hepburn up-do.

That day, Johnnie felt confused. If someone as beautiful as Mama could feel short-changed, then what did that say about a pudgy girl like her?

"Mama, remember when you picked me up from school and took me to the beauty parlor on South Main? You told the beautician, 'Feather our hair just like Farrah Fawcett's.' "

Mama tilted her head, her eyes gazing out into nothingness. "Lord, baby girl, that was a long time ago. Remember how she thought we were sisters?"

"Of course I remember. I cherished every moment I spent with you!" *'Cuz I never knew when you were going to up and leave me.*

Mama brushed a strand of hair from her eyes. "You talked to Whit? What does she have to say about Michael Jackson's death?"

Johnnie rubbed her nose, trying to hide her smirk. Did Mama actually assume Whit had a different spin on Michael Jackson's death, just because she was black?

"Whit's as shocked as anybody. She's sad that people will remember the way he died and not his music." Johnnie paused. "Who can forget his dance moves on 'Thriller' and 'Billie Jean'?"

Mama licked her thumb and forefinger and picked at something on her eyelashes.

"I remember when he was a little kid, back when the Jackson Five were all the rage."

Johnnie glanced at Mama's attire, right down to her platform shoes. *And you look like you stepped off the cover of one of their albums.*

"I was never a big fan," Mama said, wiggling one foot. "My girl was Karen Carpenter. Lord, could she sing!"

Mama crooned the opening lines to "We've Only Just Begun." Brother crawled out from under the table and turned his head in the direction of her gravelly voice.

Johnnie fidgeted with the piping on a sofa pillow and waited until she stopped singing. "Mama, did you know another soldier got killed in Afghanistan yesterday? Two entertainers die and it's blasted all over the news. An American soldier gets killed and it barely makes headlines."

Mama played with her plastic cigarette lighter, her expression pained. "Tell me about it. Your daddy got blown up on the seventh anniversary of President Kennedy's death. Which date you think folks are gonna remember? November 22, 1963 or the one in 1970?"

Johnnie sighed and threw down the pillow. "Famous people die and the media has a heyday. Regular folk keel over and we're lucky if we get an obit. By the way, that soldier who got killed . . . he was a young *lieutenant,* same age and rank as my daddy."

Mama's mouth twitched, and she shuddered and looked away.

Silence stretched between them. Brother plopped down near the fireplace and gnawed on a toy bone, the only sound in the room.

After a while, Mama stood up. "Brother Dog, let's you and me go outside. I need a cigarette." Brother dropped his bone, picked up a tennis ball, and followed Mama to the back door.

Johnnie headed for the computer to check her email. "You feeling any better?"

Mama turned as Brother snaked past her out the door. "Yeah, must have been too much carbonation on an empty stomach. Guess a Coke and a smoke at my age don't cut it anymore for breakfast."

With one click, Johnnie opened her email and scanned her inbox, impatiently deleting SPAM until she spotted the one special address she'd been waiting for since early May. Her heart quickened at the sender's name: Camp Cade.

For Johnnie, it was easier to think of her son as a fortress than a fragile human being made out of flesh and bone, so she'd changed his email to reflect that.

She stared at the subject line, “How’s ’Merica?” Smiling to herself at the way he butchered the name, she took a deep breath and opened his message:

Hi Mama,

D.J. told me what happened at the war memorial. Why didn’t y’all tell me about that peckerhead? Don’t keep stuff from me, okay? If something happens back home, I need to know about it. We’re headed back out on patrol so I’ll be out of pocket for a while. I’ll try to send another email next time I get to a computer and we have Internet.

Ask Daddy if he’ll send me more dip — Copenhagen Long Cut. Can you send more wipes? There’s times I don’t get a shower for weeks. Tell Callie Ann thanks for the granola bars and packets of drink mix. For now, keep sending care packages to the address I gave you before I left.

Y’all don’t worry, okay? Give Brother Dog a kiss for me.

Cade

She read his email three times before she hit *print* so she could have a hard copy. She quickly fired off a reply, telling him how much they missed him, to be on the lookout for another care package with the items he'd requested, and to keep his head down. As for the peckerhead of Portion, she said they hadn't seen hide nor hair of him since Memorial Day, but if he ever showed his face again, he was going to be sorry.

No sooner had she hit *send* than her computer dinged, alerting her that a new email had landed in her inbox. She didn't recognize the sender's address, but she knew immediately that it was from a reader. The subject line grabbed her attention:

Prejudice in Portion

Dear Miss Johnnie,

Confession: I'm the wise guy who signed his letter Jim Crow. I hope the good citizens of Portion got a yuck out of that one. At least the ones who still read the newspaper. I wonder if young people today even know what that hateful name stands for?

I'm a part-time caretaker for Mourning Glory Cemetery. It sits directly across the road from Holy Ghost Temple of Love, where I'm also the custodian. Since my letter got published in the paper, we've had a little problem with vandalism. I'm wondering if that white boy in the pickup you wrote about might have something to do with it. Got all my people buried here, so this is a bit personal.

I called the police and they sent an officer out, but so far nothing's been done about it. Lots of good folks around here like to pretend that these kinds of things don't happen anymore, especially not in Texas. But it wasn't too long ago that a brother got dragged behind a pickup in Jasper.

In the meantime, I'm keeping my eye out for vandals. I look forward to reading your next column.

Yours truly,
Mr. Roosevelt Hill
Longtime resident of "The Pasture"

Johnnie stared at the email, her bottom lip resting against the tips of her steepled fingers as her hands pressed together in prayer. *Dear Mr. Roosevelt Hill. Whoever you are. You sound like a man with a story to tell.*

As she began to formulate in her mind how to respond, the back door opened and Brother and Mama tramped in. Brother sneezed and Mama hacked up phlegm.

Johnnie glanced over her shoulder. "Mama, come quick. There's a message from Cade, along with an email from a lovely gentleman name Roosevelt Hill. He says he's a caretaker at an old black cemetery where there's been some vandalism. He wonders if the kid in the pickup truck might have something to do with it."

Mama scurried over and peered over Johnnie's shoulder, the scent of cigarette smoke lingering in the air. "Mourning Glory Cemetery, huh?" She leaned against the back of Johnnie's chair to get a closer look. "Isn't it out there by the lake? I think I heard Ma mention it a time or two."

Johnnie stared at the computer screen, afraid to move. Mama's hands rested on Johnnie's shoulders, and she closed her eyes, savoring her mother's tender touch as the warmth penetrated her cotton T-shirt. She didn't want to disturb this sacred moment that might never come again.

Chapter 9
The Window People

Two weeks later, Johnnie fired off an email she'd been composing in her head all morning.

To: Camp Cade
Date: Wednesday, July 8, 2009
Subject: Twenty years ago today. . . .

Dad and I left the house in a tizzy to head to the hospital. As I waddled out the door, I held my tight belly like a beach ball, afraid of the tiny creature punching my insides. I worried that I wouldn't love you as much as I loved your brother. D.J. was five, and I ached for him as he stood next to Granny Opal at the top of the driveway, the hem of his dinosaur shorts falling past his knees. He waved at me with a Lego man gripped in each hand. An hour later, and no time to prep, you charged out of the chute like a wild steer going full speed ahead. Even before I could catch my breath, I took one look at your dimpled cheeks and shaking fists and my heart went all a-flutter. In that instant, I had always been your mother.

When we brought you home from the hospital, D.J. met us at the door and said, "It's Cape, my baby brother." We laughed at his mispronunciation of your name. I know you've heard this story a dozen times growing up, but I've been thinking about it all morning. It hit me now how I've always associated the word "cape" with superheroes. You've always been a superhero in my eyes. You don't have to prove yourself by doing anything heroic. Just come home safe.

Happy Birthday, Son!

Love,
Mom

Later that day, Whit rummaged through Johnnie's computer desk searching for a piece of paper to scrawl out a note. "You'd think a writer would have a packet of sticky notes handy. And what do you want me to say, anyway? That you're too chicken to answer the door?"

In her sports bra and gym shorts, Johnnie

glanced up from the kitchen island where she was assembling spinach and turkey bacon salads, a paring knife poised in midair. "Very funny. Just say we changed our mind. That without a callback number, we couldn't cancel in time." She went back to slicing green onions, occasionally peeking over her shoulder out the window above the sink for the sight of some strange car or pickup gliding up next to the curb. "Oh, and say we are so sorry for the inconvenience."

Whit cocked an eyebrow. "*We,* huh?" she joked, then pulled out another drawer and rifled through its contents. "You mean *you,* Ladybug."

Johnnie grinned sheepishly at her friend, clad in canvas walking shoes and summer sweats. The two had gone power walking earlier at a new rec center in town because the July heat and humidity made it miserable to exercise outdoors. With Johnnie between summer school sessions, she didn't have to dash off to class. Since Whit had hired a college girl to fill in on occasion, she had time for a quick bite to eat before she changed clothes and headed back to the shop.

Johnnie glanced at her watch. "They'll be here in fifteen minutes."

Whit held up a blank index card. "This'll have to do. Now to find the Scotch tape."

While Whit scribbled out the excuse, Johnnie sprinkled black olive slices on each salad and wondered if Cade had received his birthday message. If his platoon was out on patrol, he might not get it for days. This was Cade's first birthday away from home, and she realized it was probably harder on her than on him.

No wonder she had forgotten about the window people until it was too late.

The smooth-talking woman had phoned the house yesterday around seven a.m., right after Dale left for work. Still half-asleep, Johnnie had stumbled into the kitchen and glanced at the caller ID: Private Caller. She'd plucked up the receiver, halfway hoping to hear Cade on the other end. Instead, a woman plowed through her spiel, announcing they'd be on Merriweather Street the next day, washing windows for the low price of ninety-nine dollars per household. Hesitating, Johnnie started to hang up, but then her gaze caught the morning sunlight filtering through the filmy windows in the den. "Does that include the insides and screens?" And before she knew it, she'd said, "Yes," to the stranger on the other end. "See you at one o'clock." About two seconds into her first jolt of coffee, Johnnie realized she didn't catch the name of the business, and with no callback number, she couldn't call to cancel. Red flags went up. *Were they genuine window washers or scam artists coming to case the joint?*

But then the day got away from her and she forgot all about it until she was hoofing it around the gym earlier and noted the sparkling windows on one end of the building. "Oh crud!" she blurted, stopping midstride. "I forgot about the window people." Five minutes later, Whit's Saturn lurched to a halt behind Johnnie's Suburban at the top of the drive, and they scrambled inside to come up with a plan.

"Lord, girlie, this is enough to bring on a hot flash." Whit pushed up from the computer desk and fanned herself with the index card. "How's this?" She waved the note with a flourish. "Dear window-cleaning experts, we regret to inform you —" A car honked twice out front, and Whit stopped reading and glanced at Johnnie. "Is that them?"

Johnnie slammed the fridge with her foot. "Sounds like Mama. She always honks twice." Brother's high-pitched yelp on the other side of the back gate bounced up the east side of the house, an indicator that someone had parked in the driveway.

A few seconds later, Mama tapped at the double French doors leading out to the portico. The same doors Dale had replaced a few years back after the house got burglarized while they were on vacation in Florida. Still clutching a bottle of vinaigrette dressing, Johnnie went to let her in.

Mama held a platter of what appeared to be rocks slathered in green icing. She bustled inside. "Cupcakes in honor of our soldier boy's birthday. I baked them right after I got off my shift this morning."

Johnnie's mouth fell open. Breathing in the scent of buttercream frosting, she tried to conceal her shock that her mother had gone out of her way to do something nice. "Well, they sure smell good."

Mama glanced at her, and for a split second, their eyes locked. Then Mama looked away and laughed. "Let's hope they taste better than they look. Guess I forgot the baking powder. You know Ma's spinnin' in her grave." She balanced the platter on one hip and jutted her chin at the door. "You expecting company? There's an old Plymouth station wagon out front with a ladder strapped to the luggage rack."

"Crap, they're here." Johnnie glanced at Whit, who still held the note in her hand.

Whit made a face and flicked the index card nervously against the tips of her manicured nails. "Guess it's too late to tape this note to the door."

Mama's eyes darted back and forth between the two women. "What's going on? Who are they?"

"It's a long story," Johnnie hissed, peeking out the kitchen window. A husky woman in workpants trudged up the walkway, a rag dangling from her back pocket. Even from this distance, Johnnie could see a large gap between the woman's front teeth. It was hard to tell her age. A middle-aged man about Dale's size brought up the rear. He wore a tool belt strapped to his waist, and Johnnie zoomed in on the box cutter on his belt, the same kind Dale kept handy for scraping residue off surfaces.

Mama scooped up a blob of icing and sucked the tip of her finger. "Hope they're not them *Irish Travelers.* I hear they prey on old people."

"Did you see any kind of advertisement or the name of their business on the side of their car?" Johnnie caught a whiff of Mama's last cigarette. The one she probably stubbed out in the driveway, leaving the lipstick-smudged butt for Johnnie to pick up later.

Mama licked her front teeth. "Nope. I

didn't see nothing on that station wagon but bird crap and dents."

The doorbell rang and everybody froze but Brother Dog, whining and prancing out on the deck. He scratched at the back door, wanting in.

Johnnie figured he was hot, but she'd left him a bowl of ice water on the deck. After a while he would get fed up and rest under the shade of the big oak where the kids' tree house rotted away, plank by plank.

Whit tiptoed toward the back door. "You want me to let him in?" she whispered, as if the people on the porch could hear her.

Johnnie shook her head. "He'll make a beeline to the front door and scare the big heck out of them."

"Exactly," Whit mouthed. "Then they'll leave and you won't have to deal with them."

The doorbell rang again, followed by a loud knock.

"They saw me come in," Mama said. "They know someone's home."

Johnnie thought about the man with the box cutter and how it would only take a second for him to slice open her throat. Then he'd grab Mama and Whit while the woman ransacked the house and Brother barked helplessly out back, unable to defend his family since he wasn't allowed inside.

Another knock, this one a polite rat-a-tat-tat.

And then Johnnie's brain switched gears. Visions of poverty-stricken families appeared before her mind's eye — all those desperate people who filed through the food pantry during her tenure as a volunteer. She could still see the little brown-haired girl in a tattered yellow dress as she twirled before Johnnie and said, "You're pretty."

Maybe they're really hard up. "What if I give them a twenty and send them on their way? It should at least cover gas." Before Mama and Whit could say anything, Johnnie dashed over to the computer desk, snatched a bill from her wallet, and headed for the entryway.

Pulling open the front door, she stepped out onto the welcome mat.

Hot steamy air and a woman with an overzealous smile greeted her, her teeth rotting from lack of dental care or drug abuse. "Miz Kitchen? We're here to wash your windows."

Johnnie had seen her type among the door-to-door solicitors that used to roam through the neighborhood selling items you could live without. They all had the same look — too eager to please. A face that was hard to say no to.

Already damp with sweat, Johnnie took a deep breath and offered a kind but firm smile. "I'm so sorry. I tried to cancel yesterday, but you didn't leave a callback number."

The woman blinked in confusion, and then her smile flattened into a hardened grimace. "You had us drive all the way out here for nothin'?" She swatted at a pesky mosquito.

The man stood at the bottom of the steps, his thumbs in his tool belt, eyeballing Johnnie.

"Ma'am, I'm sorry. You didn't leave a callback number," Johnnie repeated, clenching her left fist with the money as she tried to explain. "I had no way to cancel since my caller ID said only 'Private Caller.' "

The woman leaned forward and scowled, her round face reddening by the second. "Then why did you say *yes*?" she shrieked, inching closer.

Johnnie's hackles went up. She glanced at the man, but he made no attempt to move. He stood there watching in silence.

Desperate to explain, she measured her words carefully. "Look, ma'am, you cold-called me at seven o'clock in the morning. I was half-asleep. I hadn't had my coffee yet. The only reason I answered the phone is because my youngest son is a soldier in a war zone . . . and I thought he might be calling."

The woman jabbed her finger at Johnnie, less than two feet away. "I don't care about your son," she spat, her tone cold and heartless. "I don't give a shit if he's in a war zone."

And that's when Johnnie snapped.

The verbal missile slammed into her heart, fracturing her manners and good will.

Shaking, she put her right hand up like a shield and fired back with all the ammo her voice could muster, "My son is over there, putting his *life* on the line for people like *you*!"

The woman fumed, yelling louder, "I don't give a hoot about your friggin' son."

In her exasperation, the woman said the one thing that could harden Johnnie's heart. She desecrated what Johnnie held most dear: her son.

Any chance of Johnnie forking over the twenty was gone.

Whit stepped out on the porch, nudging Johnnie on the shoulder. "Ladybug, come back inside."

The woman smirked, and thrust her double chin at Whit. "Yer hired help?"

Whit's head snapped up and her nostrils

flared. "Excuse me?"

Johnnie sucked in her breath, shocked at the woman's snub. Without taking her eyes off the intruder, Johnnie grappled over her shoulder for Whit's hand, giving it a reassuring squeeze.

Mama came out on the porch, carrying the cupcakes. "Would you folks care for a snack? I baked these in honor of my grandson's birthday, but he can't be here to *enjoy* them because he's in a foreign country getting *shot at*!"

The woman took one look at the green blobs then snarled at Mama, "I don't want your darn cupcakes, lady, and I don't give a rat's ass about your grandson."

Mama's eyes narrowed to slits. Brushing past the woman, she shoved the platter toward Whit, muttered something under her breath, and stalked off around the side of the house. Whit stood holding the platter, her lips puckered to the side.

By now, the man had backed away and stood in the middle of the yard, yelling, "Come on, Carla, they ain't worth it."

The woman turned toward him, throwing her hands up in the air.

Johnnie appealed to her one more time, telling her how sorry she was. She offered them water, but the woman kept shrieking,

"We came all this flipping way for *nothing*!"

In that moment, Johnnie realized this was the couple's only stop in the neighborhood, and they probably didn't have a large customer base, at least not in Portion. As her gaze darted back and forth between them, she saw herself through their eyes. She was some privileged, middle-aged woman who had time and money to work out at a gym, had funds to pay other people to do her dirty work. A part of her felt sorry for the couple, but the woman had crossed the line, first, when she said, "I don't care about your son," and then she was so rude to Whit.

Out of the corner of her eye, Johnnie spotted Mama trooping back around the side of the house, a soldier scarecrow on a stake slung over her shoulder. This was the scarecrow Whit, Callie Ann, and Johnnie made out of rags and a surplus uniform two years ago October when Cade shipped off to Army basic training. Johnnie had hauled it out of the storage unit under the portico the other day and forgot to put it back. Mama must have seen it propped against the side of the house when she pulled into the driveway.

Without saying a word, Mama paraded past and stopped abruptly at the edge of the flower garden that skirted the porch. With a strength that belied her wispy frame, she shoved the stake into the ground, and the soldier scarecrow sprang to attention, his camouflage arms dangling by his side.

Mama stood back and dusted her hands, shouting in their direction, "Y'all need to show some respect. You are standing on hallowed ground."

The woman looked at Mama like she was crazy.

"My daughter's daddy was killed in Vietnam. And now her boy is over fighting the Taliban." She stopped to catch her breath. "Sergeant Scarecrow here don't take too kindly to trespassers and folks talking trash about the military."

"You people are nuts!" the woman exclaimed. "Besides, your daughter *invited* us here."

"Only because you cold-called me at seven in the morning," Johnnie seethed.

Whit floated down the steps, still holding the platter. "Miss Victoria, I think the sergeant is missing something." She leaned over and whispered in Mama's ear.

Mama broke out in a sly grin. "Good idea." She snatched a bobby pin from her hair, bent the scarecrow's right arm at an angle, and pinned his hand to his forehead in a salute.

"Smartass!" the woman hissed, speaking loud enough for everyone to hear and adding the N-word for good measure. Despite her girth, she scrambled quickly down the steps past Whit and headed toward the car.

The wounded look on Whit's face triggered something primal in Johnnie. She figured Whit might have endured this vulgar language as a child, but it was 2009 and Johnnie was shocked by the woman's foul mouth. Shaking her fist, she dashed down the steps two at a time and chased after the woman. "Get off my property, before I call the cops."

At the hood of the station wagon, the woman whirled, still cursing, and spit in Johnnie's direction. "Screw you! And your little colored friend, too. Get *her* to wash your windows."

Johnnie thrust the crumpled twenty at the man. "I'm sorry for your trouble. This should cover your gas."

He pocketed the cash, jerked the passenger door open, and glared at Johnnie. "May God have *mercy* on you people."

He slammed the door and the woman cranked up the motor. It died once before it started up again and the car lurched forward.

Trembling, Johnnie stood at the curb as Mama rushed by, carrying the platter of cupcakes. Covering her mouth, she watched Mama run into the middle of the street near the spot where young Edwin Marvel was hit and killed by a vacuum salesman late for an appointment. Cocking her arm back like a pitcher, Mama lobbed one cupcake grenade after another toward the fleeing station wagon as it sputtered away, the muffler dragging the asphalt and sending sparks into the air.

Moments later, Whit sidled up next to Johnnie and patted her on the arm. "You okay, ladybug?"

Johnnie nodded, leaning against Whit's shoulder. "I'm sorry about what that lady said, what she called you." She didn't want to say it, much less think it.

Whit breathed through her nose, exhaling through her mouth. Flinging a hand in the air, she admired her nails, filed to perfection and painted the same plum as her lips. "These hands have done their share of hard work. . . ."

Johnnie held Whit's hand up to her cheek. "You have the hands of Jesus," she said, before glancing down at Whit's sweatpants and tennis shoes, and then up at her regal profile. Her skin glistened in the heat. "That lady doesn't know a saint when she sees one."

Whit elbowed her, and they leaned into each other as they waited for Mama to calm down.

Spent, Mama turned and started for the house, tucking the empty platter under one arm while she swiped her brow with the other. Her hands were covered in green icing, and her eyes flashed a warning: *You don't insult my daughter and friends and not expect a fight.*

Johnnie flicked away a tear that dribbled out of nowhere. As the three women went to go inside, Johnnie hesitated at the bottom step. Gazing at the soldier scarecrow standing guard, she came to one conclusion: *Sometimes in the middle of a calm day, we create our own wars. And under certain circumstances, those wars are justified.*

Chapter 10
In Broad Daylight

From: Mom
To: Camp Cade
Date: July 20, 2009
Subject: The Moon

Dear Son,

As I write this on my new laptop, Brother Dog is stretched out on the deck, soaking up rays. It's about a hundred degrees in the shade. The heat makes his joints feel better. The older he gets, the more time he spends in the sun. The cicadas are abuzz, and I can smell that new barbecue joint up on Main Street. Maybe that's why Brother wanted to come outside, to get a whiff of smoked meat.

A chalky half-moon hangs high in a cloudless blue sky. I'm not sure why, but I've always found the sight of the day-time moon reassuring. Today is the fortieth anniversary of the first moon landing. I was five years old when Apollo 11 touched down on the Sea of Tranquility. Grandpa Grubbs, Granny, Mama, and I huddled around the black and white TV when Neil Armstrong climbed down that ladder and set foot on the moon. Talk about boots on the ground.

I turned to Mama and asked, "Can Uncle Johnny see the astronauts from Heaven?" You would've thought I'd ask if the Martians had landed. Mama looked horrified, and Grandpa Grubbs told me to hush, but not Granny Opal. She patted my knee and mumbled something about how all God's angels were watching over the astronauts and that we needed to pray for their families back here on earth.

Since you're nine and a half hours ahead, I bet the moon is aglow in the night sky where you are. If you're able to peek outside and see it, know that I'm looking at it too.

Saw on the news where the Taliban captured some private from Idaho who went missing a few weeks ago. The Army's not saying much. There's speculation that he either walked away from his unit or he got snatched. You've always been a team player so stay close to your buddies. Now's not the time to go solo.

Love you to the moon and back,

Mom and Brother Dog

Chapter 11
To Glory
Mid-August

Johnnie pressed the phone to her ear. Mama sounded rattled as she said, "I need you to meet me out by the old turnoff to Glory. Just down the road from Ma's place."

Glory. The black settlement now buried under Portion Lake.

To Johnnie, the town had existed in name only on a crude wooden sign with an arrow pointing into a grove of trees off Lakeside Drive. Once, when they were driving to church in Grandpa's Studebaker, Granny had commented as they passed the sign, "It's a shame those poor colored folks lost their homes when the lake came in." That morning Johnnie sat in the backseat, clutching her coin purse in her white-gloved hands, while Grandpa snorted, "The government took care of them. Got them all resettled over at the Pasture."

Granny had twisted in her seat and glared at Grandpa. "An entire community squeezed onto four tiny acres and no mule. That's not what I call being generous."

That long-ago conversation vanished when Mama said, "Johnnie girl, did you hear me? I need you to come PDQ." Then Mama went off on a coughing jag.

What kind of crisis did Mama have now? Ever since Victoria Grubbs had returned to Portion, it seemed to Johnnie that the roles were reversed and Johnnie was always dropping everything to help Mama.

Johnnie had just stepped inside Whit's Whimsies when Mama called from her cellphone. The last thing Johnnie wanted to do was cancel her plans. She and Whit were going to enjoy a glass of wine at the Grapevine and celebrate Whit's grand opening. As Johnnie gazed past the display of window chimes, silver crosses, and pottery by local artisans, Whit walked her last customer to the door and flipped the sign from open to closed.

"Be with you in a minute, ladybug," she said, seeing that Johnnie was occupied.

While Johnnie waited for Mama to stop coughing, she caught her reflection in a large antique mirror. In her haste to leave class at Portion Community College, she hadn't checked her appearance. As soon as she got off the phone with Mama, she'd apply a fresh coat of cinnamon-colored lip gloss, which matched her hair, swept up in a pretty comb. A peacock-blue gown with a plunging neckline caught her eye, and she pictured herself modeling it for Dale, turning this way and that, showing off a hint of cleavage.

Finally, Mama stopped coughing.

Turning away from the mirror, Johnnie tried to keep the irritation out of her voice. "What's wrong, Mama? Did the El Camino break down again?"

Mama sighed, and for a second Johnnie thought she'd crossed the line. Mama had bought her El Camino for a bargain, but it had already left her stranded by the side of the road twice. Both times Johnnie went to her rescue.

Mama cleared her throat. "Johnnie girl, Callie Ann's been in an accident —"

"An accident!" Johnnie's throat went dry. An earthquake rocked her heart, and she reached for the nearest shelf to keep from falling. For nearly three months, she'd been dreading the sight of a green Army staff car creeping up to her curb. Preparing herself for the worst news of her life, the kind that would knock her into a sinkhole she couldn't crawl out of. But a phone call from Mama, telling her Callie Ann had been in an accident? *That* she wasn't prepared for.

"She got run off the road. Hit the old hanging tree just past the turnoff."

Johnnie dropped into a tufted, gold-velvet wingchair, hugging her purse and trying to process what Mama had said.

She heard herself calling for Whit to take the phone.

Whit scrambled across the dark hardwood floor and plucked the phone out of Johnnie's trembling hand. Pacing circles around the gold wingchair, Whit stopped every few seconds to change direction as she talked. Even after a long day at the shop, she looked like she'd just stepped out of the pages of a fashion magazine. Her manicured fingernails were painted the same coral as the flower pattern on her long flowing dress, and the matching coral polish on her brown toes peeked through spiky heeled sandals.

By focusing on Whit, Johnnie forced herself to breathe through her nose.

After a moment, Whit interrupted her conversation with Mama and relayed pertinent information to Johnnie.

"Callie Ann's fine . . . a little shaken up. She and Brother had just left Granny Opal's. They were helping your mama sort through Granny's things. Your mama stayed to lock up. She didn't see what happened."

Johnnie's teeth chattered when she spoke, and her voice came out all jittery. "Was she in Granny's car?"

Whit nodded. "Your mama says to bring a couple of blankets. Callie Ann is freezing. Probably from shock."

Johnnie pulled herself out of the chair. "I've got a couple of old quilts in the back of the Suburban."

At that moment, Whit averted her eyes and lowered her voice. "Oh . . . I see. Okay, we're on the way." She hung up the phone and handed it to Johnnie. "Give me your keys. I'm driving."

They locked up the shop and raced for the Suburban, parked half a block away.

Whit jumped in behind the steering wheel and fiddled with the keys in the ignition. Johnnie strapped on her seatbelt and glanced at her best friend. "Haul ass!"

As Whit sped north on Main, she stared straight ahead, not looking at Johnnie. "Ladybug," her voice sounded strained, "your mama said for us to stop by the house and grab a large garbage bag."

Johnnie frowned. "A garbage bag? What for?"

Whit took a sharp right at Merriweather and stepped on the gas, acting like she hadn't heard the question. They flew by the same cottages and bungalows Johnnie had seen for nearly a quarter of a century, many of them restored by Dale's company. But with a son at war and a daughter in an accident, Johnnie understood that her comfortable neighborhood — lined with leafy pecans and sturdy oaks — could never offer true shelter.

As they approached the charming red bungalow where the soldier scarecrow now pulled duty 24/7, two thoughts hammered through her mind: *Who would want to hurt my baby girl?* And *what was that about a hanging tree*?

CHAPTER 12
THE TURNOFF

"You wouldn't lie to me, would you, Whit . . . about Callie Ann?" Johnnie rocked back and forth in the passenger seat, the strap of her seatbelt straining against her chest each time she pitched forward. Her feet slid on the garbage bag she'd stashed on the floorboard.

Whit kept her gaze on the narrow blacktop, the same road Johnnie had traveled over her entire lifetime, back and forth from her grandparents' home out by the lake into Portion proper. "Johnnie, how long have we been friends? Since Callie Ann was a baby, right?"

Johnnie kneaded the spot between her eyes. *Had it been that long?*

Her mind flashed to the old Cotton's Grocery Store off Redbud Lane. She'd left two-week-old Callie Ann screaming her head off at home with Dale and the boys after supper while she dashed to the store to get diapers and milk. As she approached the checkout, feeling frumpy in sweatpants and stinking of spit-up, Johnnie stopped short. The most exotic woman she'd ever seen was chatting up the pimple-faced cashier. She was wearing an orange and red sundress. Smelling as sweet and soothing as her voice, the woman turned to Johnnie and smiled, "Hi there, ladybug. Are you having a blessed day?"

Before Johnnie could find her voice, she burst into tears. Then the stranger in the sundress handed her a tissue and glanced at the diapers and baby wipes on the conveyer belt. "Whoa, sister girl, looks like you could use a break. Can I buy you a cup of coffee?"

Johnnie blew her nose into the tissue and joked, "I'd rather have wine." Right there, in front of the teenage cashier, both women giggled like truant schoolgirls.

Seventeen years later, Whit held both hands on the steering wheel as she navigated the curves of Lakeside Drive. "Ladybug, your mama said Callie Ann has a knot on her forehead from hitting the steering wheel, but other than that. . . ."

Johnnie pushed her hands against the dashboard as if she could block some blunt trauma, an emotional asteroid hurtling straight for her heart.

Whit had the AC cranked on high, but Johnnie rolled down her window, letting warm air brush her face. Closing her eyes, she breathed in the smells of early evening, catching a whiff of Portion Lake, hidden beyond the trees.

When she opened her eyes, they were passing the old wooden sign that read TO GLORY. They weren't far from the cove where her life had begun and the place in the road where Callie Ann's life could have ended.

"Look, there's your mama now."

Puffing on a smoke, Victoria leaned against the El Camino parked a few feet off the road. Johnnie watched as Mama stubbed out the butt with the heel of her shoe and went to flag them down. The crumpled front of Granny's Lincoln rested against the trunk of a massive oak tree, the driver's door ajar.

Whit eased the Suburban onto the shoulder of weeds and gravel. Johnnie grabbed the quilts and was halfway out the door before the vehicle came to a stop.

"Mama, where's Callie Ann?"

Victoria took the quilts and gestured with her head toward the El Camino. "I put her in the cab of my truck in case the dang thing blew up. Ol' Abe was hissin' and steamin' and leakin' body fluids when I got here."

Abe? Mama's lame attempt at humor, probably to cover her fear.

Late afternoon sunlight filtered through the trees. Two deep ruts cut through the tall grass where the Lincoln left the road before it slammed into the tree.

Whit approached, the large garbage bag wedged under one arm. She nodded at Victoria then glanced around, clasping her hands together and mumbling, "Merciful Lord."

On the other side of the bug-spattered windshield, Callie Ann stared out at all of them as if in a daze.

Johnnie opened the passenger door. Years of cigarette smoke and old car smell wafted out into the late afternoon. "Sis, what happened? You okay?" Johnnie took one of the quilts from Mama and draped it over Callie Ann's bare legs.

Callie Ann's teeth chattered as she attempted to talk. "I thought it was Cade. For a split second, I forgot he was deployed."

Johnnie caught her breath. "Why did you think it was your brother?"

Callie Ann rearranged the quilt on her lap. "Because the truck looked like Cade's. Except it had fat tires."

Mama made a funny noise, like she was choking. "What did that fella look like?"

Callie Ann shook her head. "I didn't get a good look. I only saw him for a sec as he tried to pass. But he had on a cowboy hat and sunglasses."

Johnnie swallowed. The kid from the war memorial.

Whit leaned into the cab and patted Callie Ann on the hand. "Sister girl, did you see a Confederate flag on the back of that truck?"

Callie Ann glanced up at Whit, both of them sniffling. "I don't know, Miss Whit. It all happened so fast. One second Brother Dog and I were driving along, his head hanging out the window, enjoying his ride. The next second this big truck comes out of nowhere and starts riding my bumper. The guy kept blasting his horn and Brother went crazy. The last thing I remember, before I hit the tree, was reaching to calm Brother. . . ."

And that's when you lost control, Johnnie thought. Despite the heat, she shivered and went to wrap herself in the extra quilt, but noticed Mama shaking in a thin blouse and said, "Here, Mama, put this on."

Victoria started to object, but Johnnie insisted. Victoria Grubbs took no time shrugging into the faded quilt, a bargain at the church's annual rummage sale.

Callie Ann brushed hair out of her eyes, and for the first time Johnnie saw the knot on her daughter's forehead. "When I looked up, Brother wasn't there."

Johnnie swallowed hard, a new kind of fear clutching her throat. She glanced over at the passenger side of Granny's car. The seat was empty. "Wait, where's Brother?"

Callie Ann stared straight ahead, her fingers clawing her forehead. "He's over there." Her voice sounded slow and flat, like she'd been drugged.

Johnnie scanned the area, the shadows growing deeper as dusk approached. "Where?"

Mama tapped her foot and seemed to study something on the ground. "He's next to the tree. Lying on a patch of bluebonnets."

Johnnie's gaze followed Mama's words until she saw a dark clump on a blanket of blue.

Mama tried to stop her, but Johnnie broke away, running through tall weeds and wild grass until she found him.

He was lying on his side on a bed of the prettiest bluebonnets Johnnie had ever seen, his legs stretched out as if he was resting. His eyes were open and his tongue drooped out one side of his mouth, his teeth exposed in a forever grin. Except for a few droplets of blood around the crown of his head, he looked peaceful.

Bending, Johnnie patted him gently on his side, and then kissed the top of his head. His fur felt like velvet, but his body was starting to cool. "Brother," she tried to say. It came out all wrong. She sensed someone beside her.

Whit teetered in her strappy sandals around the border of wildflowers that cradled Brother's body, her spiky heels digging into the weeds. "Bluebonnets have been gone for months. These are growing out of season. It's like they sprung up overnight."

Callie Ann came up behind them and offered to share the quilt with Johnnie and Whit. "I'm sorry, Mom. It's my fault."

"It was an accident, Sis." But that boy in the pickup is going to pay.

"When I realized Brother wasn't with me, I looked out the window . . . and that's when I saw them — seven little black girls holding hands in a circle around him."

Whit frowned and looked over her shoulder toward the road. "Say what? Were those little girls out here all by themselves?"

Callie Ann shrugged. "I don't know, I didn't see anyone else with them. But when

I called to them for help, they turned and walked away."

Mama scissored a cigarette between her shaky fingers. "Which way did they go?"

Callie Ann pointed toward a thick grove of trees. "They went that way."

Mama stared hard at Callie Ann. "But there's nothing on the other side of those trees but the lake."

Johnnie and Mama exchanged glances. Was Callie Ann seeing things? How long had she been knocked out?

Johnnie examined her daughter's forehead. "Sis, I think you need to see a doctor. Does your head hurt? What if you have a concussion?"

Callie Ann brushed Johnnie's hand away. "I'm fine, Mom. I just want to take Brother home."

Mama fidgeted with her lighter and lit another cigarette. She held the smoke in her lungs for a long time, like she was thinking hard. After a moment she looked over at Johnnie and said, "Guess we better call 911."

"Wait, you haven't called them yet?"

Mama put her hand on her hip. "The last thing I need is getting hassled by one of Portion's finest."

Johnnie went to punch in 911 on her cell.

"We at least need to have the EMTs check Callie Ann's vitals and make sure she's okay."

Still holding the large garbage bag, Whit asked, "You want me to call Dale and have him give us a hand?"

Johnnie took a deep breath. "Tell him to meet us at the house. We can handle this."

They huddled around Brother's body, waiting for the EMTs and the wrecker.

As the light started to fade, Johnnie glanced at the big oak that Callie Ann hit. She'd wanted to ask Mama why she called it the hanging tree, but now was not the time.

Chapter 13
The Funeral

It was dark by the time they pulled into the driveway. A gentle breeze picked up, and Johnnie was grateful for the hint of cooler air as they faced the unpleasant task ahead.

Under the glow of the porch light, Dale lifted Brother's body from the back of the Suburban and carried him to the front porch. Kneeling, he placed Brother near the rocking chair where he liked to curl up and nap. While Johnnie clung to Mama and Callie Ann, Whit scurried into the house and brought out several small votive candles. She placed them around Brother's lifeless body and lit them, then they all gathered to murmur their goodbyes.

Callie Ann dropped in a heap on the porch and sobbed into the blanketed mound.

"I'll play with you again someday."

Whit sniffled and blew her nose. "You know I'm not much of a dog person, but

Brother was the only dog I ever let slobber all over my feet."

Whit's remark brought a quiet chuckle among the group. Johnnie recalled all the times Brother would rest his head on Whit's manicured feet, her strappy sandals kicked to the side.

Johnnie put on a brave face for her friend and offered a weak smile. "That silly boy worshipped you, Whit."

Dale stood, feet apart. His right hand covered his left fist just below his belt buckle. After clearing his throat, he said in a scratchy voice, "You were a good watch dog. The squirrels and I will miss you."

Mama stared at her feet, avoiding eye contact. "I was just getting to know you." Her voice cracked, and she fumbled with the buttons on her ruffled blouse — one of Granny's garments she'd taken from the house.

A neighbor dog barked in the distance, and Johnnie looked up, half-expecting to see a chocolate Lab bounding up the steps. "Our sweetest boy," she whispered, resting her chin on her clasped hands. She already missed the feel of him brushing against her leg and the way he let her rub the top of his head, as if he understood that all of life's answers could be found in that firm spot between his ears.

An owl hooted from a nearby tree and Johnnie shivered, despite the warmth of the worn cardigan she'd retrieved from the backseat of Granny's Lincoln before the wrecker hauled it away. For a second, Johnnie could've sworn she heard the boys calling, "Brother, Brother, come chase us." But of course that was ridiculous because the boys were grown, and Brother was gone.

After Dale went around back to start digging Brother's grave, Johnnie left the others in charge to scrape together a late supper. Under the beam of a floodlight mounted under the eaves, she watched from the deck as Dale hunched over a shovel, his strong back and muscular arms already tired from a full day's work. And yet he dug and dug and dug. She was acutely aware of the thud of metal hitting earth, the sound of his heavy breathing as the pile of fresh dirt grew higher and higher.

Even from where she sat, Johnnie could smell the dampness of the hole, the same pungent scent she remembered before Granny was lowered into her grave. Johnnie started to get up, to go in search of one of Brother's doggie toys to bury with him, when the back door opened and the aroma of cooked food wafted through the air.

"Hey, Sis, what's for supper?"

Callie Ann clomped across the deck in Granny Opal's red cowboy boots and dropped into a chair next to Johnnie. "Fried okra, mashed potatoes, and fried chicken. Whit said we need comfort food, but who can eat at a time like this?" She sighed, the toes of her boots tapping against each other.

Johnnie glanced at the boots, then into Callie Ann's bloodshot eyes. "Remind me to pay Whit back for the takeout."

Callie Ann nodded, and then stared at her dad, bent over the hole. "How could Brother be alive one second, his head hanging out the window, so happy to be going for a ride, and dead the next second? I was talking to him, telling him to hang on. The next thing I remember, I lifted my head off the steering wheel and the passenger seat was empty. That's when I looked out the window." Callie Ann paused, trying to choke back her grief. When she resumed talking, her voice came out all gravelly. "How are we going to tell Cade? Guess there's no nice way to deliver bad news from home to a war zone."

Johnnie hugged herself tighter in Granny's sweater. "We'll figure it out. Whatever we do, we can't lie to him."

"I should tell him, Mom. If I'd left Brother

home today, he'd still be alive."

"It's not your fault, Callie Ann. You got run off the road." Anger and fear churned in Johnnie's gut.

Callie Ann rubbed her earlobe just like Granny used to do. "D.J. called me a few minutes ago. He's sad about Brother, but glad I'm okay." She paused, her eyes cast downward. "Mom, D.J. wants to know why we never removed the Obama/Biden bumper sticker."

Johnnie nodded, not at all surprised that her oldest son would bring this up now. "Did you tell him?"

Callie Ann stared at the red cowboy boots in defiance. "Yeah, I told him the same thing I told Dad. Not my job."

Johnnie couldn't help but feel proud of her daughter, yet she also felt guilty. Dale tried to warn them it might cause more problems. *Now look what happened.*

Callie Ann stood, reached into a back pocket of her denim shorts, and removed a small white envelope. "I found this note tucked inside Granny's boots today when I was cleaning out her closet." Callie Ann handed Johnnie a white note card embossed with the letter O.

Under the glow of the floodlights, Johnnie recognized Granny Opal's uneven scrawl.

The note was written in two colors of ink, as if Granny started out with a black pen, then changed her mind halfway through and purposely switched to red:

> To my great granddaughter, Callie Ann Kitchen:
>
> If you're reading this, my dear, I've kicked the bucket. Unlike the song made famous by Nancy Sinatra, these boots aren't made for walking. They're made for more important things: to ward off haints, summon the saints, or when you need to feel brave.
>
> All you have to do is believe.
>
> All my love,
> Granny Opal

By the time Johnnie finished reading the note, Callie Ann had stepped off the deck and was halfway across the yard. She turned to gaze at her mother. "I was wearing these boots when I hit the tree. I wasn't afraid."

Johnnie gaped at her daughter, her dove gray eyes so bloodshot with grief. Maybe by morning they would be clear again.

Granny's words "summon the saints" rolled through Johnnie's mind.

"Sis, you know those little black girls you said you saw?"

Callie Ann bowed her head for a moment, her hands clasped together like she was praying. "They were glowing, Mom, and singing hymns."

Johnnie felt the hairs on the back of her neck stand on end.

"And one more thing, Mom. Before Granny V got there, I could'a sworn I saw Brother Dog get up and follow them."

Chapter 14
Portion Telegraph
"Roundtable with Johnnie Kitchen"

We buried my dog last week. It could have easily been my daughter. She was run off the road right before dusk, out by the old turnoff to Glory. A young man driving a jacked-up gray pickup and fitting the same description as the driver who desecrated the war memorial back in May came up behind my daughter's car and started blasting his horn. My daughter lost control of the vehicle and slammed into a giant oak at the edge of a grove off Lakeside Drive.

Brother Dog was hurled through the open passenger window and killed. We hope he didn't suffer. My daughter dreamed about him last night. She said he stood at the edge of a clearing and waited for her to come chase him — like when he was a puppy.

After my husband went to bed that night, exhausted after a long day of work and digging the hole, my daughter and I sat vigil by Brother's grave. With flashlights in hand, we swapped stories about him through the night. Fearing she might have a slight concussion from hitting her head on the steering wheel, I wanted to keep her awake since she'd refused to go the emergency room after the accident. After much cajoling the next morning, she agreed to see a doctor. He said she's lucky she walked away with nothing more than a knot on her noggin. The driver of the wrecker, who hauled off my granny's Lincoln, said that between the seatbelt and the long front end, that old car probably saved my daughter's life.

The next day, not even twenty-four hours after we laid Brother to rest, my husband, my daughter, and I dipped our hands in his water bowl as we walked along the fence line in the backyard, sprinkling droplets here and there like holy water on all his favorite places. Then we sat down and tackled the chore we'd been avoiding all day.

How do you tell a son deployed to a war zone that a member of his family has died? A four-legged member, but a member all the same. You can't call the Red Cross, so you do the only thing you know how to do — you write him a letter via email. We heard later that he got so upset he tore off his helmet and threw it against the side of the communication shack. A battle buddy quickly retrieved it, stuck it on his head, and walked him outside to let him grieve in private. No sooner had Cade relayed to his buddy what happened, they learned an IED took out another patrol from their unit. One soldier was killed and several were injured.

I know the death of every service member killed in combat demands our respect and attention, more so than the death of a four-legged critter. But my dog was killed in an accident caused by a young man with road rage, a young man set off by a bumper sticker left over from the last presidential election. A young man terrorizing the streets of Portion while my youngest son is driving around in a Humvee in a land planted with IEDs that could blow whole soldiers and their families to smithereens.

When my daughter came to after getting knocked out that day, she saw seven little black girls gathered around Brother's body. She called to them for help, but they left the scene. Skeptics might say my daughter was seeing things, that these little girls were simply a figment of her imagination. But what if they weren't? What if they are real and saw the guy who ran my daughter off the road? Maybe they can help identify him. Or maybe they had a parent nearby who saw something. My family is asking the public for help.

Brother was our sweetest boy. Our family will never be the same. I will never be the same. I talk to him every day, and stare dumbly into the empty spaces he once occupied.

But thank God my daughter is okay.

~Columnist Johnnie Kitchen can be reached by email or by phone. Please refer to our staff directory for contact information.

CHAPTER 15
A TIP AND A JAB

The next morning, Johnnie received the following email:

Dear Miss Johnnie,

It's me again, Roosevelt Hill. About those seven little girls your daughter saw . . . I might know something about that. If you have the time, I'd like to meet with you to discuss a few things. Genie's Books on Main Street is a nice place to talk. Nobody gives you the evil eye if you get a little loud, and the owner, Miss Ruby, doesn't mind if you sit a spell and read without buying. Rumor has it she won the Texas Lottery. Maybe that explains why she runs her bookshop more like a library.

If you need to verify who I am, you may call the church office. Our secretary, Osa Lee Davis, can vouch for me.

Thank you kindly. I hope to hear from you.

Roosevelt

P.S. Please accept my condolences on the loss of your dog.

She dashed off a reply:

Dear Roosevelt,

Thank you for reaching out to me. Are you available to meet up at the bookshop this Friday at 3:00 p.m.? I have class until two, but that should allow me to leave campus and arrive on time. My friend Whit and I visited with Miss Ruby right after she opened Genie's Books. We never did get a straight answer about how she plans to compete against the big chain bookstores. That being said, she's filling a much-needed niche in Portion.

I look forward to meeting you.

Johnnie

P.S. I hope you haven't had any more vandalism at the cemetery.

After hitting *send,* she pushed away from the computer and went to refill her coffee.

Roosevelt Hill's latest message more than made up for a letter to the editor Dale had circled in red before he left for work. She thumped her finger against the newsprint. She didn't know what irked her more: the writer's opening statement or Dale's red highlighter.

> I'm not saying anybody who voted for Obama deserves to get run off the road . . . That's not what I'm saying. But if it had been my daughter behind the wheel, that bumper sticker would have never been there in the first place. I'm praying for the Kitchens' son over in the 'Stan. I feel sorry for the family dog. He didn't deserve to go out like that.
>
> Chet Barnes
> VFW (Portion Post)

CHAPTER 16
THE MEETING

"Enchanting." That's how Whit described the indie bookshop the first time they visited on opening night two years ago. Housed in a turn-of-the-century building next to the gazebo, Genie's Books had the feel of a well-appointed living room and library all in one. "It must be magical to live above the bookstore," Whit had whispered to Johnnie as they hobnobbed with local dignitaries and sipped complimentary wine.

"What if all the storybook characters come alive every night?" Johnnie giggled back. "While Miss Ruby's asleep upstairs, all these characters sit around in the shop telling each other their stories."

Before Johnnie tugged open the old-timey door with its rectangular glass pane, she craned her neck and admired the massive arched window that overlooked the second floor apartment above the shop. She imagined the space filled with whimsical artwork, colorful walls, and more books.

As she stepped inside, the aroma of new and used books mingled with the scent of lemon polish and a festive bowl of spicy vanilla potpourri placed on a round, carved-oak table in the middle of the room. Books of every shape, size, and color lined the floor-to-ceiling shelves. Deep plush rugs over a gleaming hardwood floor and comfortable seating invited visitors to pull out a book and start reading.

Miss Ruby looked up from an antique writing desk where she clicked away on a computer. She pushed up from her chair and pattered over to greet Johnnie. Not more than five feet tall, Miss Ruby wore a black tunic over her barrel-shaped body and black leggings on her sticklike legs. Her dainty feet, in velveteen black flats studded with silver rhinestones, pointed outward.

"You get your bestseller written, and I'll showcase it up front in the bay window," she teased, straining her neck to look up at Johnnie. "One of my regulars is waiting to see you."

Johnnie thanked Ruby and scanned the long narrow shop. A young mother holding her newborn in a sling perused the children's section, and a few customers clustered around a sales table.

An elegant black gentleman in a pink dress shirt, gray slacks, and black Justin Ropers rose from a club chair where he'd been reading. Average in height and build, with an ageless, oval face, Roosevelt Hill was *not* what she'd expected. What had she expected? An old black man in a maintenance worker's uniform, missing some teeth?

Her face grew hot as she remembered the time in first grade when Mr. Beachum, the school janitor, picked up her baby doll — it had corn-colored hair and lake-water eyes — from the cafeteria floor where she'd dropped it trying to balance her tray. As he handed it back, Johnnie stared at his ashy fingers, then up at the whites of his eyes. His kindness forgotten, she rushed to the restroom, where she washed her dolly's arms and legs with soap and water. Thank goodness she'd been alone in that bathroom, the only witness to her shame a white toilet in an empty pink stall, reflected in the mirror over the sink.

Until this moment, standing before Roosevelt Hill, Johnnie had buried this humiliating memory under the silt of time. Did that make her a racist, a bigot, or just a confused little girl? The question bothered her.

She stepped forward to take Roosevelt's

outstretched hand. "Good afternoon, sir. I'm Johnnie Kitchen. It's so nice to meet you." She hoped he hadn't read her thoughts. *Why had she stereotyped him in the first place, just because he mentioned that he worked as a custodian at his church?* Granny Opal would be so disappointed.

He flashed a pearly white smile, his kind brown eyes as reassuring as his grip. "Hello, Miss Johnnie. Portion's own Lois Lane."

She chuckled at his remark, at the merriment in his deep, smooth voice.

A book tucked under one arm, he gestured for her to sit in the leather club chair opposite where he'd been seated when she walked in. "Thank you for making time for me."

"My pleasure, and thank you for reading my column." Her gaze fell on the book he now placed on his lap. She recognized the cover. "Ernest J. Gaines' *A Lesson Before Dying.* I read it years ago. It's one of my favorite novels."

He glanced down at the book, tapping it thoughtfully with his right hand. "I'm on my second reading. The man can write."

She studied him a moment, the way he held the book so reverently. You'd think he was holding the Bible. "Have you read his other novel, *The Autobiography of Miss Jane*

Pittman? It reads like a memoir, but it's really fiction."

A look of recognition swept over his face. "Can't say as I've read the book, but wasn't it a TV movie back in the seventies?"

Johnnie nodded. "I was just a kid, but I remember my granny commenting how they made Cicely Tyson look all wrinkled up like a hundred-year-old slave."

Roosevelt closed his eyes, and Johnnie assumed he was recalling the same thing.

But then he said, "Now take Alice Walker's *The Color Purple.* How my Nora loved that one." He looked over and winked at Johnnie. "Made me go with her when the movie came out. Turned out to be a pretty good flick, too."

Johnnie's mouth twitched as another awkward memory surfaced. She was in her early twenties when everybody was talking about the film starring Oprah Winfrey and Whoopi Goldberg. A young black preacher had been visiting Johnnie's all-white Methodist church, and when she went to shake his hand, she got all tongue-tied and said, "Have you seen *The Colored People*?"

To his credit, the young clergyman in full vestments leaned forward, broke into a wide grin, and whispered, "I believe I might be the only one on the premises." His sense of humor gave Johnnie a chance to recover and poke fun at her own blooper.

So what was it about Roosevelt Hill that revived these memories? Things she'd never even shared with Whit. Johnnie had the sudden urge to confess that perhaps she was no better than the white kid in the jacked-up truck causing havoc around town.

"Roosevelt . . ." she started to say, but Granny Opal's voice warbled in her ear, *Some things are better left unsaid, my dear.*

Johnnie flinched. Roosevelt blinked as if he were waiting for Johnnie to continue when the clock over Miss Ruby's desk cuckooed.

Miss Ruby glanced their way, peeking over the rims of her reading glasses. "Don't mind him. He's about fifteen minutes fast. It's only three fifteen."

Johnnie squinted up at the clock as the little bird flew back into his house.

She turned her attention back to Roosevelt. "So, have you always worked at the church?"

He ran a hand over his silver buzz cut, a slight smile creasing his face. "Oh heavens no. After I got back from 'Nam, I drove an 18-wheeler until Nora got sick and it wasn't feasible to leave her alone. So I sold my rig and here I am, a widower, polishing pews and caring for the dead." He folded his hands on top of the book and crossed his feet at the ankles.

Admiring the sheen on the rounded tips of his cowboy boots, she pressed ahead, "I'm so sorry about your wife. Do you have children?"

He rubbed the palm of his left hand, studying it for a second. "That's the one thing I couldn't give her — kids. But we fostered our share over the years until she got sick."

Johnnie leaned forward. "Roosevelt, can I ask you something?"

He furrowed his brow and pursed his lips like he needed to think about it. "And what would that be, Miss Johnnie?"

She fidgeted in her chair, hoping she wasn't crossing the line. "Since you read my column, you know I've got a boy in Afghanistan. I was just wondering, uh . . . were you infantry?"

He took a deep breath and crossed his arms, the leather in the chair crinkling under his weight. "Yes, ma'am, Eleven Bravo. Got drafted when I turned eighteen. Back then, the draft board would rather send a poor, colored boy to 'Nam than a white man's son. Colored boys — we were disposable." He eyed Johnnie. "It was hard on my mama. I can imagine it's hard on you, too. But I'm willing to bet your son is a fine soldier. He knows what he needs to do."

Johnnie swallowed. She vowed not to start blubbering, not here, not now.

Roosevelt scratched at something on the back of his neck. "If it's okay with you, I'll add your son's name to a special prayer list at church. We keep a little electric candle going twenty-four hours a day next to the names of young men and women from our congregation who've been to Iraq and Afghanistan."

She bowed her head for a moment, touched by his generosity. When she looked up, he was pulling out a tiny notebook and pen from his shirt pocket. As she gave him Cade's name and rank, she thought about Tutts. She felt guilty that she hadn't seen him since he'd returned to Portion. "Do you mind adding another boy to the list? He's been back from Iraq for a while. His name's Steven Tuttle, but everybody calls him Tutts. His face got pretty messed up from an IED."

Roosevelt paused, as if he needed a moment to digest this information before he scribbled Tutts' name. "You know, Miss Johnnie," he said, pocketing the notebook and pen, "our congregation is mostly poor and black. But we are colorblind when it comes to praying for our troops."

At that moment, Johnnie heard the jingle of a tiny bell, the one dangling from Genie's pink collar. The black cat with white socks slunk around the corner of Johnnie's chair and jumped into her lap. Before Johnnie could object, Genie curled up in a ball and started purring.

"Looks like you've got a friend," Roosevelt chuckled, his merry voice filling the air around them.

Ruby rushed over to apologize. "Genie, you know not to impose yourself on our guests. Unless you've been invited, of course."

Stroking the cat's rich fur, Johnnie felt the tiny vibrations each time Genie purred. "She's fine," Johnnie reassured Ruby, whose reading glasses dangled from a beaded chain around her neck. Luxuriating in the cat's warmth, Johnnie reached down and kissed the top of Genie's head. She'd never kissed a cat. Its small presence filled a hollow gap in her heart left behind when Brother died. "I love that you named your shop after her."

Ruby leaned back, seeming to balance the weight of her short, rotund body on the heels of her flat slippers. "She came with the building. Nobody seems to know how old she is or how she got in. But that little bell engraved with her name — it was tied to a piece of yarn around her neck when I found her hiding in the crawlspace under the stairs."

Roosevelt eyed the cat. "Black folks and black cats. Some days it feels like we are an endangered species, ain't that right, Miss Genie?"

They all stared at the cat as if she could speak.

Johnnie cuddled her closer. "With a name like Genie, maybe she'll grant me three wishes."

Ruby's expression softened and Roosevelt murmured, "Your wishes are her command."

Johnnie closed her eyes and offered up her silent supplications: I wish . . . for Cade to come home safely. For Callie Ann to stop blaming herself for Brother's death . . . and for the kid in the pickup to come forward.

After a few seconds, Ruby padded back to her desk, calling over her shoulder, "Just set her down when you get tired of her."

The cuckoo bird flew out of his house again, announcing the time.

Johnnie glanced at her watch. It was already a quarter to four. Where had the time gone? They'd been chatting for forty-five minutes, but it felt like she'd just gotten there. "Roosevelt, you were going to tell me about those seven little girls."

He tilted his head, his expression thoughtful. "Before my wife passed, I made her a promise." He took a deep breath. "Sometimes, a person has to go back in order to move forward."

For the first time since their meeting began, Johnnie detected a tremble in Roosevelt's voice. She scooted to the edge of her chair, causing Genie to jump to the floor and scamper away.

Roosevelt swiped his forehead with the back of his wrist and handed her a manila envelope. "Like you, I've done some writing. Mostly I dabble. Before Nora passed, she made me promise to show this to someone. But I never knew who to show it to until this week. Until I read your last column."

Her whole body tingled in anticipation. She held the envelope close to her heart. "Why me, Roosevelt? Is it about the girls?"

He stood and placed his copy of *A Lesson Before Dying* with care on the small table that separated the leather chairs. Johnnie assumed the book had a permanent home in that spot in Miss Ruby's shop so Roosevelt didn't have to hunt for it each time he visited.

"You'll understand once you read it. But you might want to wait until you're alone."

Roosevelt rose to leave. Clutching the envelope, Johnnie slung her purse over her shoulder and followed.

Miss Ruby twisted in her chair as they passed the front desk. "Y'all come back when you can stay longer." She wriggled her fingers at Johnnie. "Keep those columns coming, dear."

Out on the sidewalk, Johnnie breathed in the aroma of freshly baked bread from the bakery across the street. Once Roosevelt stepped outside, she tapped the envelope. "Is this something I can share with my readers? I would give you full credit of course."

Roosevelt toyed with the cufflinks on his shirt. "Miss Johnnie, I'd be honored if you run my story. All I ask is that you don't use my name."

She watched him jaywalk across Main as he headed for the bakery to "pick up a little sweet" for the church secretary. Once he was out of sight, Johnnie pulled out the typewritten story and began reading. With each step, she felt her breathing quicken. She had to remind herself to keep looking up to avoid bumping into other people on the sidewalk.

Instead of going home to study, she headed straight to the *Portion Telegraph* a few doors down from the old corner bank building at Worth and Main. She had to stop a few times and catch her breath, not because she was out of shape, but because of what she had read.

Every hair stood on end, as if she'd been zapped by static electricity.

Chapter 17
Portion Telegraph

Editor's note: The following story is an eyewitness account of a lynching that took place in 1952 out by Portion Lake. The newspaper has no record of the crime. The Portion Police were called to the scene, but no arrests were made. The author, who wishes to remain anonymous, met recently with Johnnie Kitchen, a columnist for the *Portion Telegraph.* Stay tuned for future installments from our mystery author.

The white goblins in hoods and robes had already vanished, taking their evil laughter with them. They'd done their ugly deed and left "Santa Claus" dangling from a tree, his charcoal body stripped naked, 'cept for the Santa hat hanging from his head. I peeked through the brittle vines from my hiding spot in the woods, too scared to breathe and trembling like a beaten dog. The air smelled of smoke and the promise of snow, but the joy of Christmas was gone. I was covered in my own slime from the snot and tears running down my face.

That's when I saw them. They flew up out of the water where the town of Glory used to be before the lake came in. Like a dark mist at first, they swirled toward the shore and formed a circle around the body.

Their faces shined like lanterns.

I'd just learned to count on my fingers, and I cried like a baby when I recognized all seven of them. The oldest shushed me ever so gently like Mama had done. Then like a gospel choir, they lifted their sweet voices to the heavens, and sang Thurman Blue home.

Chapter 18
A Town Reacts

Letters poured in to the *Portion Telegraph.* Johnnie could hardly believe the response.

Dear Mystery Author,

My first husband was a young deputy at the time this hideous crime was committed. If he witnessed any "heavenly bodies" near the crime scene, he never mentioned it. Boyd was only twenty-five when he died in a car wreck three years later in 1955, but the man he suspected was the killer sat down the pew from us on Sunday mornings. I have no memory now of who that could have been. After Boyd died, I remarried and changed churches.

I can't speak for what you claim to have seen some fifty-seven years ago, but I can tell you that for the short time my sweet husband had left on this earth, he never did enjoy Christmas much after that.

Vysta Hubbard
Lakeside Senior Living

Dear Sir or Madam,

Glad I found this story online while researching family history. Thurman Blue was my great uncle and somewhat of a family legend. I grew up hearing stories about the black Santa strung from a tree for robbing from the rich to give to the poor. From what I gleaned from listening to my grandmother and aunts, the only thing ol' Thurman stole was the heart of a girl he planned to marry.

Besides the obvious, the other crime is that the perpetrators were never caught and brought to justice. Although there's no statute of limitations on murder in Texas, the reality is that the men who carried out this horrific and cowardly deed are probably rotting in their graves or mumbling for forgiveness in some nursing home.

When I was a boy, I prayed for them to burn in hell. Now that I am a man, I pray that when they get to Heaven, they have to answer to Thurman.

V/R

Captain Delray Blue

United States Navy, Hawaii

From what I gather, that gent was out doing the Lord's work, likely giving out candy and apples to poor children. He probably came from some church party when he got snatched up like some hooligan. Bless 'em. Some folks might look at me cross-eyed for saying this, but it sure is nice to read about angels that don't look like white people's Christmas cards.

Dorothy "Dot" Washington, retired housekeeper

To the good citizens of Portion,

As president of the Portion Chamber of Commerce, I am deeply troubled by some disturbing acts of racial intolerance that have taken place in our community. While the *Portion Telegraph* has done an excellent job bringing these issues to the forefront, I worry that these reports will send the wrong impression to outsiders about our lovely town.

I'd like to point out to our residents

and potential visitors that our businesses do not discriminate due to race, gender, or creed. While it's true that the Reverend Jeremiah Harkins, a Methodist Circuit Rider from Tennessee, founded this town on Christian principles, our community is home to at least one synagogue, a Buddhist Temple, a mosque, and a coffee shop/lounge where nonbelievers gather to "have church" or so I am told.

Portion is a destination place with old-timey storefronts on a friendly Main Street that dates back to horse and buggy days. Our historic neighborhoods are populated with charming bungalows, cottages, and Victorian homes, some built in the early 1900s. We have some of the best public schools in Texas. Nearby Portion Lake is teaming with a variety of fish and wildlife, along with family friendly campsites and ball fields. We are home to Portion Community College, two museums, a state championship football team, nearby Dallas/Fort Worth Airport, a National Guard unit, and a war memorial erected shortly after WWI.

Portion, Texas: where everybody gets

an equal slice of the American Dream.

John Hammond III
President, Portion Chamber of
Commerce

Johnnie put down the paper and shook her head in wonder.

Chapter 19
Middle of the Night

Icy fingers touched her shoulder. Johnnie awoke with a start, kicking back the covers with both feet. Disoriented, she searched the dark, trying to get her bearings.

A figure loomed over her, and she sucked in her breath before she realized it was her daughter and not some ghostly vision of Cade standing next to her bed. She'd read somewhere that moments after a soldier is killed in battle, he appears at his mother's bedside to say goodbye.

"Jeez! Callie Ann. You scared the crap out of me." Johnnie sat up, cradling a pillow. She took several deep breaths to calm her racing heart.

"Sorry, Mom." Her daughter's soft breath and strands of hair brushed against Johnnie's arm. Wrapped in a blanket like she was seven and not seventeen, Callie Ann might have been a little girl afraid of the dark. She blocked the glow from the night-light plugged into the wall socket.

Dale snored softly from the other side of the bed.

"What's wrong?" Johnnie whispered, not wanting to wake him.

"I can't sleep." Her daughter's voice thrummed through the air.

"Are you sick?"

Callie Ann rubbed at something in her eye. "No, but. . . ."

Johnnie couldn't remember the last time Callie Ann roused her in the middle of the night to say she couldn't sleep. It was one thing for her to tiptoe into the bedroom on those sleepless weekend nights when Johnnie stayed awake half the night waiting for her to come home after curfew. But this was a school night, and she'd gone to bed before Johnnie. Clearly, something was wrong. Johnnie sighed and crawled out of bed, not bothering to look for her slippers. "Come on, I'll walk you back to your room."

Still groggy, she couldn't help but notice Brother's absence in the house. How his tail no longer thumped against the doorframe when he nosed his way into the master bedroom to check on them.

Back in Callie Ann's room, they snuggled under sheets that smelled faintly of fabric softener and Callie Ann's perfume, more musk now than melon. The last time they'd snuggled this close was the morning after Cade left for basic training, when Brother Dog lay between them on Cade's bed and offered his body as a sponge for their fear.

As Johnnie pulled the covers up to their chins, she realized Callie Ann was trembling. "What is it, Sis? Is it Brother Dog?"

"Uh-uh." Callie Ann shook her head and looked away.

"Is it some guy?" Johnnie probed, aware that her daughter hadn't been on a date since the accident. That worried Johnnie but not Dale. "There's not a boy around here good enough for my daughter," Dale had insisted on more than one occasion.

"No, Mom. It's not some *guy,*" Callie Ann huffed into the covers.

Well, whatever it was, Callie Ann wasn't going to volunteer it.

Johnnie bit her lip. "Is it drill team?" she ventured, broaching the subject for the first time since Callie Ann came home last spring and announced, "I didn't try out for drill team. My heart's not in it anymore." This happened weeks after Granny's funeral and days before Cade's sendoff.

Callie Ann turned to Johnnie. "I don't miss it, Mom, especially practice. And with ACTs coming up, I have more time to prepare."

Johnnie hoped Callie Ann was telling the truth, not regretting her decision at the last minute now that her senior year had started. One drill team mom had approached Johnnie in the grocery store, shocked that her long-legged daughter — one of the most popular girls in school — was missing on the dance line. At least when Cade walked away from baseball his senior year, no one approached her in the supermarket. But apparently some baseball dads had hit Dale up at the gas station, demanding to know why Cade quit.

With the exception of the coaches, no one razzed D.J., her brooding nonconformist, when he dropped out of football after his freshman year to concentrate on honors art and the garage band he'd formed with Steven Tuttle. But the Kitchen family's two athletic blonds? Why, this was Texas! It was *un-American.*

"Now I know how the boys felt when they quit sports," Callie Ann said, as if reading her mother's thoughts. "Their coaches told them they'd end up working down at the car wash. Said they'd never amount to anything because they were quitters."

"Quitters, my foot," Johnnie cut in, wishing she could rub it in the coaches' faces that one of their "quitters" had graduated from college with a 4.0 and the other was serving his country in a war zone. She was proud that she and Dale had raised three rebel souls to think for themselves. She grappled for the right words, not wanting to add to Callie Ann's troubles. "Did Coach Dixon say something like that to you? Because if she did —"

"I can take care of myself, Mom. I don't need you coming up to the school."

Johnnie glanced at the alarm clock on the nightstand. "Sis, it's two thirty in the morning. I love talking to you, but both of us have to get up for class in a few hours. You wanna tell me what's troubling you . . . why you can't sleep?"

Callie Ann burrowed her long legs deeper into the covers. She took a deep breath. "It's those little girls, Mom. I can't stop thinking about them."

Johnnie shivered and snuggled closer to her daughter. "I know. Me neither."

She heard Callie Ann swallow. "I wasn't freaked out until I read Roosevelt's story."

They both lay flat on their backs, staring up at the ceiling. The fan whirred at a low speed above them.

Johnnie fiddled with the edge of the top sheet, crinkling the cotton between her fingers. "You didn't seem frightened the night Brother got killed."

"I was in *shock,*" Callie Ann snapped, her words punching the air. She lowered her voice. "Are they angels? Ghosts? Roosevelt didn't say."

Hearing the word *ghosts* gave Johnnie the heebie-jeebies, but she tried to act nonchalant. "I ran into Miss Ruby the other day at the post office. She's pretty open about things. She thinks the girls could be spirit guides."

"Spirit guides?" Callie Ann repeated, her voice reflecting both fear and curiosity. She rolled onto her side and added, "You mean like angels?"

Another chill shimmied up Johnnie's back. "Maybe. I like to think of them as special messengers sent by God."

Callie Ann shifted in the bed. "Then if they're sent by God, why are we afraid of them?"

"I don't know, honey. I guess because they represent the unknown. Things we can't explain on a human level. Even the shepherds were scared when the angel appeared the night Jesus was born."

Callie Ann sighed. "Yeah, I remember that from playing Mary in all those Christmas pageants at church. Remember when D.J.

played a donkey and Cade played a sheep?"

Johnnie chuckled, brushing hair out of her daughter's eyes. "How could I forget? That's the night D.J. told the preacher he liked playing a jackass."

They both laughed, and for a moment, their fears evaporated.

"Mom," Callie Ann hesitated, "has Roosevelt ever seen those little girls again?"

"I asked him that the other day when he called to check on us. He said he sees them every day . . . in his mind."

Callie Ann yawned, sounding sleepy. "Who were they, Mom?"

Johnnie reached for her daughter's hand, warmer now than when she first tapped her on the shoulder earlier. "We're going to find out soon enough. Roosevelt stopped by the newspaper office the other day to meet the editor. He said he's writing about them now, and soon the whole town will know their story."

Callie Ann gave a little shudder and jerked straight up. "That's it." She gestured at something in the dark, over by the closet door, and started crawling across Johnnie.

"What are you doing?" Cowering under the covers, Johnnie held her breath, half-expecting to see seven little girls hovering overhead.

Callie Ann grabbed something and scrambled back to the bed. "Here, put one on."

The scent of worn leather enveloped Johnnie like a warm embrace.

"Granny's boots, Mom. For when we need to feel brave."

Chapter 20
Pickups

"I wanna kill some guy I don't even know," Dale fumed, his jaw clenched. He gripped the steering wheel with both hands, as if any second he might rip the whole column out with brute force. As his pickup idled in the driveway, the front bumper facing the street, he glared out the windshield. At night he occasionally backed the truck in if he had equipment he was too tired to unload, or sometimes just for the heck of it.

Johnnie squinted into the morning sun that filtered through the white crepe myrtle next to the driveway. The aroma of other people's breakfasts wafted through the neighborhood, and Johnnie felt a twinge of nostalgia for the days when she rose at dawn to cook bacon and eggs or ham and French toast for her growing brood. These days she'd convinced Dale to make do with granola and fresh fruit while Callie Ann preferred instant oatmeal or cream of wheat.

Clutching a steaming mug of coffee, she took a hit of caffeine. She was still groggy from her middle-of-the-night chat with Callie Ann. In her cotton robe and slippers, she huddled next to the driver's window and waited for Dale to calm down. She didn't like him going off to work half-cocked, especially since he worked around power tools all day.

"I chased down the wrong effing pickup yesterday," Dale went on. "I was pulling out of the bank when I thought I saw the kid drive by. I followed the truck to some doctor's office and was about to yank open the driver's door when this young woman with a pixie haircut climbed out, holding her abdomen." Dale banged his fist on the dashboard, so unlike him. "Poor girl looked about eight months pregnant."

Johnnie covered her mouth. "Oh, Dale. You must have scared her silly."

Dale's cheeks flamed crimson. "Do you know how many jacked-up pickups there are in Portion? In the whole state of Texas, for cripes' sake!"

Johnnie flashed back to the day at the war memorial. How one second the gunmetal gray pickup cruised by, blaring country music, then before they knew it, it had wheeled around and was almost on top of them.

"I'm sorry I didn't get the license plate number. It all happened so fast."

Dale nodded, but stared straight ahead. "None of this would've happened if you girls had listened to me. That bumper sticker almost got my daughter killed."

Johnnie closed her eyes against his fury. Breathing through her nose, she waited a moment before she looked up at him. "Dale, I know you worry that kid might strike again. So do I. But we can't prove that he was provoked by a political bumper sticker. And even if he was. . . ." She yawned, too tired to continue a conversation that was going nowhere.

He tapped his fingers on the steering wheel. "Well, in the meantime, while y'all are sittin' around holding hands singing 'Kumbaya' and talking about angels and stuff, some punk is out there running his mouth. And if I get my hands on him. . . ."

The idea of Dale tracking down the kid frightened her almost as much as the kid running Callie Ann off the road. She stared at her husband's powerful hands. No telling what Dale would do if he confronted him.

She leaned into the window and tousled his hair, trying to defuse his anger. "If I ever see him again, I'll call the police. I promise."

He gave a little nod, and then his lips grazed her cheek. "You think you can work me into your busy schedule, college girl? When you're not readin', writin', and doing your 'rithmatic?" He knuckled her playfully on the nose.

She tilted her head, batting her lashes at him. After twenty-five years of marriage, she was still learning how to handle her man. "Only if you promise to behave, mister."

He pressed his lips together in a half-smile and jutted his chin toward the lone evergreen in the vacant lot across the street. "We haven't had any rain in a while. Looks like Edwin's tree could use a drink. I'll run the hose over there after I get off work."

She smiled at his offer and watched him pull out of the driveway and motor down Merriweather to a jobsite where he would work alongside his men, mentoring and monitoring them throughout the day.

From the corner of her eye, she spotted Sergeant Scarecrow at his guard post. She lingered outside for a moment before going inside to put dinner in the Crock-Pot and get ready for class. While she gazed at the raggedy soldier, Dale's words hissed through her mind: *I wanna kill some guy I don't even know.* She figured Cade felt the same way about the enemy.

CHAPTER 21
LITTLE BIRD

Green chili stew simmered in the Crock-Pot, filling the house with the smells Dale loved: roasted Hatch chiles, onions, and garlic in a thick chicken broth with chunks of white meat. The meal was healthy and satisfying and occasionally Johnnie would substitute turkey for chicken and not tell Dale. Everyone in the family knew he wasn't a turkey fan except on Thanksgiving when he carved the bird or once in a blue moon when he'd order the good smoked turkey served in a barbecue joint. After Dale popped open a beer and went to water Edwin's tree, Johnnie and Callie Ann moseyed out back to check on Brother's grave.

A male cardinal swooped down and perched on a fence post a few feet away. Admiring his red plumage and beady eyes, Johnnie whispered, "Sis, remember when you kids were little and I'd see a male cardinal? What did I say about his tiny black mask and red feathers?"

Callie Ann crossed her arms, squinting at the bird in the late western sun. "You'd get all goofy and say he'd dressed up for a masquerade ball."

Johnnie glanced sideways, catching a glint in her daughter's eyes. "And when he'd fly away to join his mate?"

"You'd say, 'There goes Mr. Cardinal to pick up his date,' " Callie Ann teased. "The boys thought you were crazy, you know, talking about birds like they were people." Her daughter elbowed her gently in the ribs.

They stopped talking long enough to listen to the little bird whistling to a female, hidden somewhere in the foliage of the big oak that shaded Brother's final resting place. The female whistled back. A few seconds later, the male took off and she followed him, her subdued plumage less obvious to predators.

After a moment, Johnnie said, "You know there's a whole legend around cardinals. Some folks say when a cardinal appears in your yard, it's a visitor from Heaven."

Callie Ann bent over, hands on her knees, and studied the fake rock Johnnie had ordered with Brother's name engraved on it. "What do you believe, Mom? Are they visitors from Heaven, or just little red birds flying off to your imaginary balls?"

Was Callie Ann mocking her, or simply asking a question? Johnnie wasn't sure. Callie Ann's face was hidden behind a curtain of hair.

Would Callie Ann believe her mother's story about what she'd seen at age four? Then again, Callie Ann had witnessed something that couldn't be explained from the pulpit or in a textbook.

"Sis, I'm going to tell you something I've never told anyone. Not even your dad." She paused, feeling slightly lightheaded because she was finally going to share her secret.

Callie Ann straightened, nervously twisting her hair to one side like a rope. She retrieved an elastic band from her jean pocket and tied up the loose end. "I hope this isn't like the time you told Cade about your affair."

Johnnie stiffened; the memory of two years ago still stung. She peered at Brother's grave, avoiding her daughter's gray eyes. "Back when I was four years old, something magical happened when Grandpa Grubbs and I were strolling along the shore down at the cove."

She waited, gauging her daughter's reaction. Callie Ann leaned closer, spellbound, so Johnnie continued, "A little red bird was hopping around on the shore. He looked at himself in the water, and then he stared straight into my soul and called to me."

"Called to you? Like how?"

"He whistled my name. 'John-neee . . . John-neee.' "

Callie Ann blinked at her a couple of times, puzzled. "Did Grandpa Grubbs hear him?"

Johnnie hugged herself. The sun was setting and she suddenly felt chilled, standing in the lengthening shadows. Her teeth chattered. "If he did, he didn't say. But he kept both eyes locked on that cardinal the whole time as he said, 'That's not just any bird, young lady. That's an angel bird, sent straight down from Heaven.' "

Callie Ann stared at her, open-mouthed, her hands clasped under her chin.

Johnnie gazed at her daughter. "To this day, I believe it was your Great Uncle Johnny. Male cardinals were his favorite bird, so it makes sense that he appeared to me in the form of a red bird. He was near the dock where he drowned trying to save Mama when she was two months pregnant with me."

Callie Ann didn't move. Dusk had settled in. "Why didn't you tell anyone?"

"Who would believe me? Even Grandpa

made me promise to keep it our secret. Guess he thought Granny or Mama might tease us. Or most likely, Aunt Beryl, who lived with us more than she did in Salt Flat."

Callie Ann flinched when the spotlights came on and illuminated the backyard. They both whirled about. Dale stood on the deck, his hands in his pockets. "What are you girls doing out there in the dark?"

They moved toward the deck, arms locked around each other's waists.

"Do you think that's how Roosevelt feels? Why he doesn't want his name mentioned with his stories?"

"Could be. I think he's afraid people will make fun of him or that some nut will take offense and come after him."

"Mom, all the kids at school know about my accident and what I saw. Guess your column's gaining in popularity. One of the football players came up behind me in the hall the other day and yelled, "Boo!" and I about ripped off his face. He won't be bothering me again."

Johnnie gave her a little squeeze. "Good for you. Your brothers taught you well."

"Everyone's been nice to me — or at least not mean. Many kids want to know if we're getting another dog."

That last part made Johnnie's heart hurt.

As they clambered up the steps of the deck, Johnnie glanced over her shoulder at Brother's rock. As much as she missed him, she didn't want another soul to worry about right now.

The smell of supper greeted them, along with Dale's open arms.

Johnnie's phone buzzed on the coffee table in the den. It was nearly 10:00 p.m. Dale had drifted off to sleep and Callie Ann was in her room working on her senior thesis. The paper wasn't due for months, but Callie Ann said she wanted to get a head start. All Johnnie knew at this point was that her daughter was keeping her subject top secret.

Snatching up the phone, Johnnie read Mama's number on the caller ID with equal parts relief and dread.

"You still up?" Mama's smoky voice curled up out of the phone and wrapped around Johnnie's heart.

"I'm studying, Mama. What's wrong?"

"Does something always have to be wrong? I'm on break, sitting out on this swanky *veranda* enjoying some peace and quiet. Got all of my guests taken care of. Now it's my turn to rest."

Johnnie heard the flick of a cigarette

lighter, then Mama's breathy inhale. She pictured Victoria Grubbs swaying to and fro on the porch swing of the Dooley Mansion's massive front porch, flicking her ashes in a fancy ashtray pilfered from the smoking porch out back. Guests weren't allowed to smoke out front, but Mama bent the rules since she worked there. Knowing Mama, she had all the porch lights out and relied on the glow from the elaborate twin lamppost that illuminated the stone path leading up to the porch.

"You asked me the other day about the hanging tree and why I've never mentioned it."

Yup, and you acted as if you didn't hear me, Johnnie thought.

"Well, your mystery man and his story got me to thinking."

Johnnie tossed her notes aside on the couch and drew her knees to her chest as the antique clock on the mantel struck ten. "Go on. I'm listening."

Mama sighed and took a long drag on her cigarette. "Once, when we were kids, my brother overheard Poppy refer to that giant oak as the hanging tree. When Johnny asked him about it, Poppy got real quiet. Then he went into this big lecture about how there are some things you don't talk about in polite society, and a lynching this close to home is one of them. He said you learn to keep your mouth shut or the Klan will make sure you never talk again."

By now Johnnie had pushed up from the couch and was circling the kitchen island, her pajama bottoms flaring at her bare ankles. Seconds earlier she had felt chilled; now she was burning up. "Mama, I don't mean any disrespect, but don't you ever want to yank Grandpa from his grave and shake some sense into him? I grew up right down the road from that tree, and until my daughter hit it, I never knew its history."

Mama was silent on the other end.

Johnnie pulled a glass from the cupboard and filled it with tap water. "Are you still there?" She took a long glug and waited, worried she'd crossed the line.

After a long pause, Mama said, "Poppy was only doing what he thought was best at the time. Protecting his family. Things were different back then, Johnnie girl. Even white people were targeted if they went against the grain."

"So, Granny Opal . . . did she know about the lynching, too?"

The question was met with silence.

After they hung up, Johnnie went to gather

her notes and head to bed. On a blank sheet of paper, she scribbled in big crooked letters:

Dear Mr. Blue,

Most days I go charging up that mountain fist first, punching at the wind to get out of my way. Some days that wind knocks me on my butt. Tonight feels like one of those times. But my struggles are nothing compared to the horror you went through. What kind of twisted soul would torture and kill another human being and take pleasure in the act? Until I met Roosevelt, I never knew of your suffering. My precious pup died near the very spot where your life ended. They say all dogs go to Heaven. So if you happen to see a chocolate Lab named Brother, call to him — and he will answer with a wag of his tail and an outstretched paw.

Johnnie

Chapter 22
Day of the Dead

On the phone D.J. sounded out of breath. "Mom, glad I caught you between classes."

Johnnie clutched her cellphone. "Is everything all right?"

"Don't freak out, okay?"

She hated it when her kids started a conversation this way.

"You know the dude that followed me last October at Denton's Day of the Dead Festival?"

The memory of that crisp fall day swirled around her like a cold gust of wind. "Of course I remember. It still gives me chills."

While she power-walked across campus on this sweltering day in September, her mind drifted back.

Denton's historic town square had bustled with festival goers decked out in costume, along with their dogs. Sipping hot apple cider and strolling along the leaf-strewn sidewalk, Johnnie admired the turn-of-the-century limestone courthouse with its grand clock tower and four whimsical domes.

Breathing in the aroma of kettle corn and cotton candy, she smiled at the image of D.J. a few feet ahead. Clean-shaven and sporting Grandpa Grubbs' old trench coat and fedora, he looked as if he'd stepped off the pages of a 1960s issue of *Town & Country* magazine, except for the dried fake blood dripping down one cheek. His girlfriend at the time, a college student named Liz, wore a low-cut black ball gown and yellow wig.

Callie Ann tagged along beside them, her blonde hair piled in a beehive and half her face painted to resemble a sugar skull mask, the other half bare of makeup except for mascara and lip gloss. "Leave half my face untouched," Callie Ann had requested at the makeup booth earlier that day. "I want the skull part to honor our friend Tutts, whose face got disfigured in Iraq." As the makeup artist went to apply a mixture of pink and purple and black and white hues, Callie Ann glanced up at her big brother, seeking his approval, but D.J. turned away, biting his bottom lip to keep it from quivering.

Johnnie had the urge to tell the makeup artist that her other son was at Fort Irwin for pre-deployment training and that her husband had to work, but something in D.J.'s expression stopped her. She wondered, too, if his feelings were hurt when Mama turned down his invitation to the festival, claiming she needed to stay with Granny Opal. Johnnie knew Mama hated going to Denton — too many memories in a town where she'd given birth as a teenager.

With the kids still several feet in front of her, Johnnie stopped to read a poster advertising a ghost tour. Out of the corner of her eye, she spotted an older man in the crowd following D.J. and the girls. Every time they stopped to look in a shop window, the man in the tan corduroy jacket stopped, too.

He followed them into Recycled Books, the old pink opera house on the northeast corner of the square. Johnnie was right behind him, keeping her distance. When D.J. paused to leaf through a bin of vinyl records, the old man stopped a couple of bins over. He stuffed his hands in his pockets, trying to look nonchalant. Every few seconds, he glanced their way, eyeing D.J.

Crossing her arms and leaning against a wall of books, Johnnie observed the man. He was average in height, with a distinguished air — an aristocrat, D.J. might say. He had a white goatee and wore a matching turtleneck. There was something familiar about him, yet Johnnie had never seen him before.

At one point, D.J. looked up. He must have sensed the stranger was watching him. Her son's voice was polite but guarded. "Is there a problem, mister?"

The second D.J. spoke, the man stumbled back, turning pale. He grabbed at the rolled collar of his sweater, as if D.J.'s words caused him to choke. "I, uh, I'm terribly sorry. I thought I saw . . . I thought you were," the man swallowed, gasping for breath, "a ghost." Backing away, he bumped into a kiosk full of bookmarks and scurried out the door.

D.J. pulled out an album cover and studied it. "Dude's probably tripping on 'shrooms."

Johnnie frowned at her son. " 'Shrooms?" Even in the cavernous space, she felt hemmed in. Usually, a maze of floor-to-ceiling books brought comfort, but as she gazed at the fake blood caked on D.J.'s cheek and tried to process what the man had said, she fought the urge to flee.

D.J. smirked and stuffed the album back in the bin. "Mushrooms, Mom. You know, psychedelics."

Liz giggled, but Callie Ann didn't take her

eyes off the front entrance. "That was creepy."

For the rest of that day, Johnnie had shivered every time she thought about the man.

Now, taking a deep breath, she adjusted her book bag and put one foot in front of the other. "Have you seen that man around town?" she asked, glancing at her watch. Fall semester had only been in session a couple weeks, and she was still trying to make a good impression by not showing up late to class, which started in three minutes.

D.J.'s baritone voice boomed through the phone. "He's here in the shop, Mom. I'm talking to him right now."

Fear sent her heart rocketing straight up her throat.

"He tracked me down after he saw my photo in the newspaper announcing the shop's grand opening."

Dizzy, she staggered off the sidewalk into the grass. "What does he want?" *Was the man a nut job?* Right then, on her way to American Lit, she leaned against the side of the English building and braced herself for whatever D.J. said next.

His deep, throaty laughter rang in her ear — the kind of laughter he reserved for those he trusted. "He wants to meet you, Mom."

"Me? What for?"

"I can't tell you that over the phone."

"But . . . I don't understand."

"You will. Why don't you skip your next class and get up to Denton. *Now.*"

"D.J., you're scaring me."

"Sorry, Mom. There's nothing to be afraid of." He paused for a moment as if he'd forgotten how frightened she could get at times. "Just get up here as quick as you can, and come by yourself."

Chill bumps covered her body.

She heard D.J. tell someone to have a seat, and then he said, "We'll see you in a few. Be careful driving."

Johnnie was gulping air, and her head swam with a thousand questions as she stuck her phone back in her purse, hoisted her backpack, and went to tell her professor she was skipping class.

Who was the man in Denton? And why did he want to meet her?

Chapter 23
The Man on the Square

Approaching the outskirts of Denton on 377, Johnnie eased up on the gas pedal as a freight train chugged past, going clickety-clack in the opposite direction. Any other day, she would have rolled down her window and waved, hoping the engineers in the locomotive waved back. Instead, she broke out in the lyrics to "Little Red Caboose Behind the Train."

She did that sometimes when she was nervous — sang childhood tunes and silly rhymes to calm her racing heart. Tapping the steering wheel, she continued on.

By the time she finished, the freight train had long passed, with *no* little red caboose bringing up the rear. My, how times had changed.

Maneuvering north on Carroll Boulevard, she passed the Odd Fellows Cemetery. Its towering gray monuments, visible from her driver's side window, competed for her attention. Before she and Dale dropped out of North Texas State and got married, they used to roam the cemetery, reading names from century-old tombstones and making up stories about the people buried there. One time they stumbled upon "Suzanna and infant" chiseled in a crude chunk of stone. Even now, all these years later, Johnnie still pictured a young mother and child, cuddled together for eternity.

A bright orange bread truck lumbered by, followed by a ratty compact car with no hubcaps. Two young men in cutoffs and tank tops pedaled on their bikes against the flow of traffic, their backpacks bulging. A young woman walking her dog had one hand on the leash; the other clutched her cell as she texted, head bent.

The closer Johnnie got to downtown, the more she noticed how apartment buildings gave way to older homes with front porches crammed full of plants, bicycles, grills, and the occasional "For Rent" sign out front. A young man on a skateboard whizzed by, a large black case flattened at his side. *An art portfolio,* Johnnie thought, picturing D.J. not that long ago, rushing to get to class. In a town that boasted two universities, transportation took all forms.

At East Hickory, she hung a right on the

one-way street and scooted into the left lane. Up ahead, the green and white neon CAMPUS THEATRE sign welcomed her to the square. Rolling past the grand movie house, now a venue for special events, she glugged half a bottle of water, trying to chase down the jitters that had been building since D.J.'s phone call.

The light turned green at Elm and Hickory, and she proceeded through the intersection. Cars and people packed the square in the middle of a weekday afternoon. On the courthouse steps, a curvaceous model in eveningwear posed for a photographer hunched behind a tripod, but Johnnie's eyes were drawn to the Confederate soldier atop a gray marble arch on the south side of the courthouse lawn, still green in the heat of Indian summer and shaded by towering pecan trees starting to change color.

"Why, you're just a boy," she whispered as her gaze swept over the youthful face with a strong jaw line that reminded her too much of Cade, "and I'm just like Mama, talking to statues." Before glancing away, she noted the two water fountains left over from the days of segregation that flanked each base of the arch.

Instead of circling the square, a favorite pastime when she came to town, she went straight through the intersection at Locust and Hickory and coasted downhill until she came to a single-story building on the right. A bright orange awning over a large picture window offered shelter from the elements. As she swung into a parking slot in front of the building, her gaze shifted to the company's hand-painted logo on the matching orange door: Denton's House of Ts, Screen Printing & Design, Established 2009. With her foot on the brake and the engine still running, she sat there a moment, remembering a text message Cade sent Callie Ann right before he deployed. "Hey, baby sis, that's cool about D.J.'s new job at Denton's House of Tease. Sounds like a strip club? Ha! Ha!"

Johnnie would give anything to have her jokester boy home, and to hear his sister give him grief, "It's Ts, you moron. Didn't you learn how to spell?"

Her heart raced ahead of her as she slammed the gearshift into park and cut the engine. Checking her lipstick and hair, she dropped her keys into her purse and got out of the Suburban.

The heavy odor of Chinese food from the restaurant next door hung in the humid air. Usually, she savored the scent of ginger, hot peanut oil, and garlic, but today it made her queasy. She steadied herself against the driver's door, waiting for the feeling to pass.

Until that moment, she hadn't realized she was shaking.

"There's nothing to be afraid of," D.J. had told her on the phone. But he was wrong. There were so many things in this world to be afraid of. So many enemies. She tried to reassure herself that the man waiting on the other side of the orange door wasn't the enemy. The enemy was someone halfway around the world trying to kill her youngest son.

When she looked up, D.J. stood in the open doorway, all six feet two inches of him in black jeans and a T-shirt, his arms crossed over the bib of his work apron, his mouth set in a tight-lipped grin. She slung her purse over her shoulder and offered her bravest smile. "Hey, son. I love the orange awning. You can see it all the way from the square."

D.J. bent to give her a one-arm hug. "That's the idea, Mom." Then he ushered her inside the small, air-conditioned lobby furnished with just a couple of vinyl-covered chairs, a large plant, and a display of T-shirts with various designs on a wall behind the central counter.

The man from the square rose from his

seat where he'd been sipping coffee. He ran his hands up and down the sides of his relaxed fit jeans. A cream-colored camp shirt had replaced the white turtleneck and tan corduroy jacket he'd worn when he followed them into Recycled Books. On his feet was a pair of casual boat shoes.

He hesitated, and then stepped forward. "You must be Johnnie." His gravelly voice gave away his age; he had to be somewhere in his early eighties. But it was the glimmer in his deep-set eyes when he spoke her name that caught her off-balance.

Dry mouthed, she swallowed and glanced up at D.J., but his dark eyes cut away before she could read them. Her son's hand rested in the center of her back, his sweaty palm pressed into her thin cotton blouse. He seemed to be coaxing her forward.

She took a step and stuck out her hand. "And you must be from Publishers Clearing House." The joke tumbled out unbidden, her voice gruffer than usual. "Have I won a million dollars?"

The old man took her hand, and he began to tremble at her touch. "You're the little girl in the photo." Tears welled in his eyes.

Her pulse quickened and she searched his lined face, his white goatee so trim in contrast to his dark, bushy eyebrows. "What photo?"

He released her hand and fished a hanky from his back pocket, the kind Grandpa Grubbs used to use, and blew his nose. Then he and D.J. exchanged glances.

"Mom, you might want to sit down." D.J. led her to one of two chairs in the lobby and the old man followed.

With shaky hands, he retrieved a business-sized envelope from his chest pocket, lifted the flap, and pulled out a faded photograph. Her heart misfired and time came to a standstill as her gaze swept over the familiar images of a dashing Army officer in uniform, standing by a picnic table. Over his shoulder, a chubby-cheeked girl in pigtails peeked out from behind a tree trunk.

"Where did you get that?" Her voice exploded inside her head as she stared dumbfounded at the same photo framed on her entry table back home. The photo Dale found taped to the underside of a drawer two years ago in Uncle Johnny's old bedroom. The photo Mama had taken at Fort Hood when Johnnie was five. Mama had led her to believe the lieutenant leaving for war was Uncle Sam, and not *Daddy.*

The old man's voice faltered. "It was among my son's personal effects." He paused and dabbed his eyes with his hanky. "They were shipped home after he was killed in Vietnam."

All the air in her lungs gushed out at once, and she bent forward to keep from toppling out of the chair. Leaning on her elbows, she hung her head between her legs and stared at her feet. They were laced into comfortable walking shoes and planted firmly on the tile, but the tile was spinning.

The ceiling fan whirred above her, stirring the air around in the tiny lobby, yet a sudden heat moved through her body. In a matter of seconds, cold beads of perspiration dampened the skin beneath her peasant blouse and white jeans, and she swiped at her wet forehead and flipped her ponytail off her sweaty neck.

She heard a door swish open behind the counter and a young man's voice call out, "Hey, D.J. Have you seen the. . . . Oh, hey, sorry, man. Didn't mean to intrude."

Through her blurry vision, Johnnie recognized one of D.J.'s bosses, a chubby fellow with black eye glasses to match his dark beard and beefy forearms covered in tats. He'd graduated from college a couple of years ahead of D.J.

From somewhere above her, she heard her son say, "It's cool, dude. Be there in a sec.

Just having a family powwow."

The door closed and her son patted her on the shoulder. "You okay, Mom?"

Slowly, Johnnie lifted her head and stared in confusion at the old man. "I don't understand. Mama told me a long time ago that y'all had died — that I had no family left on my father's side, so don't even bother looking."

The old man sagged in his chair and stared out the picture window, shaking his head.

D.J. pounded his fist on the counter. "Unfricking-believable. Queen Victoria strikes again." He stomped across the room. "I need a smoke." Right before he pushed through the door, he stuck his head back inside. "My deepest apologies, Arthur. My Grand*maw* Victoria, Mom's *mother* — and I use that term loosely — well, let's just say she's got a thing for family secrets."

Through the picture window, Johnnie watched her son light a cigarette, take a long drag, and release his anger each time he exhaled. One thing was certain: as soon as she left Denton, she and Mama were going to have a little chat. Mama had some explaining to do.

"May I?" She reached over and gently tugged the photo from the man's fingers —

the man D.J. had called Arthur. She sat back down and flipped it over and studied Mama's handwriting on the back: *Francis and Johnnie, Fort Hood, 1969.* "Mama must have gotten duplicates made and sent this to him."

Arthur Murphy's sigh filled the room with decades of regret. "After we found the photo in his footlocker, we contacted the Army, wondering if he had been secretly married, but they had no record of a wife or a daughter. Without a last name, we had nothing to go on. Well-meaning friends told us the little girl in the photo was probably another soldier's daughter, but I knew in my heart that wasn't the case . . ." his voice trailed off and he gazed longingly at Johnnie. Finally he said, "I never gave up hope that I would find you one day." His eyes glistened.

Johnnie took a deep breath. She was still in shock over this revelation. This man sitting right in front of her, this stranger, was her grandfather. "I'm forty-five years old. My Grandpa Grubbs has been dead for years. He's the man who helped raise me. What should I call *you*?"

He rubbed his thumb against his goatee. "You can call me whatever you want, but my students called me Arty behind my back." He paused and chuckled. "I taught high school art and they thought it was funny, like they were getting away with something."

Johnnie smiled, trying to picture him as a young art teacher. "I like Arty."

They both gazed out the window as D.J. stubbed out his smoke and tossed the butt in a nearby trash can. "You know, Arty, before my husband found the photo, I didn't trust my memory. I was only five; it's the only memory I have of my father. But looking back, I realize D.J. has always resembled him, even when he had long hair and a beard."

Arty nodded. "I'm eighty-four years old. My wife, Mae, has Alzheimer's. Francis was our only child. This morning, when I saw your son's picture in the newspaper, I darn near choked on my coffee." He stopped to rub his eyebrows before he went on, "The same thing happened last fall when I spotted him on the square. It's like I'd lost my mind. I thought he was Francis. But then he spoke, and I remembered that my son was dead. Thirty-eight years last November."

"November twenty-second," Johnnie said as D.J. pushed through the door, the smell of cigarette smoke trailing him. "The anniversary of JFK's death."

D.J. glanced at his watch then rubbed his hands together. "Well, kiddies, I hate to break up the party, but I've got to get back to work."

Johnnie's gaze shifted from her son to Arty. For the first time, she noticed his hands. They were larger than average, with long elegant fingers and specs of paint on his yellowed nails. *D.J.'s hands, only older.*

D.J. went to help him out of his seat, but Arty waved him off. "I'm not crippled yet, son, but thanks."

They exchanged nervous laughter, then Johnnie scribbled her address and cellphone number on a piece of paper and pressed it into Arty's palm. "We live in the historic part of Portion, right off Main Street. There's so much for us to talk about. I would like to know more about my father and what kind of person he was."

Arty glanced at the paper then slipped it into the envelope with the photo and stuck it back in his shirt pocket. Pulling out his wallet, he handed Johnnie a business card. "I'm looking forward to meeting my other great-grands. D.J. filled me in on everybody's whereabouts."

Johnnie scanned the glossy card: Arty's Art — Original Paintings of North Texas. "I'd love to see your work. Maybe next time

I come to Denton?"

He fumbled with his wallet. "I'd like that very much. I have a special series I devoted to Francis," he added, a catch in his voice.

As Johnnie gazed into her grandfather's eyes, she saw past the friendly retired art teacher to the grieving father of a dead soldier. She shivered, and then gave him a hug. His wrinkled neck smelled of Aqua Velva.

After they embraced, he held her at arm's length. "I must say, the little girl in the photo sure grew into a beautiful woman."

She rubbed her nose, hiding behind her shy smile. He had no idea who she was or what she had been through in life. Until today, all he had was the image of a little girl in pigtails and his hope of finding her, but it had been enough. His kindness reached deep into her heart, mending the broken threads of her life and hopefully his too.

He patted her on the shoulder. "Try not to worry yourself sick about your boy, Cade. We both know he's got a guardian angel going into battle with him."

Her throat clutched. He'd picked up on her fear.

From the corner of her eye, she saw D.J. bow his head. She wondered if he was crying or praying.

A blast of hot air blew into the room as Arty opened the door to step outside. As soon as he was out of sight, she reached for her phone to call Mama.

Chapter 24
Missing in Action

Clutching her purse in one hand and her cell in the other, Johnnie stared at the tile floor as Mama's smoky voice came on the line.

"Sorry I missed your call, y'all. Leave me a message. I'll get right back atcha." *Beep.*

Johnnie's chest tightened. She blew out a lungful of air and gritted her teeth. "Mama, it's me. We need to talk. Call me back the second you get this. Bye."

"Ever notice how the moment you need her, Queen V's conveniently out of pocket?" D.J. leaned against the doorframe behind the counter, his arms crossed and his head tilted in that way that told Johnnie he'd already made up his mind. His grandmother was guilty of something.

Johnnie wanted to give Mama the benefit of the doubt. "Maybe she's checking in a guest. Or overseeing housekeeping." She pictured Mama dashing up and down the stairs of the Dooley Mansion, barking out orders to the maids and counting down the minutes until her next cigarette break.

Her son's dark eyes flashed with disapproval. "Quit making excuses for her. You've been doing that since the moment she hit town." Johnnie winced and his face softened. Out of the three kids, D.J. seemed the least tolerant of his grandmother's shortcomings. "I'm sorry, Mom. Text me when you get home." He gave her a half-wave then disappeared behind the door.

Out on the sidewalk, Johnnie tried Mama's number again. "Sorry I missed your call, y'all. . . ." Frowning, Johnnie mashed the *end* button on the keypad, aborting the call.

Throwing her purse in the front seat, she slid behind the wheel, threw the Suburban in gear, and hustled back to Portion, seething the whole way but too mad to cry. Two hours later and still no word from Mama, Johnnie flipped open her cell and tried again. "Mama, I need to talk to you. It's really important. Please call me back."

After leaving a second message, she poured a glass of iced tea and went to check her emails. Holding her breath, she plopped down at the computer station and peeked at the screen, hoping for a new message from

Cade. Nothing. With a heavy sigh, she massaged the spot between her eyes, fighting back the sinking feeling that threatened to rob her of all joy. The computer dinged and she jumped at the sound of a new message in her inbox.

Please be Cade.

She didn't recognize the sender's address, but she clicked on the subject, *your column:*

How you doin'?

I write science fiction with a twist of erotica — robots having sex. I would love to send you a copy of *Man of Steel Shows His Metal* in exchange for a mention in your column. I've been trying to set up a book signing at Genie's Books on Main Street, but the gal that runs that place told me she's not interested. I thought maybe if you wrote about my book, she might change her mind.

Rex the Rocket

What the heck! If I weren't so upset, I'd laugh. Instead of hitting *reply* or *delete,* Johnnie forwarded the email to her editor:

Don't know if this guy's a wannabe wrestler, writer, or some dude getting his jollies, but sounds like ol' Rex would do better pedaling his book at those adult bookstores out on Northwest Highway in Dallas.

Johnnie

Next she sent her professor a brief note apologizing for ditching class. As she went to get her literature book out of her backpack, her cell rang.

Please let it be Mama . . . or Cade.

Dale's number appeared on her screen. Leaning against the kitchen island, she pressed her cell to her ear. Dale's voice competed with the tap-tap-tapping of hammers on the jobsite. "Any word from your mama?"

She started to tell Dale about the sleazy email but decided against it. She didn't want another lecture about how she needed to be careful now that her name was in the public arena. "Nope. I think she's avoiding me."

"Maybe her phone's dead. She forgets to charge it sometimes. It's only been a few hours."

Johnnie glanced at her watch. "I hope you're right, but I don't have a good feeling about this."

"If you don't hear from her soon, give me a buzz. I can stop by the Dooley Mansion on my way home from work and see if the El Camino's parked out back. I'll check your granny's place, too."

"Dale?" She hesitated, trying to sound braver than she felt. "I just got off the computer. There's nothing new from Cade either. It's been a couple of weeks since that last email."

Dale sighed. "Try not to worry. They're probably at some outpost without Internet."

Dale sounded so confident, so sure of everything, but Johnnie knew in her heart that while he was trying to reassure her, he was reassuring himself.

She fidgeted with the seam of her jeans. "Dale, you're going to like Arty. He's the nicest man."

Dale cleared his throat. "D.J. called a couple of hours ago when he was on break. We're trying to figure out the best way to tell Cade. It was hard enough when Brother died."

She peeked out the kitchen window over the sink, checking to make sure no government vehicle pulled up next to her curb. "Yes, but the news about Brother was bad. This is different." She touched the Blue Star banner in the window, sending her silent petition to God: *Please keep Cade safe.*

"It will still be a shock," Dale said, "learning he's got a great-grandfather waiting to meet him back home." As Dale talked, Johnnie noted the screech of power saws in the background. The house was too quiet without Brother.

If he were alive, she would curl up next to him and pour out all her fear and heartache into his rich, brown coat. He had the kind of thick skin that could shield him from the emotional pain of others. His body could withstand human suffering — he never judged — but it wasn't strong enough to survive being hurtled through a car window.

Glancing at Brother's favorite spot on the braided rug in the den, she walked into the entryway and picked up the duplicate photo on the table. Staring at the picture of her father, its colors faded with time, she shuddered at the mental image of Arty and his wife getting the bad news about their only child. *Did it come via telegram? A phone call? A knock at the door?*

The clock over the mantel chimed six o'clock. She sat the photo down and went back into the kitchen. She knew she should start dinner, but she also needed to study. And she needed to know that Cade was okay and that Mama hadn't skipped town.

Her stomach somersaulted when she tried Mama one more time and the call went straight to voicemail.

"Mama, answer your darn phone! You're starting to scare me."

Johnnie tossed her phone on the table and pulled out a chair. She wasn't in the mood to read, but she didn't have a choice, especially since she'd missed class that morning.

Flipping through her literature anthology, she came to "The Harlem Renaissance" section. Today's assignment: read Langston Hughes' bio (1902-1967) and six of his poems, starting with "Mother to Son." As Johnnie began to read, she visualized a poor, hardworking woman climbing the rickety stairway of a tenement, a young son in tow. The mother's lesson to the boy: keep climbing, keep plugging away no matter how weary, and don't ever turn back.

Chin in hand, Johnnie rested her elbow on the table and stared at the page. In the margin next to the poem, she scribbled, "Never give up." Twirling her finger through her ponytail, she imagined Brother Dog curled up at her feet, his warm presence keeping her company while she studied. "Never give up on my dream to finish college," she murmured, wishing she could reach under the table and feel his firm head. "Never give up hope that Cade will come home alive. . . ." She paused for a moment, letting it sink in, then added, "And never give up on Mama."

The last part caught her by surprise, and she sat up straight as D.J.'s voice thundered in her head, *Quit making excuses for her.* Johnnie's gaze drifted to the top of the page, to the poem's title, "Mother to Son." She closed her eyes for a moment, switching the words around in her head, *Son to Mother.* She began to visualize D.J. leading her up the rickety stairway. Her adult son was now the teacher, and she his student. And she saw Mama through his eyes: an aging woman who could no longer use her beauty to charm her way through life.

Mama, you better check in and not check out. If you can't do it for me, do it for your grandkids.

Cade's pickup roared up the driveway. She glanced up expectantly. For those few seconds while the engine idled, she forgot he wasn't driving.

The side door burst open and Callie Ann appeared, breathless and smelling of french fries and catfish from her new afterschool job at the Marina Café. "I wanna hear all about Grandpa Arty. D.J. said he's a doll. But first I wanna know why Grandma V would lie about this." She ripped off her apron, her eyes hard as iron as she stood in the middle of the room, slapping the apron straps against her leg. "She can't mess with people's lives. It's not right."

Johnnie pushed away from the table, her studies on hold. "Sis, I've been trying to call her all day. I want to ask her the same thing, but it seems that Mama is missing in action. Again."

Johnnie stalked past Callie Ann to the computer station.

"What are you doing?" Callie Ann followed her.

Johnnie opened her email and began clicking the keys. "I'm writing to Cade."

Callie Ann peeked over her shoulder, resting her chin on the top of Johnnie's head. "How are you going to tell him?"

"The same way we told him about Brother Dog. 'Straight up,' as D.J. would say."

From: Mom and Callie Ann
To: Camp Cade
Date: September 2009
Subject: News from home

Dear Cade,

We hardly know where to begin. This is good news, but you might want to sit down. It seems we have gained a new family member. It's a long story, and we don't even know all of it yet, but here goes. . . .

After Johnnie composed the email with her daughter's input and hit *send,* Callie Ann tugged on her mother's ponytail. "Mom, do you think Granny Opal knew about your other set of grandparents?"

Johnnie leaned her head back and stared up at her daughter's face. "Oh, Lord. I haven't a clue. All I know is that Mama led me to believe they died a long time ago, and that their ashes were scattered over my father's grave at Arlington."

Callie Ann reached down and kissed Johnnie on the cheek. "I'm sorry, Mom. And all this time they've been living in the same town where you were born, and where D.J. went to college."

Johnnie gripped her daughter's hand and pulled her onto her lap. "Sis, I will never lie to you the way Mama lied to me." Johnnie couldn't remember the last time Callie Ann sat on her lap, and she relished the moment until her daughter pulled away. "Where're you going?"

"To change out of these stinky clothes and go look for Granny V. You coming with me?"

Chapter 25
The Text Message

Before she scurried out the door the next morning in a new pair of brown leggings and a long orange cardigan, Johnnie left another voicemail for Mama:

"We've searched everywhere for you. The Dooley Mansion, the war memorial, the cemetery. Dale checked Granny's place twice last night. . . . We talked to your boss, Mr. Fred. He says you took off in the El Camino yesterday after you got a phone call. He's worried about you, too. Is everything okay? Callie Ann says she taught you how to text, so please send me a message if you don't feel like talking. I just need to know you're okay." She gulped back a knot of fear. "I love you, Mama."

And if I don't hear from you in a couple more days, I'm filing a missing person's report.

Five minutes before her Texas Government

class let out, Johnnie's cell phone vibrated. Trying to be discreet, she peeked down where she'd wedged it between her thighs. D.J. had been badgering her to get a smartphone, but she wasn't ready to learn the new technology, plus it cost money. Since Mama had gone missing, she hadn't let her phone out of her sight. If she flipped it open now, she could see who was calling or texting. But today Johnnie sat in the front row, five feet away from her professor, Delores Richards, a woman about Johnnie's age. Kind as she was, Professor Richards didn't tolerate cell phones in class. Johnnie could raise her hand and asked to be excused, as if she were back in elementary school and needed a hall pass to pee — younger students did it all the time — but Johnnie was the oldest student in class and she didn't want to call attention to herself. So she jiggled her foot, watching the clock as her professor droned on.

Finally, class was over. Bolting out of her seat, she dashed from the lecture hall and tore down the corridor toward the exit. Outside, she held her breath as she passed through the gauntlet of students puffing away on cigarettes before they headed indoors. A cold front had blown in overnight, clearing the sweltering air and lowering temperatures to a breezy fifty degrees.

Flipping open her phone, she read the text: Gonna finish what I started. Check glove box for note. Luv u, baby girl.

Finish what she started? Johnnie stared at the cryptic message. A second later, her heart turned over. It could only mean one thing. She hoped she wasn't too late.

Tears clouded her vision as she charged across campus, bumping into a couple of students on her way to the parking lot. Too upset to call Dale, she barely noticed the weight of her backpack as it jostled from side to side. Hands shaking, she fumbled to insert the key in the ignition. Firing up the engine, she barreled out of the parking lot, ignoring the twenty-mile-per-hour speed limit on campus.

Without giving it another thought, she headed straight for the cove — the secluded cove far from the marina and dam, sheltered on one side by a high bluff. The cove where Uncle Johnny drowned while saving his sister and her unborn baby.

Ten minutes later, a memory rippled through Johnnie's mind as she navigated the curves and straightaways of Lakeside Drive. A gray morning at dawn, the ghostly image of Mama in her cotton nightgown at the edge of the dock, sobbing at young Johnnie to "stay away from this place. It'll bring you nothing but heartache."

If Johnnie hadn't snuck up on Mama that morning, no telling what she might have done.

Driving with the window down, Johnnie spotted a whirlwind of pumpkin- and squash-colored leaves alongside the road. October was right around the corner. Despite the heat of Indian summer, the leaves had been changing colors all along.

As she sped past the turnoff to Glory, she glanced at the hanging tree to her left, its mottled canopy a mixture of green, yellow, and brown. The last time she saw it, the day Brother died, the leaves were still green. Back before she knew the tree's tragic history.

Passing by Granny's, she slowed down to make sure Mama's car wasn't parked in the long, narrow driveway leading up to the sprawling white house. Dale had driven by here twice last night and could find no sign of her. Johnnie's gaze traveled over the big picture window, the empty glider and geranium pots on the long front porch, her abandoned playhouse in the side yard. She hadn't stepped foot in her childhood home since Granny's funeral. Until Callie Ann's accident, Johnnie had left it up to her daughter and Mama to sort through Granny's things. Maybe it had been too much for Mama. Maybe it had done her in. Along with that phone call.

Pressing her foot on the gas, Johnnie held her breath and raced the quarter-mile around the bend, following the same path a teenage Victoria Grubbs had pedaled on her bicycle in 1963.

At the cove, Johnnie eased the Suburban onto the wide shoulder and cut the engine. She spotted the El Camino parked nearby and wondered if Mama left it in the same spot where she'd dropped her bike before running into the water. Poor Uncle Johnny, throwing down his fishing rod and diving off the dock to save her, the cast on his leg acting like the sinker he'd tied to the end of his line.

Mama's slender form at the edge of the dock caught Johnnie's eye. At first she thought Mama had on a hospital gown, but as she strained forward, she realized it was one of her calico dresses. Hadn't she stopped wearing those when Granny died?

Instead of flinging open the door and jumping out, Johnnie sat frozen behind the steering wheel, unable to move. It would be so easy to let Mama end it. For a second, all Johnnie felt was release. Because once Mama jumped, it would all be over. Then she remembered the promise she'd made to Granny Opal to take care of Mama. She tried to move, but so help her God, she couldn't budge. She didn't have the energy to get out of the car. Her body turned to jelly. It was too late to call 911. Mama needed help *now.*

Then she heard Granny Opal calling from somewhere nearby. "All you have to do is believe," as if she'd been out hanging wash on the clothesline and had seen Johnnie's predicament.

Johnnie's scalp tingled as she peered over the curve of the steering wheel, half-expecting to see Granny standing at the edge of the bluff, waving a white hand towel in her direction.

I hope you're right, Granny.

Blinking once, Johnnie "summoned the saints."

Seven dark figures swirled out of the water and encircled Mama, forming a barrier so she couldn't jump. The tallest one held a hand a few inches above Mama's head like she was imparting a blessing. With her other hand, she beckoned Johnnie. *Hurry now,* she seemed to say.

Johnnie watched herself kick open the car door, rushing now on sturdy legs made strong from years of running and power walking. Unencumbered by stiff jeans, her legs were encased in tights that freed her to run fast and hard, her feet in comfortable Sketchers. She would tackle Mama gently so as not to scare her.

As she shrugged out of the cardigan, she looked up, and the seven were gone.

Mounting the dock, she rushed toward Mama, wrapping the sweater around a ghost. A ghost of a woman whittled down to nothing but skin and bones.

"It's okay, now, Mama. I'm here."

As they fell backward, Mama began to sob, and Johnnie cradled her like she was one of her children.

"I'm no good to anyone!" Mama wailed, her voice tortured.

Johnnie rocked her mother, smoothing matted hair off her forehead. "What happened? Your boss said you seemed upset after you got a phone call yesterday."

"Does he hate me, too?"

"Who, your boss?" Johnnie wrapped the cardigan tighter around Mama's emaciated form. She'd been so caught up in her grief for Brother and worry for Cade that she'd failed to notice Mama wasting away.

"No, Arthur Murphy!" Mama cried, her body convulsing in Johnnie's arms.

Arthur Murphy! So Mama knew about him after all.

Johnnie grasped for the right words, picturing how the whole thing went down. Before she'd arrived in Denton yesterday, D.J. had given Arty the scoop on all the family, including Victoria Grubbs. Once Arty left the shop, he'd called the Dooley Mansion, looking for her.

Johnnie took a deep breath, inhaling Mama's scent of too many cigarettes and unwashed hair. She kept her voice even. "No, Mama, Arty doesn't hate you. He wants to meet you."

Mama burrowed deeper into the sweater, like a naughty child who'd been caught red-handed. "I only did what Poppy told me to do."

Poppy! Johnnie thought. Sometimes she found it hard to believe that Grandpa Grubbs and her mama's Poppy had been the same man.

Johnnie gazed up at the sky to keep from crying. Not a cloud in sight. Off in the distance, a silver airliner passed over the lake on its approach into DFW Airport. Water lapped against the side of the dock from the wake caused by a speedboat racing too near the shore. Two mallards paddled by; the drake's glossy green head matched Mama's eyes. The hen's brown-speckled feathers reminded Johnnie of the changing leaves, the changing seasons of their lives.

"We can talk about Poppy later. Let's get you back to my house." She kept her tone gentle and soothing. "You can soak in a nice bubble bath, and later I'll help you fix your hair."

Mama sniffled, "What about my car?"

Johnnie glanced over at the El Camino, wondering about the suicide note in the glove box. "We'll get Dale and Callie Ann to come pick it up before supper. It should be safe here . . . as long as it's locked."

As she started to help Mama up, Johnnie spotted a rough carving on a section of planks, a pocketknife tossed aside near the design. Mama was no artist, but Johnnie could tell she'd been whittling on it for some time.

Johnnie didn't need an explanation for what it symbolized: a love triangle like no other. Her family's tragic history chiseled into wood. Each tip of the triangle contained a name: at the top was Johnny, then Francis to the left and Victoria on the right.

Etched in the center of the triangle was a crude baby's face.

Johnnie choked back tears. She was the baby in the middle.

Chapter 26
Them Bells

Whit pulled the Saturn into a small lot behind the Dooley Mansion and shoved the gearshift into park. "Guess this was the servants' entrance back in the day." She gestured toward the back porch, half the size of the wide veranda out front. The western sun faded as the gray and purple hues of dusk settled over the manicured yard, dappled in shadow from century-old trees starting to drop their leaves.

Johnnie crawled out of the backseat and held the front passenger door open. "Mama says they call it a smokers' porch nowadays, right?" Mama acted as if she was deaf, like she hadn't heard a word. She seemed so small and frail in Callie Ann's gold warm-up pants and one of the boys' old sweatshirts with Portion Bandits stitched across the chest.

"Listen to them bells." Mama sighed as she grasped Johnnie's hand and struggled out of the car. It took a second for her to straighten up.

Whit shut the driver's door and came around the front of the Saturn, her long skirt swooshing against brown leather boots with spiked heels. "You like those wind chimes, Miss Victoria? I carry them down at the shop."

All three women turned to admire the large tubular wind chimes hanging from the crooked branch of a towering post oak a few feet away. "They sound like church bells," Mama said in a faraway voice.

Wedging sunglasses on top of her spiked hair, Whit looped an arm through Mama's and they ambled toward the steps leading up to the back porch. "Watch your step," Whit advised. "These flagstones are pretty, but they're a little uneven and hard to see this time of day."

"I can see just fine, Whit. I'm not blind yet," Mama sniffed, sounding like her old self again.

Thank You, Lord, Johnnie thought, bringing up the rear. Mama's laundered dress flopped halfway out of Johnnie's purse. That afternoon, while Mama soaked in the big-jetted bathtub Dale had installed during the last renovation, Johnnie washed and dried her things and made a few discreet phone calls. “Mama tried to kill herself today,” she began, as if this was an everyday occurrence and she was just reporting in.

Whit dropped everything and left her shop in the hands of her assistant to lend Johnnie moral support. Dale offered to leave work early, but Johnnie told him to stay put; she and Whit could handle things. D.J. said he’d check on Arthur Murphy in case “the old man flipped out after Queen Victoria hung up on him.”

Mama stopped midway up the walk and turned to Johnnie. “We should hang some of them bells up at the war memorial. There are plenty of trees. . . .”

Even in the fading light, Johnnie could see a sparkle return to Mama’s eyes. The breeze picked up and the melodious sound of bells filled the cool, smoky air. Wrapped in her long orange cardigan to stave off the evening chill, Johnnie pictured a set of wind chimes hanging from a sturdy branch next to the old soldier. Each time a bell tolled, it would ring a death knell for the fallen. The idea both haunted and comforted her.

At the bottom step, Whit pivoted and her gaze lingered on something in the distance. “Johnnie, remember how you talked about wanting to put a memorial plaque at the base of the hanging tree?”

"Yeah, and after two glasses of wine I realized no one would see it from the road."

Whit pursed her lips, thinking hard. "But they might hear chimes clanging in the wind."

Throwing her head back, Johnnie flung her arms skyward. "Because sometimes music speaks louder than words," she sang, casting off the doom and gloom pent up since getting Mama's text earlier that day.

Mama's gaze shifted back and forth between the two women. "Those bells probably cost more than I make in a week."

Whit squeezed Mama's shoulder. "Don't worry about the cost, Miss Victoria. I can get 'em wholesale."

As Mama and Whit mounted the concrete steps, Mama's slumped shoulders squared and a spring returned to her step. She patted Whit on the arm. "Thanks for bringing me home."

Home, Johnnie thought. Mama considered this place home, not the house on the bluff overlooking the lake where she grew up. Johnnie had the strangest sensation her mother had navigated these steps for years. Once they got her settled, Johnnie planned to ask her what she meant that day in June about getting her old room back. Johnnie had yet to see it since Mama moved in.

Stepping onto the porch, Mama glanced over her shoulder and poked her brass room key at Johnnie's purse. "You can burn that dress. I never want to see it again."

Johnnie fingered the soft cotton. "Would you like me to donate it to charity?"

"No, just throw it out. It's bad luck now."

Johnnie nudged Whit in the side, and the two friends exchanged glances. "Dale and Callie Ann should be along any minute now with your El Camino," Johnnie said, changing the subject. Before they'd left for the Dooley Mansion, Johnnie had said, "Maybe you should speak with a member of the clergy or a counselor."

Swaying to and fro in the porch swing, Mama had pointed her lit cigarette at Johnnie and huffed, "I ain't talkin' to no preacher or shrink. I know what's wrong with me. My life's been one big screw-up since I turned fifteen."

The back door opened and a tall, bony gentleman in a white dress shirt, slacks, and running shoes stepped out, his salt and pepper hair slicked back in a short man bun. His wire-rimmed granny glasses enhanced his hazel eyes. "Good evening, ladies. Looks like autumn rolled into North Texas overnight. Yesterday we had on the AC. Today we cranked up the furnace."

Whit extended her hand. "Hello, Mr. Fred. I'm Whit Thomas, a friend of the family."

His thin face broke into a warm grin as they exchanged greetings. "Good evening, Ms. Thomas. I'm Fred Johnson, but everybody calls me Mr. Fred."

To Johnnie, he looked more like an eccentric law professor than a guy running a bed and breakfast. He had an old-fashioned formality about him, but he didn't put on airs. Of the three owners, he was the only one who lived at the mansion fulltime. Mama said he was single, about Johnnie's age, and ran marathons.

He took Mama's hand like she was a guest and not one of his employees. "Welcome back, Miss Victoria. Have you ladies eaten yet? There's some roast beef, mashed potatoes, and green bean amandine in the kitchen. All you have to do is heat it up in the microwave."

Mama clasped her hand over his, craning her neck. He towered over all of them. "I'm sorry I ran out like that."

"You don't owe me an explanation. Why don't you take a couple of days off since it's the middle of the week? I can get someone to cover your shift."

As they filed inside, Johnnie's stomach

rumbled with hunger pangs at the smells coming from the kitchen. She hadn't eaten since she and Mama heated up a can of beef and barley soup hours ago. Mr. Fred's offer sounded good, but Johnnie would leave it up to Mama, who thanked her boss but told Johnnie and Whit she needed to rest.

While Whit ushered Mama into her room, directly to the right of the back door, Mr. Fred took Johnnie aside, out in the wide central hall that ran the length of the house. "Is your mother all right?" he asked, sounding concerned.

"She had a little episode, but she's better now."

Lowering his voice, he spoke out of the side of his mouth. "She's a hard worker, your mother, but I'm afraid she's running herself ragged trying to do the job of two people. That's why we have a housekeeper."

That old familiar ache returned to the pit of Johnnie's stomach. "Sounds like she's trying to prove herself."

Mr. Fred gave a quick nod. "She doesn't have to prove anything to me. We haven't had one complaint since she started working here."

Johnnie pictured Mama brushing hair out of her eyes as she scurried up and down the staircase, cleaning bathrooms and changing sheets, as if this could make up for all the years of neglect and God knows what kind of life she'd led outside of Portion.

"Mrs. Kitchen, without sounding presumptuous, may I ask what your mother's connection is to this house? Besides the fact that your husband is her son-in-law and the general contractor for the renovation."

Johnnie glanced at the hand-scraped wood floors, high ceilings, white crown molding, and the gleaming wood banister of the wide stairs leading up to the third floor landing where Dale's company had converted the attic into a honeymoon suite. "You know about Mama hiding out in the attic before the renovation?"

Mr. Fred nodded. "The day your mother inquired about a job, I realized I'd seen her before. As she was filling out her application, I recognized her as the woman in the attic, the one gazing out the dormer window the day the other owners and I stopped by to look at the property." His eyes twinkled at the memory. "Your mother has a striking face, you know. She's hard to forget." He cocked his head slightly. "You resemble her."

Johnnie's heart softened. She started to disagree, to tell him that her daughter actually got Mama's good bones. But instead, she simply replied, "So you're the one who saw Mama in the window that day. . . . My husband told me the story."

He pressed his finger to his lips. "She doesn't know I know. I'd like to keep it that way."

She studied him. "Weren't you afraid to hire her? I mean, she was *trespassing,* after all."

He rubbed his nose, hiding a shy smile. "I had a hunch she was a woman who'd been through a lot. I wanted to give her another chance."

Crossing her arms, Johnnie glanced at the toes of her Sketchers then back at him. "You're a good man, Mr. Fred. Thanks for taking a chance on her."

He turned to go. "You know, I can't put my finger on it, but sometimes I get the feeling she's lived here before. And I don't mean when the house sat vacant."

Time stopped for Johnnie. "Why do you say that?"

"I don't know." He shrugged. "One time I overheard her telling one of our guests that she and Mrs. Overby ate lunch on TV trays in the den so they could watch their soaps, but they always ate breakfast and dinner in the dining room."

Mrs. Delthia Overby. . . . So she and Mama were more than casual acquaintances. Johnnie wondered if Mama had worked for her at one time.

Fingering the shoulder strap of her purse, Johnnie said, "Mrs. Overby owned this place back when I was a kid. Every Halloween, she dressed up as a witch and served hot apple cider from a black cauldron on the front porch. She always spoiled me with extra treats, but I don't recall Mama and me ever being invited inside."

Mr. Fred rocked back on the heels of his running shoes and stuffed his hands in his pockets. "Well, except for that phone call yesterday, your mother seems to feel safe here."

The last part of his statement echoed in her mind — as if this was all the explanation required for hiring a woman with a shady past.

"And you deserve a medal," she told him as she turned and caught her reflection in a big silver mirror over the large walnut buffet.

A younger version of Mama gazed back.

Rounding the corner to Mama's bedroom, Johnnie stopped abruptly when she overheard Mama tell Whit, "Then I felt something touch the top of my head, like a rush of energy. It moved through my body, but no one was there. Not until my daughter grabbed me. I've never felt anything like it. . . . Well, maybe an orgasm," she quipped under her breath.

Whit let out a chuckle and Mama whispered something. Johnnie strained to listen, but she couldn't make it out. After a moment, Whit murmured, "Miss Victoria, what you felt was the hand of God, the Holy Ghost washing over you."

Mama gasped and started wheezing. Whit's serene voice floated through the air, and Johnnie heard the sound of footsteps, the rustle of a long skirt, then Whit cooing, "It'll be okay, Miss Victoria. We all fall short of the glory." Then Whit started humming the opening lines to "Blessed Assurance," one of her favorite hymns.

Leaning against the doorjamb, Johnnie shuddered. All afternoon, while pampering Mama and fixing her hair and sipping hot tea together, Johnnie had convinced herself that she'd conjured the whole thing up — that what she'd witnessed on the dock was a figment of her imagination. At one point, she'd even asked Mama, "Did you see anyone else at the cove . . . before I got there?" Mama had looked up from her mug of spiced tea, batted her lashes, and said, "Nope. Just me and them ducks . . . a few squirrels. Thought I saw a buzzard circle once, though."

Dizzy, Johnnie pushed away from the doorframe and entered the room, her legs wobbly as she looked around. Mama sat on the edge of a wrought-iron bed, a white quilted coverlet tossed back to one side. "Baby girl, come here," she motioned, dabbing her eyes with the corner of a pillowcase.

Whit looked up from a ladder-back chair where she was seated in front of a small antique roll-top desk near the bed. "Ladybug, you okay? You look a little pale."

Soft light glowed from a hurricane parlor lamp on the nightstand. A banged-up dresser stood next to the window, the curtains drawn. The small, bare-boned room might have served as a storage area at one time or the maid's quarters.

"I need to sit down," Johnnie said, glancing at twin black picture frames propped side by side on the dresser. Her eyes stung when she realized the frames didn't contain photographs but her last two columns from the newspaper.

Mama bit her lip, the aging stage mom caught in the act. "So I'm proud of you. Now don't go getting all mushy on me."

For a few seconds, all the pain of Mama's neglect and suicide attempts over the years faded away. At that moment, it didn't matter to Johnnie how many times Mama had done her dirty or the twenty-three years she'd estranged herself from the family. Johnnie plopped down on the bed next to her and cupped her mother's face in her hands. "Mama, that's about the sweetest thing you've ever said or done." A part of her wanted to tell Mama what she'd overheard in the hallway, but something held her back.

Mama's eyes watered and she looked away. "You two probably better head back. It's been a long day for all of us. Don't forget to stop by the kitchen on your way out and grab some supper to take home."

Whit started to get up. "Miss Victoria, you want me to fix you a plate and bring it to your room?"

Before Mama could answer, Johnnie heard herself cut in, "Hang on, Whit. Before we go. . . ."

Despite all the *God talk,* Johnnie wasn't letting Mama off the hook that easy. She took her hand. "Remember at the dock, when you were going to tell me about Poppy, and why he told you to lie about my other set of grandparents?"

Mama pulled away, and the serenity in the room vanished. She stood up and started to pace, jamming her hands deep into the pockets of the warm-up pants. "Poppy's the one who should'a joined the military . . . always barking orders," she began in that voice that was scratchy and soft at the same time. "He made it real clear. 'Your boyfriend was a *West Pointer.* How's that going to look if you and your illegitimate child show up on his grieving parents' doorstep? You are the last person they want to see, much less your daughter. Those people are heartbroken, and they'll think you are looking for a handout.' "

Those people, Johnnie thought, picturing poor Arthur and Mae Murphy huddled over their son's footlocker when they discovered the photograph of their son with a little pigtailed girl. All those years they cuddled up to his memory — unaware he'd fathered a daughter who lived less than an hour away.

The room grew quiet when Mama stopped to catch her breath. She peeked out through the curtain then spun around and started pacing again, this time illustrating her words with broad gestures. "The whole time Poppy was yapping and telling me how to live my life, Ma kept right on washing the dishes like she didn't have a brain in her head. Did you know Poppy even tried to tell her how to vote back then? Anyway, as usual, Aunt Beryl was visiting and woodpeckered her way into the conversation. She told Poppy he was dead wrong, that it wasn't fair to Francis' parents. She said he was smart as a whip when it came to him being an engineer, but he was dumb as a stump when it came to people. The only reason he didn't kick her out — she was his only sister."

Johnnie sat on the edge of the bed, repelled and fascinated at the same time. She crossed her feet. "Where was I?" she interrupted, having no memory of the conversation where Grandpa Grubbs instructed his daughter to lie — in essence, to deny his beloved granddaughter part of her heritage.

Mama flashed a desperate look her way and rolled her tongue around like she had a piece of hard candy lodged in one cheek — like she was trying so hard not to show any emotion. "Lord, baby girl, I suppose you were taking a bath. All I'm saying is I should've listened to Aunt Beryl that night. For once the old biddy was right."

Yawning, Mama stared straight at Johnnie, but she might as well have been back in the house overlooking the bluff, trapped between grieving parents who never got over their own son's death — much less the death of his best friend. "Can your daddy's parents ever forgive me?"

"Arty seems like a fair man. As for his wife, Mae, well . . . don't think it matters much. According to Arty, she won't remember anyway."

Mama yawned again and it echoed across the room. She turned down the lamp and stretched out on the bed. "You girls don't mind me, but I'm too tired to eat."

"Mama . . . ?" Johnnie started to ask about her connection to Delthia Overby, but realized she'd already pushed her enough for now. Within seconds, Mama was fast asleep. Whit and Johnnie tiptoed across the room and quietly shut the door.

Out in the massive gourmet kitchen, complete with off-white cabinets, honed granite countertops, a porcelain farmhouse sink, and two dishwashers, Johnnie and Whit watched in awe while Mr. Fred divvied up enough leftovers in carryout containers to ensure that neither woman had to cook that night. And it was a good thing, too, because Johnnie was too exhausted to think, much less throw a meal together when she got home. Her mind couldn't process everything that had happened since D.J. had summoned her to Denton. First a surprise grandfather. Then Mama's attempted suicide. Johnnie needed to rest.

Later, as they opened the back door to leave, a soothing chorus of bells rang into the night.

Chapter 27
Mama's Note

Dale tapped the long white envelope against his palm. "Aren't you at least curious what it says?" He sat on the edge of their king-sized sleigh bed, clad in nothing but boxer briefs and a warm throw Johnnie had draped over his bare shoulders.

She curled up next to him and leaned her head on his shoulder, breathing in the scent from his evening shower. Under the glow from Dale's bedside lamp, she stared at Mama's uneven scrawl on the back of the envelope: *Last Will and Testament of Miss Victoria Grubbs.* Ever since Dale retrieved the note from the El Camino's glove box and brought it into the house, Johnnie couldn't bring herself to open it. "You think Mama really wanted to kill herself?"

Dale sighed and propped one foot up on the bedrail. "Part of me says yes, but then why did she send you a text. I think she knew you would come."

Johnnie reached under the throw and caressed the inside of Dale's muscular thigh. He stirred, and she felt his muscles flex. It wasn't a tease but an invitation for another time when their lives weren't turned upside down. She gained strength from just being next to him, and she appreciated his years of hard work to build his business and provide for his family. It took her almost losing him two years ago to appreciate his goodness. She searched his blue eyes, and ran her fingers through his short, wavy hair. "Are you saying it was all a stunt? Because it sure looked like she was fixing to jump. And then there's the note."

He balanced the envelope in his callused fingers. "Maybe it was a cry for help. All I'm saying is she had plenty of time to jump before you got there."

Johnnie glanced at the clock radio on Dale's nightstand. Ten thirty p.m. glared back. All she wanted to do was crawl under the covers in her silky pajamas Dale had given her and go to sleep. She didn't want to deal with Mama's note or stay awake until Callie Ann got home. The day had worn her down.

After Dale and Callie Ann dropped off the El Camino, Callie Ann left in Cade's truck to meet up with friends for supper and to study for a test. Johnnie expected her home by now, but she held off calling her. She didn't want Callie Ann to think she was checking up on her, especially since she was supposedly studying for a test.

Gnawing her thumbnail, Johnnie tried not to fret. She wanted to trust her daughter, but too many of Cade's high school shenanigans played tricks on Johnnie's mind. Her heart quaked at the memory of Brother Dog waking her at dawn, his growls alerting her to a shiny black hearse parked in front of the house. The sight of the hearse about did her in, until she saw Cade puking in the jonquils and the hearse's driver, Steven "Tutts" Tuttle, backing away so he wouldn't get his dress shoes soiled. Tutts had been on his way to gas up the hearse for Farrow & Sons when he spotted Cade stumbling home drunk from his senior party. Not wanting D.J.'s little brother to get picked up for public intoxication, Tutts loaded Cade up in the hearse and dropped him off at the house, hoping to get away before Johnnie woke up. A week later, Tutts deployed to Iraq.

D.J.'s senior year proved just as stressful, but in a different way. While Dale went to bed early and slept with earplugs most nights, Johnnie stayed up reading in case the cops showed up to issue noise complaints. On school nights, D.J., along with Tutts and the rest of the band, practiced aggressive metal in the Kitchens' attached garage. On weekends, the band traveled all over Dallas/Fort Worth playing gigs in various venues, navigating the freeways past midnight. Johnnie spent many restless nights waiting for her oldest son to walk through the door.

Johnnie had tried to shield Dale from all those late nights spent worrying about their kids. Because his job was so physical, he was usually the first one to bed and the first one to rise. All those nights while Dale snoozed away, Johnnie waited. Waited for her children to come home alive.

Lost in thought, she jumped when Dale touched her on the knee, his coarse thumb going in circles on the shiny fabric. "Do you want me to open it? It's getting late."

About then, Cade's pickup roared up the driveway and the engine cut off. Relieved, Johnnie listened for the side door to open and close, the sound of her daughter's footsteps clopping through the house and down the hall. For a second, Johnnie thought she heard the rattle of tags and Brother's claws clicking on the hardwood floor, as if he'd waited up, too. But then she remembered he was dead.

Dale's weight shifted on the mattress, and he eyed the bedroom door.

Callie Ann's footsteps softened, and Johnnie pictured her tiptoeing down the hall to her room where she would quietly shut the door. But instead, she stuck her head in their doorway, looking surprised. "Hey, Dad, what are you still doing up?"

Dale studied her. "Your mom and I were just talking. How was your study group? You ready for your test?"

For once Johnnie was grateful Dale was the parent asking the questions.

Callie Ann took a few steps into the room and gestured at the envelope. "Is that Granny V's suicide note?"

Johnnie nodded and motioned for her to join them.

Callie Ann dropped her book bag on the floor and slouched in a chair next to Dale's side of the bed, her feet turned inward as if she were pigeon-toed. Tossing her hair back, she leaned forward on her elbows. "Yeah, we studied for like two hours." She glanced around the room, then back at her parents. "Sorry I'm late. I ran into an old friend as I was leaving the coffee shop. We got to talking and I lost track of time."

Johnnie perked up, eager to hear more

about it. "Oh, was it one of the girls from drill team?" Minutes earlier, Johnnie had studied her daughter's every move. Her speech wasn't slurred, she walked a straight line from the door to the chair, and she didn't reek of alcohol when she sat down. Johnnie hated that she'd doubted her.

Callie Ann brushed off her question and gazed at her dad. "So you haven't read it yet?" Then her eyes cut to Johnnie. "And no, Mom. I haven't been drinking if that's what you're thinking. I can tell the way you looked at me when I walked in the room. Just because Cade put you through hell . . ." her voice trailed off as she turned back to Dale. "Come on, Dad, open it."

Johnnie blinked, feeling the old familiar sting. For all her beauty, Callie Ann could be so abrupt. She peered at her daughter, seeing three generations in Callie Ann's face: Grandpa Grubbs' steely eyes, Mama's haughty cheekbones, Dale's blond eyebrows — and something else, too. Determination. Admiring her daughter's features, she speculated about the grandmother they'd never met.

Johnnie cleared her throat. "Actually, Sis, I was wondering if you look anything like Mae Murphy." She paused to let it sink in.

Callie Ann lowered her lids. Her voice

cracked. "Sorry I'm so edgy. Between Granny V trying to kill herself and my test tomorrow and always worrying about Cade. . . ." She hesitated and glanced up at Johnnie. "Do you think we can call Grandpa Arty soon? I'm dying to meet him and Granny Mae."

Granny Mae. She'd already picked out a name. Not Great-grandmother Murphy, not Great Grandma, but Granny. Callie Ann hadn't even met them yet, but she'd already accepted them as family.

At that moment, Johnnie longed to tell her daughter how she'd summoned the saints, just like Granny Opal suggested in her note to Callie Ann. But something held Johnnie back: that part deep inside that still questioned. She reached around Dale, grabbed a pillow, and hugged it to her chest. "I'll call Arty tomorrow and arrange a time for all of us to get together."

All of us, that is, except Cade, Johnnie thought.

Dale retrieved a pocketknife from his nightstand. "You girls ready?" He slit open the envelope, pulled out a handwritten note on yellow legal paper, and handed it to Johnnie.

With trembling hands, she took the note. Her voice faltered a few times then gained momentum as she began to read:

Because I loved a boy with my whole self, I brought shame to my family. When my brother died, a part of me went with him. Then Francis died, and my spirit dried up and flew away. My body's been looking for it since. Maybe in death I can be whole again — the carefree girl I was before everything changed.

Below are my instructions for my daughter to carry out in the event of my death. I don't hardly own much anymore, but these items deserve a good home.

1959 El Camino: to Dale Junior (Title is stashed in a box in the roll-top desk in my room at the Dooley Mansion. The other items on this list are also in the box.) I'm betting a smart guy like D.J. knows how to drive a stick shift.

Ma's long string of pearls: to Callie Ann. About the only thing of value I haven't hawked. Before they belonged to Ma, they belonged to her mother, Hannah Rose, my grandmother.

Lieutenant Francis Murphy's butter bars: to Cade. Francis gave them to me after he made 1st Lieutenant. Only a fellow soldier will truly value the rank.

My upright piano: please donate to a worthy cause rather than sell it in the estate sale. It needs to be tuned.

My body: cremate me and scatter my ashes at the war memorial since that's where I was when Poppy told me of Francis' death.

My portion of Ma's estate: Divide evenly between my three grandchildren, Dale Junior, Cade, and Callie Ann. I never want them to struggle.

My daughter's baby teeth: to Johnnie girl. I carried them with me everywhere I went.

And last but not least, my apologies to Arthur and Mae Murphy; I was only following orders from Poppy. He didn't want my daughter and me to become anyone's burden.

Victoria Grubbs
Portion, Texas

After Johnnie finished reading the letter, she handed it to Callie Ann. Squeezing Dale's bronze neck, Johnnie went to grab a wad of tissues from the master bath.

From over her shoulder, Callie Ann's voice clanged out across the room, "Granny V's not dead yet! Our job is to love her."

October 2009
From: Camp Cade

Holy guacamole, Mama! I've got a great gramps! I go off to war and folks start creeping out of the woodwork. Ask Papa Murphy if he's up for a special trip to Arlington National Cemetery when my time's up. It's high time we visit the lieutenant's grave.

Johnnie shuddered at Cade's choice of words. She knew what he meant — when his deployment was over. But still, his mention of Arlington National Cemetery felt like a bad omen.

Before she drifted off to sleep, she reminded herself to call Grandpa Arty in the morning and arrange a time when they could all get together.

Chapter 28
Portion Telegraph
"Roundtable with Johnnie Kitchen"

"Imagine sending two sons to war and not knowing if you'll ever see them again. Will both come home unscathed? Or will one get killed . . . or God forbid, both come home in body bags?"

These are the musings of a Marine mother whose two oldest sons are currently serving in Afghanistan. She contacted me last week to talk about what it's like to have two sons in a war zone at the same time. Besides the day-to-day fear, she said one of the most difficult aspects of sending her sons to war is the anger she feels when coworkers and friends complain about minor inconveniences. "While they rant about this or grumble about that, our young men and women are dying overseas! And I'm in a holding pattern, waiting for the plane to either land or crash."

"Sometimes people can be plain insensitive," she says. Most days she bites her tongue, but the other day she'd had enough and unleashed her fury on an unsuspecting person.

Her third son still lives at home and attends community college. When the weather is nice, he rides his Harley to class. One day last week as she went to retrieve the morning paper, she waited by the curb and watched him roar off down the street, his long hair whipping in the wind behind his helmet. Meanwhile, her neighbor (a sleek-looking woman in a business suit) came outside and remarked offhandedly, "I don't know how you sleep at night." The neighbor, of course, was referring to the biker son with long hair and tats. As the neighbor turned to go inside, the mother lost it and stormed across her yard, yelling, "Why, because my youngest son rides a Harley? I've got *two* other sons in Afghanistan. That's what keeps me up at night."

Shocked by the woman's outburst, the neighbor lady didn't have a comeback and scurried inside. A few hours later she tapped politely at the woman's front door. When the woman answered, the neighbor held out her version of "humble pie." Biting her lip, she smiled shyly and said, "I hope you like blackberry. It was my husband's favorite."

The woman invited her inside, and over

pie and coffee, they compared stories of heartache and loss and vowed to stay better connected.

Do you have a story you'd like to share with Johnnie Kitchen? Contact her at j.kitchen(at)portiontelegraph.com

Chapter 29
Chat with the Chief

"You're selling newspapers," the editor-in-chief called out across the newsroom. Her chipper voice bounced off hundred-year-old brick walls with black and white photos of Portion when horses trotted through town, kicking up dust.

Halfway out the door, Johnnie whirled and grinned at Glenda Hunter, a big-boned gal in her late fifties with short-cropped hair and an easy laugh. "Thanks for giving me a chance, Glenda."

"One of the smartest moves I've ever made," Glenda chuckled, twirling a pencil in both hands as she sat behind her desk in the center of the newsroom.

A young reporter with his back turned glanced over his shoulder and waved in Johnnie's direction. She envied how he could speak into his cellphone and jot notes at the same time, all with such ease, and then churn out a story by deadline. Johnnie, on the other hand, struggled over every word. At least she had the additional luxury of time that a daily reporter didn't. And yet Glenda had hired her.

Fifteen minutes earlier, Johnnie had stopped by the *Portion Telegraph* to chat and pick up her meager paycheck. Glenda had motioned her over to her desk. "People are reading your column, Johnnie, both online and in print. Subscriptions have picked up and copies are selling out at newsstands around town. Keep this up and you might get a small bonus at the end of the year."

Johnnie stared at her boss and tried to appear calm, but her heart jumped in her chest like a little kid in a bounce house. "A *bonus*! Imagine that." Johnnie knew she'd be lucky if it was twenty bucks, but it wasn't the money so much as the fact that people were reading her work.

Glenda sprang forward in her squeaky chair, a sly grin spreading across her handsome face. "People love controversy," she said in a breezy tone. "They eat it up. And you've been writing about some pretty controversial subjects lately."

Slowly, Johnnie glanced up at the high ceiling with exposed pipes then back at Glenda. "I can't take all the credit. Roosevelt's guest column really stirred things up."

"True, but you paved the way," Glenda replied before Johnnie could disagree. "Your column gave him the courage to speak out."

Standing in front of her editor's desk, watching Glenda toy with a thick yellow wristband, Johnnie recalled the day she waltzed into the newsroom over a year ago looking for a job.

Glancing around that day, Johnnie didn't see a door to an office with a sign out front that said "Editor." So she approached the first person she saw, a woman with bulky shoulders. She was tapping away on a keyboard, the stubby tips of her fingers flying over the keys. Johnnie had never seen anyone type so fast. The woman's wrists were encircled with bracelets supporting one cause or another. At first Johnnie thought the woman hunched over the keyboard at the gray desk was a reporter. But then the woman glanced up, and a twinkle in her eye gave her away, along with a nameplate on the desk that said, "Editor-in-Chief." Somehow Johnnie had missed it.

"Howdy, I'm Glenda Hunter, chief cook and bottle washer. How may I help you?"

Her humor put Johnnie at ease . . . almost.

Offering her bravest smile, Johnnie

stepped forward and introduced herself. "Do you have any openings for a local columnist? I've been reading your newspaper for years, but the only columns I see are either written by preachers, famous people, or are geared toward high society folks."

The editor stopped typing and swiveled in her chair, both eyebrows raised. "Do you have any experience?"

Gulping, Johnnie pressed ahead. "In 2007, you published my letter to the editor about my thoughts on war and my role as a military mom. A short time later, the community college published my story 'Granny Opal's Cake Factory' in their literary magazine, and . . ." she paused to steady her breathing and choose her words carefully. What she said next could make or break the deal. "I've been journaling most of my life, and occasionally I write letters to dead people."

The editor eyeballed her over the rims of her glasses. "You write letters to dead people?" Her forehead creased in a frown.

Johnnie kept a straight face. "I don't *mail* them," she deadpanned with more confidence than she felt. "It's a whole lot cheaper than therapy. When I was nineteen, I wrote a letter to the singer Karen Carpenter, the day after she died. I was struggling with bulimia, and her death was a wakeup call."

You can forget about writing your column now, an inner voice taunted. You've blown this whole interview, Johnnie girl. But since you're already making a fool of yourself. . . .

Clearing her throat, she continued, "I've been recovered for years, and I'd welcome the opportunity to write about it in a future column. That is, if you're interested. It's not just a young woman's disease. I go to school with a lady in her sixties who's been battling it for forty years." An image of Beverly Hills in baggy pants and running shoes jogged through Johnnie's mind, the back of Beverly's right hand covered in scars from years of teeth sinking into flesh when she stuck her finger down her throat. The last time Johnnie had seen her, Beverly was running laps around the campus parking lot in between classes.

Glenda Hunter's expression softened. She leaned back in her chair and stuck a pencil behind her ear. "I'll say one thing, Ms. Kitchen. You've got *chutzpah.* I admire that. Why don't you bring me some samples of your writing, and I'll be happy to take a look. But I must warn you — it doesn't pay much."

Johnnie had expected the part about low

pay; she'd done her research. But *chutzpah* — no one had ever told her that.

Taking a deep breath, she reached into her satchel-sized purse, pulled out a manila folder and placed it politely on the corner of the desk.

Glenda Hunter reached over and slid the folder across a desktop covered in paperwork and newsprint. "I see you've come prepared."

Johnnie thanked the editor for her time as she left. Two hours later, after Johnnie had looked up the word *chutzpah* in the dictionary, Glenda Hunter called with an offer. "Give me seven hundred fifty words about your battle with bulimia and how you overcame it. And include that woman you go to school with. Just don't mention her name."

For the first time in Johnnie's life, someone was going to pay her to write. The money wasn't much, but it was the *byline* she was after. Story by story, she would build her professional portfolio.

Out on the sidewalk, Johnnie tucked her paycheck in her bag and strolled south on Main. Glancing over her shoulder, she caught a glimpse of Genie's Books to her left. Even from this distance, she could see

Genie the cat slink past a display of books in the store window, her ebony tail curled around a pumpkin sporting a witch's hat. The cat looked like one of the props. "You get your bestseller written, and I'll showcase it up front in the bay window." Miss Ruby's words tap-danced around Johnnie like a dare.

Two years ago, Johnnie didn't think she was smart enough to get through college biology, much less algebra. Working with tutors at the math and science labs proved her wrong. Passing those challenging courses had given her the courage to approach an editor. Now, with a year's worth of published columns under her belt, the idea of writing a book began to bubble up inside of her. She smiled to herself, empowered by the possibilities and her editor's words: "You're selling newspapers." For now, she stashed her secret away, protecting it from others' expectations.

Her ponytail swinging, Johnnie hummed Karen Carpenter's mega hit "Top of the World" as she bounced along in leather clogs and brown leggings that showed off her slender but shapely legs. Passing a storefront window, she caught a fleeting glimpse of her long orange cardigan swinging behind her like the coattails of a drum major. Despite the nip in the air, the noon sun blazed in the blue October sky and warmed Johnnie's face. For now, nothing could stomp the joy dancing in her soul. Not Mama's suicide attempt, or Brother's death, or even her worry over Cade.

The storefronts were decorated with harvest colors of yellow, red, and deep orange. A wheelbarrow full of gourds rested next to the grand entrance of the Preacher's House, a bar and grill housed in the stately old corner bank building at Worth and Main. The place where she and Dale celebrated their twenty-third wedding anniversary two years ago, and where Dale finally relented and gave Johnnie his blessing so she could go back to college.

A guy with a black mustache and good-looking as all get out drove by in a souped-up hotrod. He grinned at Johnnie and revved his motor. Throwing her head back, she laughed and kept walking, ignoring his flirtatious nod.

The noon traffic drowned out the hum of the freeway that separated Portion and the railroad tracks from the Dallas/Fort Worth Airport. The aroma of freshly brewed coffee from the Daily Grind, a new coffeehouse in the former drugstore, hit all her senses at once. A piping hot cup of coffee would hit the spot. She'd pick up a to-go cup for Whit and head down to Whit's Whimsies. She hadn't talked to Whit in about two weeks, not since the day Mama tried to kill herself. As she was about to push open the door, lulled by a memory of herself and Grandpa Grubbs seated at the soda fountain slurping milkshakes and spinning on shiny stools, the twang of country music pulled her back. Frozen in place, she felt her skin prickle from head to toe.

Rushing to the curb, she saw a gunmetal gray pickup trundling south on Main Street, the chassis jacked up on fat tires. *It could be anybody,* she told herself as Dale's words rolled through her mind: "Do you know how many jacked-up pickups there are in Portion? In the whole state of Texas, for cripes' sake!"

The pickup approached, and Johnnie caught her breath at the familiar tune that blared from the cab's speakers. The lyrics to "If I Don't Make It Back" by Tracy Lawrence played havoc on her heart. Before Cade shipped off to Army basic training, he'd crank up the stereo in his room and blast that song throughout the house. One time Callie Ann came home from drill team practice and marched into the kitchen with her hands on her hips, demanding, "Mother, make him turn that dang song off. Don't you know what it's about?" And Johnnie had turned with tears in her eyes and said, "Yes, baby, I do. It's about a soldier killed in war."

As the pickup cruised past, Johnnie looked for a young man in a straw cowboy hat and dark sunglasses, with ropey tanned arms, and a Confederate battle flag waving like a middle finger behind the cab. Shielding her eyes from the glare of the sun, she squinted to get a better look at the driver. Blond bristles covered his scalp and a long-sleeved white dress shirt shielded his arms.

Was it the same kid? She wasn't sure, but she took off, clopping down the sidewalk, wishing she'd worn walking shoes instead of clogs. If she could just read and memorize the license plate number, then she would have something to report to the patrol officer who responded to Callie Ann's accident. What she would give for a pair of binoculars right now.

But her clogs were clumsy and slowed her down. The pickup was getting away. Feeling defeated, she was about to turn back and go get coffee when the truck flashed its right turn signal and veered into an open slot in front of the Trading Post. Even from this distance, Johnnie could see the store's permanent resident, a life-sized wooden Indian seated on a turquoise bench in front of the store's entrance.

She picked up her pace and then ducked behind a sidewalk sale sign two shops away from the Trading Post. The driver got out of his truck, came around the front bumper, and stepped up on the curb. Outside of his truck, he barely looked old enough to drive. From her vantage point, Johnnie thought he looked about sixteen and maybe five feet eight inches tall and a hundred forty pounds if you counted his scruffy boots with riding heels and the big silver belt buckle holding up his trousers. She fumbled in her purse for her journal and pen to jot down his license plate number. He stopped midstride to check his reflection in the store window, tucking in his dress shirt and adjusting his collar.

From the second he emerged from the truck's cab, Johnnie had begun to form a plan. She would follow him into the shop, tag along close enough to keep an eye on him, and then confront him in the open. If the kid ran, that would prove his guilt. But then what? She couldn't tackle him. That would get her thrown in jail. Well, she hadn't thought that far ahead, but a surge of heat fired through her core and the anger over

Brother's death ignited all over again. She couldn't wait to give the punk a piece of her mind and demoralize him like he'd demoralized Whit.

If it's the same guy, that is.

She was about to step out from behind the sign and follow him when the kid walked right past the wooden Indian and headed next door to the recruiter's station.

The place where Dale signed Cade's life away to the United States Army.

The heart-tugging lyrics about a young warrior who didn't make it back strummed through her mind as she gawked after the kid. No wonder he had that song blaring from his truck's speakers. Nothing like that kind of message to get a young man all fired up to go fight for his country.

Taking a deep breath, she looked up at the large letters that formed the word ARMY on the face of the building. Stalling for a few minutes, she looked around, thinking she should just go home. But then Cade's words in an email egged her on: "Why didn't y'all tell me about that peckerhead?"

"God forgive me if I'm wrong," she muttered under her breath as she swung open the door and breezed inside.

The first thing she noticed was the plain,

no-nonsense atmosphere of the place, more austere than a doctor's office but warmer than a bus station. Posters of uniformed men and women of all races greeted her as she glanced around to get her bearings. For a millisecond, the air felt too still to breathe, although a ceiling fan pulled duty overhead. As she clung to her purse strap, her mind tumbled to the day she and Mama took the Greyhound bus to Fort Hood when she said goodbye forever to the handsome soldier who didn't make it back — her father. Swallowing, her heart slingshotted up her throat as she tried to dismiss the image of Cade waving with his whole arm out the passenger window, hollering, "Y'all be good. I'll see you when I get back."

Taking a few steps forward, she wondered if the African American soldier seated behind the desk was Sergeant Jackson, Cade's recruiter. She'd never met him in person, only talked to him on the phone once or twice when he called the house looking for Cade before he left for basic. The kid from the pickup stood in front of the desk, partially blocking Johnnie's view of the soldier's nametag.

Stepping to the side, she heard the kid mumble, "Sergeant Jackson, I'll do whatever it takes. I'll sell my truck if I have to."

Johnnie tilted her head, catching a glimpse of Sergeant Jackson's square, thoughtful face, his strong chin resting on clasped hands, his thick lips closed in a serious expression as he appeared to gaze intently at the young man before him. "Now, son, hopefully that won't be necessary. I'm just waiting on your background check before we send you to get your physical. You been eating right and working out?"

The kid hitched up his trousers, and was about to say something when Sergeant Jackson interrupted him and turned his attention to Johnnie. "Hello, ma'am. Can I help you with something?"

Johnnie hesitated. "Sergeant Jackson? I'm Cade Kitchen's mom —"

At the mention of Cade's name, Sergeant Jackson jumped up from his desk and stuck out his hand. "Mrs. Kitchen! Good to meet you."

But as Johnnie went to shake his hand, she saw a look of concern wash over his dark face. His head tilted ever so slightly. "Everything all right with your son? He stopped by here a few months ago before he left for the 'Stan."

Oh God, she hadn't expected the corners of her mouth to twitch or her eyes to mist up. She looked away, trying to regain her composure. Of course an unannounced visit from a deployed soldier's mother might cause that soldier's recruiter to be alarmed. She let out a sloppy laugh, sniffing in embarrassment. "Cade is fine . . . uh, last we heard. You know how sporadic communication can be."

Sergeant Jackson nodded and the alarm in his sympathetic eyes vanished. "Would you like to have a seat?" He gestured to an empty chair a few feet away. "If you'll excuse me for a few minutes, I need to get this young man squared away."

For those few seconds, as Johnnie and the sergeant bantered back and forth, she glanced politely at the kid a few times, but he didn't acknowledge her. He stood erect in his cowboy duds and stared straight ahead, his small, tanned hands clasped behind his back like a good soldier.

Johnnie started to back away, waving off Sergeant Jackson's offer. "Sorry to bother you. I was down at the newspaper office when I figured I'd drop by and thank you for the Blue Star banner. It's been hanging in our window since May."

Sergeant Jackson paused and scratched behind his ear. "Say, Mrs. Kitchen. Did they ever catch the varmint who threw the beer bottle at you near the soldier's statue back on Memorial Day? I read about it in your column right after it happened."

At that moment, she wanted to give Sergeant Jackson a high-five. Because the second he asked the question, the kid began to fidget and sweat profusely. She watched him from the corner of her eye. When Brother had been afraid, he gave off a funk, a stink like no other. Johnnie could smell a similar stink coming off the boy; he reeked of fear from every pore.

She turned toward him. His ruddy cheeks were inflamed and big red blotches broke out on his neck above the collar of his faded white dress shirt pressed into service for a visit to the recruiter. On closer examination, Johnnie could see crinkles around his startling blue eyes and the hint of blond fuzz above his upper lip, now dotted with perspiration. The kid was probably about Cade's age or a year younger. Something about him reminded her of the young men who came and went when she worked at the food pantry. Along with sweat, he reeked of desperation.

You remember me now, don't you? she thought. She'd nabbed him. Now what?

Slowly, her gaze drifted back to Sergeant Jackson. "No, we never did catch the fella, but we're pretty sure he's the same guy who ran my daughter off the road back in August. I wrote about it in my column."

He squinted, as if he was trying to remember. "I must've missed it. I was out of the office most of the summer, TDY to Georgia. I hope your daughter's okay."

"She's fine. But my dog got killed in the accident. He was riding in the car with my daughter when she smashed into a tree." Johnnie's eye panned to the kid. He looked like he was about to throw up.

Sergeant Jackson's hands went to his heart. "Oh, Mrs. Kitchen. I'm so sorry. I'm a dog lover myself."

Johnnie let out a heavy sigh, the kind that lingered in the air. "Thank you, Sergeant. Life isn't the same without *Brother Dog.*" She paused, wanting his name to sink in. "Well, I better scoot. I've taken up too much of your time." Readjusting her purse strap, she glanced at the kid. It was all she could do to restrain herself from grabbing him by his stiff collar and throwing him across the room. As much as she wanted to hate him, she heard herself say, "Good luck with the Army. I hope you survive basic."

She heard him gulp as he stared straight ahead. "Thank you, ma'am." His voice was barely audible.

Halfway to the door, Sergeant Jackson

called out, "Give my best to your son."

Once outside, she took a deep, cleansing breath, strolled over to the turquoise bench, and sat down next to the wooden Indian to wait for the kid. No sense embarrassing him in front of the sergeant.

"Hey, Chief, how you doing?" She swiveled on the bench, and her eyes swept over the likeness of a Navajo man in faded jeans, a denim shirt, scuffed work boots, and a red bandana tied around his forehead. His jet-black hair hung past his shoulders, and a beaded necklace dangled from his neck. She leaned back, studying his earthen features, the way his palms rested on his lap as if they were tired from a day's labor. The artist had sculpted his facial expression in ambiguity. Johnnie couldn't tell if he wore a half-smile or a frown.

At that moment it struck her as silly. His hands and face weren't made out of wood, but *pottery.* Underneath his clothing, his limbs and torso were probably a combination of wire and papier-mâché. Yet everybody in town called him "The Wooden Indian."

She patted the back of his lifeless hand in apology. "You've been sitting on this bench through rain or shine all these years, and until today, I've never taken the time to see what you're made of."

Stunned by this sudden observation, she reached into her purse and pulled out her journal. "Glenda says people like controversy. What you say we shake things up a bit, hey, Chief?"

Flipping to a blank page, she jotted the following lines: "We get something stuck in our heads — like a name or an idea — and we start calling it that, whether we believe it or not . . . or ever take the time to investigate if it's true. Take 'The Wooden Indian' parked outside the Trading Post on Main Street. He's no more wooden than the rest of us, and yet. . . ." Biting the end of her pen, she looked off in the distance, trying to come up with a few more lines to make her point clear. After a while, she bent over her journal and scribbled, "We're all just made out of clay. Some lighter, some darker. And yet we get caught up in name-calling over our shades."

There, she had the framework for a new column.

She glanced at the kid's pickup, noticing scrapes, dents, and *wash me* written on the grimy back panel on the right side. The N-bomb from Memorial Day whistled through her memory like a mortar attack.

Dropping her journal back in her purse, she glanced at the weathered tips of the Indian's boots and thought of the kid's worn boots and trousers. And a plan began to form in her mind.

Twenty minutes later, the door opened and the kid strutted out, whistling as he started for his truck.

Johnnie jumped off the bench and called after him, "Excuse me, young man. Do you have a minute?"

The kid wheeled around, startled. His mouth formed a snaggletooth O. "Yes, ma'am?" His eyes shifted back and forth between Johnnie and the door he'd just exited. He stuffed his hands in his pockets and waited.

"Mind if I ask you a few questions?"

He pulled a toothpick from his pocket and stuck it between his teeth. "I have to get to work."

She offered her brightest smile. "This won't take long. So, you want to be a soldier?"

He chomped on the toothpick. "Yes, ma'am."

Pursing her lips sideways, she gave a slow nod. "That's real patriotic of you, but what would Sergeant Jackson say if I waltzed through that door and told him you might be the little varmint who desecrated the war memorial?"

He hung his head and shuffled his feet. Sweat dripped off his forehead and dropped in fat blotches on the sidewalk. "I don't know what you're talking about."

"I wasn't completely sure at first but now I can see guilt dripping off of you."

All the color drained from his tanned face.

"I've got your number, kid. All I have to do is mosey back inside and tell Sergeant Jackson what you're really made out of. 'Cuz the last thing the military needs is another skinhead."

His head jolted up. He removed the toothpick. "I ain't no skinhead."

"Sure didn't appear that way the day you threw a beer bottle and hurtled your obscenities at me and my mama and friend. Or when you ran my daughter off the road."

He ran the toothpick under his fingernails, avoiding her eyes. "I was drunk, ma'am."

"In the middle of the afternoon? Well, at least somebody taught you manners. The way you throw *ma'am* around like you do."

He stopped picking at his nails. "Yes, ma'am, my grandmother."

Johnnie waited a second. "She teach you how to hate, too?"

He groaned and rolled his eyes. "She was

a good Christian woman. Look, ma'am, I'm real sorry about your dog. I was late for work. I was only trying to pass that old Lincoln when —"

Sergeant Jackson stuck his head out the door. "Jordan, glad I caught you before you left." His gaze shifted between Johnnie and the kid. "You forgot your Army swag." He grinned and handed the kid a plastic bag that said *Go Army.* "Couple of ballpoint pens and some travel mugs . . . just a little sumpin' for signing up."

Jordan. Was that the kid's first name or last name?

Jordan's hands trembled as he took the bag from the recruiter. "Thank you, Sergeant."

After Sergeant Jackson ducked his head back inside, Johnnie ambled over to the bench and sat back down. It was time to put her plan into action. "Hey, Jordan, you ever read the newspaper?"

The kid stood in the middle of the sidewalk, holding his bag of goodies. He looked absolutely terrified of Johnnie. "No, ma'am."

"Start reading it," she ordered. "Be on the lookout for a story I write about this guy." She patted the Navajo man on the knee. "It'll probably run in the *Portion Telegraph* in a week or so. I'll be checking in with Sergeant Jackson from time to time. Once my story runs, I'm going to have him give you a pop quiz. You are dismissed."

The kid stuck the toothpick back in his mouth, turned, and half-staggered to his truck. Johnnie could've sworn he was shaking in his boots.

Chapter 30
Drive-by

Right after the kid climbed up in the truck and pulled away from the curb, Sergeant Jackson strolled outside and sat down on the bench opposite the Navajo man. "He the kid you wrote about in your column?"

Johnnie leaned forward on her elbows and glanced in Sergeant Jackson's direction. "Was it that obvious?"

Sergeant Jackson brushed at something on his lap. "The kid's usually pretty cocky when he comes in. But the second you showed up and started talking, he looked like a rabbit caught in a trap."

Her gaze drifted from Sergeant Jackson, whose skin was several shades darker than the Navajo, to the predominately white window shoppers strolling up and down Main Street. At that moment, Johnnie tried to put herself in Sergeant Jackson's place. What did it feel like to be in the minority? She and Whit had danced around the subject, but they'd never discussed it. Maybe it felt akin to being the oldest student in class. When it came to going back to college in midlife, Johnnie went out of her way to blend in. But of course she didn't. She was still the *old mom* wherever she went. Just like Sergeant Jackson was the only black male out on the sidewalk on this section of Main Street.

"You showed some kind of restraint," he continued when Johnnie didn't say anything. "If it had been me, well. . . ."

She swiveled about on the bench. "Will this ruin his chances of joining the Army?" She didn't want to be responsible for that. What if the Army had rejected Cade? It would have crushed him. Something about the kid gnawed at Johnnie's heart. "Sergeant Jackson, I've come up with a plan to make him pay for what he did and teach him a lesson at the same time. But I'll need your help."

He propped his elbows on his knees and studied his hands. "What are you proposing?"

Reaching into her purse, she pulled out her journal and pointed to the Indian. "Take Mr. Navajo, here. Everybody calls him the Wooden Indian. But do you see any wood?"

The sergeant studied their silent companion. He thumped his knuckles against the Indian's clay cheek. "Guess we can't knock on him for good luck, can we?"

Johnnie chuckled at the sergeant's joke. No wonder Cade liked him. Then she set out to explain her plan of action.

The recruiter rubbed his chin, gave a little nod, and looked in the opposite direction. "So you want me to drill the kid about your column? Ask him what he learned from reading it? I can do that."

She stashed her journal back in her purse, eager to go home and get started. "I'll keep you posted when it runs."

The sergeant stood up and stretched his legs. "You got time to take a ride with me out by the lake? Now that you've shown an interest in young Mr. Rivers, I'd like you to see where he lives. One drive by that place, and you'll see why he acted like he did."

Johnnie hesitated, but only a second. "Let me call my husband and let him know what I'm doing."

After Sergeant Jackson went to lock up and leave a note on the door, Johnnie punched in Dale's number. When Dale came on the line, Johnnie practically broke into song. "Honey, you're not going to believe this. Not only do I have the punk's name and license plate number, but I'm here with his recruiter, Sergeant Jackson. He's going to show me where the kid lives."

Dale was silent for a second. "Tell Sergeant Jackson I'm coming with you. I wanna see that kid who hurt my daughter and dog. I want to look him in the eye and have him tell me why it happened!"

She closed her eyes. "Dale, calm down. Let me handle this. The last thing I need is to have you thrown in jail."

"That's the hanging tree," Johnnie pointed out as Sergeant Jackson eased up on the gas pedal. The massive oak with the gaping gash in the trunk stood out among the other trees at the edge of the clearing. Most of its coppery leaves had fallen to the ground, exposing a gray skeleton.

Sergeant Jackson nodded with his chin to a section of road up ahead. "Is that where my man, Jordan Rivers, started tailgating your daughter?"

Johnnie sat in the front passenger seat of the nondescript government minivan and fidgeted with a loose strand on the sleeve of her cardigan. "Yes, on the other side of that bend." As they wove along Lakeside Drive, Johnnie filled Sergeant Jackson in on what she knew about Callie Ann's accident and also about the lynching Roosevelt Hill witnessed when he was young.

From the moment Sergeant Jackson had pointed his key fob at the silver minivan and held the door open for Johnnie, she'd fought the urge to tell him she'd been living in terror of an Army green sedan pulling up to the curb in front of her house. Running her hand over the nubby upholstery at the edge of the bucket seat, she realized bad news could travel in a minivan full of soldiers and not the dreaded staff car. Now every time she saw a plain minivan coming up Merriweather, she would have to brace herself. Would she ever stop living in fear?

Cool air blew from the AC vent even though it was chilly out. Cade told her once that their camouflage uniforms could get hot, and she figured Sergeant Jackson needed to cool off more than she needed to warm up. Besides, he was in charge and she was only a civilian along for the ride.

As they rounded the next bend, the sprawling white house surrounded by towering oaks and pecan trees came into view on their left. "That's where I grew up." She swept her hand through the air in a grand gesture. "You can't tell from here, but the back of the house sits on a bluff overlooking the lake. I need to get it ready to sell. Been putting it off since my grandmother died in April."

Sergeant Jackson glanced out the driver's window. "Nice place. I bet you'll make a bundle since it's lakefront property. But I know what you mean. My buddy's been gone a year, and his wife can't bring herself to clean out his closet."

She wondered if his buddy died in combat. She patted him on the shoulder and hoped it was okay to ask. "I'm sorry. Was he a soldier?"

The sergeant nodded. "One of the best. He got killed a week before he was supposed to come home. Left behind a wife and two kids." He kept staring straight ahead and refused to look at her. "No one said this job is without risk. That's for sure."

She focused on the trees flashing by outside her window and choked back the torrent of fear swirling from her gut to her throat. The last thing her son's recruiter needed was a blubbering mother riding shotgun on military business. *Buck up,* she told herself, but her words tumbled out as they rounded another bend and headed away from the lake. "Sergeant Jackson, I have a confession to make. I didn't want Cade to join the Army. I live in fear every single second, and I don't know how to handle it." Clasping her hands under her chin, she looked at him, hoping he wouldn't judge her for being weak.

Sergeant Jackson pressed his lips together and glanced at her, his eyes full of compassion. "Mrs. Kitchen, being the mother of a soldier is a tough job. If it makes you feel better, my mama checks on me all the time, and I'm thirty-five years old."

She let out a nervous laugh. "I bet she's proud of you though."

His face broke into a boyish grin. "Yeah, when I first joined the Army, she made me wear my uniform to church every time I went home to visit. Showed me off like a new pair of shoes."

Johnnie smiled. "You're a good son. I can tell."

Tipping his head, he twitched his brows in a jaunty fashion. "Ya only got one mama."

His words caused her face to crumple so she smiled until it hurt. Sergeant Jackson had no idea about her mother's history, and it wasn't fair to burden him. Johnnie looked the other way as they passed the narrow turnoff to the left that led down an embankment to the cove.

About two miles later, they hooked a right down a one-lane dirt road surrounded on both sides by thick brush and tall trees.

Johnnie rolled down her window, breathing in the smoky air from a nearby chimney. A couple of dogs barked, and the sound ricocheted through the cold air like a stray bullet.

The van rolled to a stop. "Okay, this is as far as we go. Look over there." He pointed to a rickety shack hidden behind tangled vines. A large Confederate battle flag flapped in the wind, a no trespassing sign bolted to the tall, skinny flagpole. Smoke curled from a pipe jutting out of the jagged roof. Barbed wire strung between rough-hewn cedar posts served as a barrier between the occupants and outsiders. KEEP OUT signs were nailed to every other post.

Sergeant Jackson draped his arms over the steering wheel. "Don't it make ya all warm and fuzzy?"

Her gaze swept over sheets of corrugated metal that served as siding on the structure. An older model truck, its flatbed trailer piled high with junk, stood parked near a side yard where a few chickens pecked at the ground. No sign of the kid. Sergeant Jackson said he was at his dead-end job cleaning horse stalls at the racetrack. Johnnie tried to take it all in. "Makes you wonder if they have running water and electricity." She couldn't believe someone actually lived here.

"Get a good look, because we aren't staying long. Old Man Rivers probably has a riflescope aimed on us now. Don't expect he'll be inviting us in for vittles."

Johnnie scanned the area. "His dad?"

Sergeant Jackson shook his head. "No, an uncle. Kid's parents died years ago. He got kicked from one foster family to another. Ended up at this dump."

"Did he go to school around here? Surely my daughter would have recognized him."

"Moved here from East Texas about a year ago. Graduated from Portion High in May. I don't think he's made any friends."

Turning back toward the makeshift fortress, Johnnie narrowed her eyes as she read the words spray-painted on a large sheet of plywood: NEVER MIND THE DOGS. BEWARE OF OWNER!

"What the heck?" Before she could digest the warning, Sergeant Jackson directed her to a large block of letters plastered on a metal sign that hung from a padlocked gate. Johnnie gawked at the words that sent chills up her spine: NOBAMA! WHITES ONLY BEYOND THIS POINT!

She bowed her head and rubbed her brow. "I don't understand this kind of hate, and it's already rubbed off on the kid."

Sergeant Jackson shoved the gearshift in reverse. "It's too late for the old man, but maybe not for Jordan." They did a K-turn and hightailed it out of there.

Right before Johnnie rolled up the window, she heard a rooster crow.

Minutes later, they passed the hanging tree. Hugging herself, she visualized Thurman Blue's naked body swinging from a rope. *What did he do that caused him to get lynched?* Scanning the clearing, she could feel young Roosevelt's fear as he trembled in the woods, waiting for the men in pointy white hoods to leave.

Shifting in her seat, she was struck by the thought that she and Sergeant Jackson sat inches apart in their bucket seats, their bodies divided by nothing more than a drink console. Fifty-plus years ago, Emmett Till, a teenager from Chicago, was murdered for talking to a white woman in Mississippi. What if the Klan or Jordan's uncle snuck up on them now and forced them off the road? It would take less than five minutes to pull Sergeant Jackson from the minivan, throw a noose around his neck, and string him up like a buck left to bleed out.

Johnnie shivered and peeked at the side mirror. No carload of thugs followed them as they drove by the old wooden sign, TO GLORY.

"Mrs. Kitchen, you okay?" Sergeant Jackson's deep voice startled her as he reached inside the console for something. "You're awfully quiet." He offered her a stick of gum.

Unwrapping the foil, she stuck the gum in her mouth and welcomed the minty flavor. "Sorry, sometimes my mind drifts." She didn't dare tell him what she'd been thinking.

They rode in silence a few more minutes. Finally, Johnnie said, "Why do you care what happens to the kid? Do you get bonus points for signing him up?"

Sergeant Jackson looked over and shrugged. "Each station has its recruiting goals, but that's not why. Kid wants to better himself. Can't blame him for that."

"I overheard him say he'll sell his truck if he has to. What did he mean?"

"His truck's the only thing he owns of value, and his job doesn't pay much. He wants to go to school and get an education. He can get all that in the Army, but —"

"But if the Army doesn't work out, he has nowhere else to go except to stay with his uncle until he can afford to move out?" She paused, thinking of Brother's lifeless body on the blanket of bluebonnets. Breathing deeply, she realized that if Brother had been with her today, he'd have gone up to the kid on the sidewalk, sniffed his boots, and then sat on his haunches expecting a head pat. Brother had been a good dog, but he didn't get that way without discipline. Sighing, she stared out the windshield at the blacktop ahead of them. "Sergeant, I've reevaluated my plan."

With a gleam in his eye, the sergeant tapped his finger to his temple and grinned. "Great minds think alike. I like your idea of making him read the newspaper, but the boy's going to need a little more attitude adjustment before I hand him over to his drill sergeants at basic."

"What are you thinking?" Johnnie rolled the foil wrapper between her fingers.

"Community service. He needs to pay for what he did up at the war memorial. Even if he didn't intentionally run your daughter off the road, he's partially responsible for what happened."

At that moment, Roosevelt Hill's words floated by as if he'd been eavesdropping in the backseat: *We've had a little problem with vandalism since my letter ran in the paper.*

"I have an idea," Johnnie said. "But we'll have to clear it with Roosevelt first." She told Sergeant Jackson about the vandalism at the black cemetery located out by the lake. "The kid may have had nothing to do with it, but I don't see why that little firecracker can't put his hands and feet to use and help clean that place up."

Sergeant Jackson smiled and hit the steering wheel with the heel of his hand. "Mrs. Kitchen, you're all right. So begins the re-education of my man, Jordan Rivers. Kid won't know what hit him. Of course he'll have to keep all this from his uncle. No telling what that old bigot would do if he found out."

Settling back in her seat, Johnnie rode the rest of the way in silence as they wound through town and headed south on Main Street. As Sergeant Jackson pulled the minivan into an open slot in front of the recruiter's station, Johnnie was still trying to shake off the image of a WHITES ONLY sign and the vision of a black soldier dangling from a tree.

Chapter 31
The Imposter

A fake skeleton in overalls and a straw hat greeted Johnnie as she entered the lobby of the nursing home in Denton. On this cold Sunday afternoon in October, Johnnie was glad she'd changed out of her church dress into her favorite jeans and a warm fleece jacket with a hood. As she held the door open for Dale and Callie Ann, she removed the hood and noticed Arthur Murphy waiting nearby. He wore the same tan corduroy blazer as the first time they saw him at Denton's Day of the Dead Festival, but today he paired it with a navy turtleneck, relaxed jeans, and ostrich cowboy boots.

His eyes glimmered when he spotted Johnnie. "Good afternoon," he called as he hustled across the lobby. He moved fast for a man his age. Just last week while talking to Johnnie on the phone, he'd shared that he was a mall walker. No wonder he'd been able to keep up with them that day on the square.

She waved, nervous and happy at the same time. "Hello, Arty. Sorry we're running late."

Arty glanced at his watch. "You're right on time, dear." He grasped Johnnie's hand and held onto it for a few seconds, swinging their arms to and fro as if they were children. "I've got her all dolled up and ready for company."

Then Arty turned to Dale. "Hello, young fella. D.J.'s told me so much about you."

Dale gripped the old man's hand. "Howdy, Arthur. Boy, isn't it something how this all worked out?"

Callie Ann stood back, her fingers tucked in the pockets of her body-hugging jeans. "I like your boots," she said, tossing her hair back. She wore a gold sweater that showed off her slender yet shapely figure.

Arty stepped forward. "Hello, Callie Ann. I like yours, too. We both have good taste in footwear."

The tips of her red cowboy boots poked out the bottom of her boot-cut jeans. "These were a gift from . . ." her voice broke off and she sniffed as she glanced over at Johnnie.

"It's okay," Johnnie whispered, realizing

her daughter was afraid to mention Granny Opal.

At last Callie Ann said, "These belonged to my other granny. She left them to me when she passed away."

Arty rubbed the tip of his nose and stepped forward. "Well, you're even prettier now than the first time I saw you up on the square. You had your hair all teased up and your face painted."

Her pouty lips spread into a coy grin. "You really freaked us out that day, Grandpa Arty."

He chuckled at the sound of his new name. "Grandpa Arty, huh? I could get used to that." He touched a finger to her cheek. "You remind me of her. I didn't see it that day because I was so focused on your brother."

About then Arty's cellphone rang. He retrieved it from a leather holster clipped to his belt. "Ah, it's D.J.," he announced, and Johnnie could hear her son's baritone voice blare out of the tiny speaker, saying he was running late. "When you come in the lobby," Arty continued, "hang a left at the first hallway. Look for the sign that says, 'Memory Care.' We'll see you shortly."

He hung up and glanced over their shoulders like he was expecting someone else.

"Where's Victoria? She decided not to come?"

Johnnie glanced at Dale then back at Arty. "Mama isn't feeling too well today." Unless D.J. had blabbed it, which was highly unlikely, Arty had no idea that Mama tried to kill herself after his phone call. And Johnnie wasn't going to tell him.

Arty looked disappointed. "Well, we'll just have to plan another day. Let's go meet Mae." He hooked his arm through Johnnie's and they headed down the hallway. Callie Ann and Dale were right behind them. Just before they got to the room, Arty said, "Remember, if she says something totally off the wall, it's best if you just play along."

Entering the room, Johnnie caught her breath at the sight of an elderly woman with sapphire blue eyes that sparkled from an oval face with a flawless complexion. Mae wore a quilted bed jacket that matched her eyes. Her white hair appeared to be long and held up with a clip at the nape of her slender neck. She sat propped up in a hospital bed made homier with an embroidered pillowcase and a quilt folded at the foot of the bed. A watercolor of the historic Denton County Courthouse on the square hung on the left wall, and Johnnie wondered if Arty had painted it. Next to a hairbrush on the bedside table sat the framed photo taken at Fort Hood.

Mae took one look at Callie Ann and gasped, "You look like an angel."

"And she's just as sweet as one, too," Arty whispered, patting Callie Ann's shoulder.

Mae's eyes flashed at Johnnie. "Who are you?"

Arty nudged Johnnie forward. "Mae, this is Johnnie, the little girl in the photograph."

Trembling, Johnnie took Mae's hands and caressed her bony fingers. These aging hands once pampered a little boy who grew up and fell in love with Johnnie's mother and became a soldier. The moment felt holy, and Johnnie let it seep into her soul, knowing it wouldn't last.

Mae narrowed her eyes. "You're not the little girl in pigtails. Where's the little girl in pigtails?"

"I'm right here, Granny Mae. I grew up," Johnnie said, feeling small and out of sorts.

Mae's pink lips parted and she lifted her head off the pillow. She seemed to be scrutinizing Johnnie.

Callie Ann jumped up from the chair and scurried around the bed. "Hold still, Mom." Before Johnnie realized what was happening, Callie Ann released Johnnie's ponytail, parted the mass into two sections, and went to work braiding each side. She fastened one end with Johnnie's ponytail holder and a spare Callie Ann kept in her jean pocket. "Look, Granny Mae, here's the little girl. Only she's older now."

Dizzy, Johnnie leaned into Callie Ann for support. For a few seconds, Johnnie actually felt five again, shy and awkward in her chubby body, her cheeks hot, her armpits sweaty.

From behind them, Arty cleared his throat. "Oh, sweet child, Callie Ann. You have your grandmother's heart." There was a catch in his voice. "If only you could have known her sooner."

Mae glanced at the photo on the nightstand then blinked a couple of times at Johnnie. Her voice made a gurgling sound when she spoke. "Arthur said you would come." A tear dribbled down one cheek.

A hush fell over the room.

Before Johnnie could bend to give her a hug, Mae's body shifted on the bed. Her eyes drifted past Johnnie and Callie Ann. Johnnie turned to see what had captured Mae's attention.

Mae was staring at the blond man in the chambray shirt and jeans, standing off to the side, one hand crossed reverently over the other.

Mae crooked her finger at Dale. "Hello there, handsome."

Dale's ruddy cheeks grew a deep crimson. "Hello, Mae. I'm Dale. I belong to her." He pointed his thumb at Johnnie.

Callie Ann stepped forward and introduced herself. "I belong to them. I've been so anxious to meet you."

Mae reached up and twirled strands of Callie Ann's long blond hair through her fingers. "Did you bring me my candy bars?"

Callie Ann chuckled. "Oh, you like candy, too?"

As they were talking, D.J. entered the room, tall and lanky in his black jeans and short-sleeve dress shirt open at the collar, his denim jacket draped over one arm. He paused for a second as if assessing the situation. After he and Johnnie exchanged glances, he handed her his jacket and approached the bed.

Mae's whole face lit up when she saw him. "*Francis,* you look so handsome." She flung her arms wide. "Come give Mommy a hug."

Glancing at the others for guidance, he bent slightly and patted her gently on both shoulders. "Hello, Mae. That's a sweet jacket. Color looks rad on you." He'd softened his deep voice, and Johnnie knew he looked more composed than he felt. "You look like a Hollywood starlet from back in the day."

Mae blushed and peeked over D.J.'s shoulder and gave Arty an exaggerated wink. "My boyfriend gave it to me."

Arty bowed his head and tipped an imaginary hat. Even with his wife's declining health, he carried on like a young beau still wooing his beloved. Growing up, Johnnie had never witnessed this kind of open display of affection between Grandpa Grubbs and Granny Opal, although she knew they loved each other.

As D.J. straightened, towering over the old woman's bedside, the expression on Mae's face changed. She stared at him, glassy eyed. "How come you're not in your uniform?" Her long, slender fingers tipped in pearl nail polish grappled at the buttonless lapels of her retro-style jacket. Her gaze traveled from his face to his left forearm covered in tattoos. Her chin began to quiver.

Before D.J. could answer, Mae shrunk back against her pillow, petrified. Her blue eyes brimmed with tears. "You're not my son!" she wailed, reaching for the hairbrush. She scooped it off the nightstand and flung it at D.J. "You're an *imposter*! My son got killed in the *war*!"

D.J. ducked, dodging the brush. It sailed

through the air and hit the far wall.

Everyone froze as Mae's words descended over the room. Johnnie's lungs deflated, and she gripped the end of the hospital bed to keep from falling.

D.J. stiffened, clenching his jaw. He stared at something on the floor, refusing to look at any of them.

Dale cracked a knuckle, and the sound broke the silence. Callie Ann covered her face with her hands.

Arty rose from his chair and placed his hand on D.J.'s shoulder. "I'm so sorry, D.J. It's the disease talking. Why don't you go take a walk? I'll be along in a sec."

D.J. nodded, did an about-face, and strode toward the exit, passing Johnnie on the way out. As she handed him his jacket, his deep-set eyes cut her a look that said, "I told you this wasn't going to work." Johnnie glanced over at Dale. He jerked his head in their son's direction, a signal for Johnnie to follow him. As she filed out the door, Arty was right behind her.

Out in the corridor, D.J. slid his arms into his denim jacket and patted the chest pocket where he kept his smokes. "Well, *I* was a big hit. That went over well." He tried to sound nonchalant, but Johnnie detected the gloom in his voice.

Arty swiped the heel of his hand across the side of his head. "Mae's not in her right mind. She would never hurt you intentionally." He jiggled his wrist, adjusting his watchband.

D.J. pulled out a plastic cigarette lighter, twirling it in his long fingers. "I understand that, Arthur. But is it going to be like this every time I visit? I don't want to cause her more sorrow. I mean, her thinking I'm him, and me inadvertently cracking open an old wound?"

Arty shrugged, pulled out his hanky, and blew his nose. "Here's the thing about this disease, D.J. Today she thought you were Francis. Tomorrow she might think you're Daffy Duck."

At that instant, Johnnie fell in love with Arty. This kind, gentle soul had the ability to rise above the sadness and find humor in an awkward situation. He was a treasure for her family and her. She was so lucky they had found each other. She couldn't wait to know more about this man who was her long-lost grandfather.

D.J. chuckled and slung an arm over his great-grandfather's shoulder. "Maybe I'll try again in a few days."

Arty stuffed the hanky in his back pocket and stroked his goatee. "Next time you visit, maybe bring a picture of you with your brother and sister when you guys were young, or one of you in your cap and gown when you graduated college." He stopped stroking his goatee and stuffed his hands in the pockets of his corduroy blazer. "There's always bribery, you know. She loves Butterfingers."

Johnnie reached over and hugged the old man's neck, getting a whiff of his clean scent. "We still need to make a date to come see your art."

D.J. and Arty exchanged knowing grins, like a secret handshake had passed between them. Johnnie looked from one to the other. "Okay, fellas. What are you two cooking up?"

Arty waggled a dark brow and put his finger to his lips. "It's a secret for now, but when the time is right, you'll get an invitation."

D.J. tugged on one of Johnnie's pigtails. "Mom, I'm going to step outside for a smoke and then head out. Tell Dad and Callie Ann bye for me." He glanced at Arty. "Give me a call later, Arthur. I'll meet you at the studio."

She searched both their faces. Just because she was the mother of one and the granddaughter of the other did not mean she had to be privy to everything.

Arty slapped D.J. on the back. "I'll walk out with you. I could use some fresh air."

Johnnie started to turn, then hesitated. "Arty, what if Mae gets confused again or agitated? What should we do?"

"Just play along. Talk to her in a calm voice. If all else fails, punch the call button on the side of the bed. A nurse will come."

Johnnie nodded. She'd had a similar experience two years ago. Moments before Mr. Marvel died in her arms, he called for his mother who'd been dead for years. With the ambulance on the way, Johnnie played along and pretended she was his mother, comforting him in a soothing voice as he took his dying breath.

After D.J. and Arty went outside, she headed back toward Mae's room. An elderly man in a wheelchair rolled by, his watery eyes sizing her up. He smiled, showing a mouthful of yellowed teeth. "Hello there, sexy. Come sit on my lap."

Johnnie patted his gnarled hand and kept walking. *Poor thing!* She detected a sour odor in his wake. One day that could be her, rolling along in her wheelchair, flirting with every young man who came within range.

Outside the door to her grandmother's

room, Mae's words thundered through Johnnie's head. *My son got killed in the war!* Johnnie felt a sucker punch to her womb as she stared at the simple nameplate on the door. All it said was, "Mae Murphy." No gold star next to her name, no sign announcing to the other residents or staff or visitors, "Here lives a Gold Star Mother . . . whose son gave his life for our freedom." Maybe she would mention it to the staff and see if they could come up with a special marker for her grandmother's door.

She turned to catch a glimpse of the frisky old man in the wheelchair before he disappeared around a corner. He could be a war hero for all she knew or a draft dodger. In this place, it didn't much matter.

Halfway in the door, she paused and marveled at Callie Ann next to the bed, brushing Mae's thick mane of white hair. Years of growth cascaded over the old woman's shoulders like a glacier slipping into the sea. Johnnie could hear them talking.

With a look of adoration, Mae gazed at Callie Ann and cupped her face in both hands. "I always wanted a granddaughter."

"And I've been needing another granny." Callie Ann fussed over the old woman as Johnnie entered the room.

Mae's dark eyebrows arched in question, and her sapphire eyes pinned Johnnie in place. "Who are you?"

Johnnie's voice cracked. "I'm the little girl in the photo." She took a few steps, twisting the end of one braid.

Mae's face scrunched in confusion. "But where did Francis go? He needs to get ready for Cub Scouts."

Johnnie and Callie Ann stared at each other, stumped as to how to respond. No matter what they said, they would have to lie. From her vantage point, Johnnie could see out the window to the parking lot. Arty had walked D.J. to his Honda and the two were talking.

A toilet flushed in the adjacent restroom. Dale stepped out, still working a paper towel around in his palms. He tossed the wad in a nearby trash can.

Mae took one look at Dale and waved him over. "Mister, have you seen my son? He hasn't come home from school. I'm getting worried."

Dale pulled up a chair and sat down and took Mae's hands in his. His voice was tender when he spoke. "Mae," he paused, as if searching for the right words, "Francis is with his father. Try not to worry."

Mae blinked at him a couple of times and

a peaceful smile returned to her face.

Johnnie stared at Dale in awe. Her carpenter husband with able hands and a kind heart knew just what to say to ease Mae's muddled mind. *And it was only a lie if you chose not to believe it.*

Johnnie's cellphone buzzed. Mama's name blinked on the caller ID. Johnnie walked out into the hall to take the call. "We're still here, Mama. I hope you're feeling better."

Mama took a drag on her cigarette. "Are y'all talking about me behind my back?"

Johnnie bit her tongue. "Arty asked about you, Mama. He said he's sorry you couldn't come." *But other than that, we didn't talk about you at all.*

Chapter 32
Letter in Care Package

Dear Son,

Enclosed are a few items I thought you might need. If there's anything you can't use, please share with your fellow soldiers or needy Afghans, as long as this doesn't put you at more risk.

You told me when you first deployed not to keep stuff from you. First, there is NO BAD NEWS in this letter. Just thought I would fill you in on life on the home front. If you've already heard some of this from your brother, sister, or dad, please humor me and keep reading.

Yesterday, we visited your great-grandmother at the nursing home in Denton. Depending on how you look at it, the visit was both a huge success and an utter disaster. Grandpa Arty was thrilled to meet your dad and sister, and he can't wait to meet you when you return. D.J.'s been to his studio several times. I get the feeling they are working on a joint project, but they aren't saying what it is. As for the disaster part — remember the first time you saw a photo of the lieutenant and you asked D.J. if he believed in reincarnation because he looks so much like my dad? Well, poor Mae Murphy, she took one look at your brother and thought he was her son. And that was *before* she remembered he was dead! Now I'm contemplating whether to show her a photo of you in uniform, even though you don't look anything like my dad. Just the sight of a soldier in uniform might set her off. But Arty asked me for one, so I sent him that photo of you surrounded by all those Afghan children after you gave them candy.

Dad and I had a long talk last night after we returned from the nursing home. I decided to hold off putting Granny Opal's place on the market until you come home. All three of you kids loved spending time there when you were young, and I want all of us to be together one last time on that property before I turn the key over to someone who doesn't know its history.

Once I sell it, we won't have legal access to the cove. That place is sacred to me, despite everything that happened there. For me, it represents a place of loss, but also a place of hope. It was there that your great Uncle Johnny lost his life to spare Mama's life and mine. If he hadn't made the sacrifice, I wouldn't be here and neither would you or your brother or sister. I know you got spooked one time when you and D.J. went night fishing and you thought you saw a ghost. Maybe that wasn't a ghost you saw but an angel watching over you and your brother. I don't talk to your brother about these things because he'd say I'm full of malarkey.

Enclosed are some clips of my latest columns, along with one written by my new friend, Roosevelt Hill. He's witnessed some things in his day. He's working on a second story but not sure when it will run. He served in the infantry in Vietnam. Maybe you two can compare war stories when you get home.

I met Sergeant Jackson the other day. He asked about you. We nabbed the kid in the jacked-up truck. It's a long story and I'll share it when you get home, but suffice to say the kid needs to learn a thing or two about tolerance before he joins the ranks of the Army.

Tomorrow, when I get out of class, I'm meeting Roosevelt and Sergeant Jackson out at the old black cemetery by the lake. The kid will be there, too. Before he serves his country, he needs to do some service. Vandals knocked over several tombstones and made a mess of things. We don't know if he was involved, but he's going to put in some backbreaking work to help fix it. If Whit can get someone to cover for her at the shop, she might join us. I've been anxious for her to meet Roosevelt and Sergeant Jackson. The plan is not to "gang up" on the kid, but to teach him about service.

The colonel called your dad the other day. He asked if you've seen many B-52s overhead. You might drop him a brief email next time you get to a computer. He told your dad he wished he could have gone in your place. That's your Grandpa Kitchen's way of saying he loves you.

Better wrap this up and get your box in the mail.

Love always,
Mama

P.S. Brother's headstone looks real nice out back next to the fence.

Chapter 33
Mourning Glory

The white shepherd sat on his haunches and gazed up at his master. Roosevelt stroked the dog's ears then addressed the people gathered at the entrance to the cemetery. "This is Hal. It's short for *Hallelujah.* He showed up one day during choir practice and we couldn't get rid of him."

Johnnie huddled in her fleece-hooded jacket and looked on, bemused, as Roosevelt held court, clad in a reddish orange dress shirt and chinos tucked inside knee-high rubber boots. He didn't wear a jacket against the late afternoon chill.

Dappled in shadows, Mourning Glory Cemetery appeared small and humble compared to the larger cemetery in town with its stone pillars and monuments reaching skyward. Scanning the area overgrown with withered vegetation and littered with the last of October's brittle leaves, Johnnie viewed a statue of Jesus missing a hand, graves marked with broken stones, cement blocks with no inscriptions, and metal posts with faded nameplates. A few graves stood out because of their granite or marble slabs and upright tombstones with square or half-round tops, but those were few and far between. It appeared Roosevelt had righted most of the tombstones toppled by vandals.

Whit elbowed Johnnie and whispered, "I'm with Hal. I'd show up at Roosevelt's choir practice any day."

Johnnie giggled and jabbed her friend in the side. "Down, girl," she muttered, trying to keep a straight face. She should have known Whit might be attracted to a man like Roosevelt, a sharp dresser and easy on the eye. It didn't seem to bother her that he was seventeen years her senior. Earlier, right after everyone assembled and Johnnie made the introductions, Whit had taken her time shaking Roosevelt's hand.

Johnnie's gaze drifted to Sergeant Jackson in Army camouflage, his military bearing adding dignity to the surroundings. Slouching next to Sergeant Jackson, the kid bit the inside of his cheek and shuffled his feet, looking more like a prisoner in tan coveralls than a young man about to join the Army. Johnnie grew uncomfortable watching him. She took no pleasure in his unease.

Sergeant Jackson addressed Roosevelt. "Mrs. Kitchen tells me you served in 'Nam. Eleven Bravo."

At the mention of the war, Roosevelt's stance changed. One second he was petting Hal, the next he stood at parade rest. His left foot stepped to the side about twelve inches from his right, and he locked his hands into position at the small of his back. Johnnie had seen Cade practice this hundreds of times before he left for basic.

"Private First Class Roosevelt Hill, reporting for duty, Sergeant." For a split second, Roosevelt looked deadly serious, like forty-some years hadn't passed since he'd seen combat. Even Jordan Rivers seemed to stand taller in his dull coveralls, his slouch giving way to squared shoulders and his fists clenched at his sides. His mouth was set in a firm line, not the usual slack-jaw with a toothpick jutting out. Before Roosevelt relaxed and the men gave each other high fives, Johnnie could've sworn she saw a look of respect wash over the kid's face.

The kid stuttered then swallowed and tried again, "Mr. Roosevelt, sir, did you see a lot of action over there?"

Roosevelt narrowed his eyes at the kid. "Well, young man, I'll put it like this. I earned a Purple Heart for getting wounded.

But the guy next to me, well," Roosevelt paused as if to gather his thoughts, "he earned his Purple Heart when he got his head blown off."

Wincing, Johnnie noted that Jordan Rivers' Adam's apple bobbed a couple of times as he digested Roosevelt's words.

Whit closed her eyes and mumbled, "Sweet Lord."

Sergeant Jackson stuffed his hands in his pockets and rocked back on the heels of his combat boots.

Nobody dared ask Roosevelt where he got injured. He'd obviously recovered and moved on with his life.

Bending over, Roosevelt retrieved a weed-whacker and thrust it toward Jordan. "We're losing daylight standing around ratchet-jawing. We'd better get to work."

Johnnie listened as Roosevelt instructed Jordan as to what he wanted done in the next few days while Sergeant Jackson took notes in a small spiral notebook. Johnnie milled about, uncertain what to do. Should she offer to pull weeds, or just make small talk? For a few minutes, she tagged along beside the men.

"I spent the better part of a year building this fence," Roosevelt said as they walked past a section of the normally waist-high picket fence mowed down by a vehicle. He told the group he would buy the replacement material, and he described to Jordan how he wanted it repaired on the next visit.

Jordan "yes-sirred" him right and left. After Roosevelt and Sergeant Jackson walked off, Jordan hefted the weed-whacker, pulled the cord, and went to work trimming around the entrance then moving over to the graves. Hal followed, his tail wagging. Every few seconds he stopped to sniff, then trotted next to the kid like they were best friends. The whine of the motor didn't seem to faze Hal; Johnnie recalled how Brother used to hide whenever she hauled out the vacuum cleaner.

As Whit doled out water bottles and hummed hymns, she sashayed around, her black boots with spiked heels impractical for walking in the dirt. She looked chic as ever in a long black and white hound's-tooth skirt. Once she stopped to give the shepherd a quick, stiff-handed head pat. "Hello, Hal. I'm not much of a dog person, but my arm can be twisted." She winked at Johnnie and handed her a water bottle.

A few minutes later, Johnnie overheard Jordan Rivers tell Whit, "I'm sorry what I said up at the war memorial. I didn't mean it."

Tilting her head, Whit studied him a moment before answering. "We all fall short, Jordan. Now, can I tell you something about that flag you were flying on the back of your truck?"

He blinked and shuffled his feet. "Yes, ma'am?"

"See, for me and my people, it symbolizes oppression. Hate. When I see that flag, well, I feel . . ." her voice broke off for a moment, and Johnnie could see Whit's mouth working, how she breathed through her nose as she formulated her words. Whit squeezed a water bottle in her hand, and when she opened her mouth, her voice thundered, "That day you drove by with that flag, I felt like it was slapping me in the face and telling me I should still be a *slave.*"

Whit's words fired out across the graveyard, pinging from marker to marker. Everyone froze and stared in her direction.

The kid's mouth twisted all funny and he stared at the ground for what seemed like an eternity. Finally, he looked up and stared at something in the distance. He shrugged his shoulders several times as if he didn't know what to say.

After a moment, Whit sighed. "Well, I said what needed to be said. Now we can move on." She jutted her chin and placed a hand on the kid's shoulder. "With a name like Jordan Rivers, there's hope for you yet."

Leaning on the weed-whacker, he let out a nervous chuckle. "Yes, ma'am. My mama was a druggie and wanted to name me Mississippi, but my Grandma threw a fit and said, 'No grandson of mine is gonna be named Mississippi Rivers.' So Mama's second choice was a river in the Holy Land. I get teased about it sometimes."

Whit had worked her magic. The kid had opened up. Johnnie leaned against a tree, mesmerized by their conversation.

"Well, you be proud of your name, Jordan Rivers. You got nothin' to apologize for." Whit turned and brushed past Johnnie. "I don't know if he's playing me, but I got my point across," she said out of the side of her mouth.

Johnnie retrieved her journal, stashed in her bag. She sat down on a small boulder and scribbled: "Hal the former stray and Jordan the recovering troublemaker." She studied what she wrote. It might be good fodder for a future column. Biting her pen, she swept her gaze once again over Mourning Glory Cemetery. Then she bowed her head and began to write: "So we come to the cemetery hoping to hold on to something tangible — a name, a date, an endearment inscribed in stone, anything to remember a loved one by. Because how do you wrap your arms around a spirit? That's like trying to hug the air."

As she contemplated what she'd written, Hal appeared in front of her, only inches from her face. She could smell his warm doggie breath. "I'd give you a mint if I had one," she laughed and razzed him. Running her hands through his thick fur, she felt something stir deep inside. Dropping her journal on the ground, she threw her arms around Hal and clung to his warm body, breathing in his scent. "Glory, glory, hallelujah," she sang, staring into his golden eyes. His pointy ears twitched. "You've got bunny ears," she teased, noticing the pink interiors.

Smoothing her palms over his face, she kissed his forehead while he panted. "I bet you're thirsty, big dog." Pulling the water bottle from her bag, she cupped her hands and dribbled water into her palm. Hal lapped away. When he'd had enough, she nuzzled her head in his fur. The dam broke, and her grief spilled over. Hal looked so noble sitting there in the middle of the graveyard watching the others work while Johnnie stroked his back and baby-talked him.

After a while, Hal licked her face and his

black nose sniffed at her jeans. Then he trotted off, stopping at the base of an old pecan to hike his leg and pee.

Pushing up from the boulder, Johnnie ambled from grave to grave, reading whatever names and dates were legible.

At one grave enclosed in a border of bricks, her heart quickened at the jagged inscription made in the slab of wet cement before it had hardened:

Thurman Blue
1927-1952
A saint among men

The man who played Santa was twenty-five years old when he was murdered. *D.J.'s age.*

"I see you found Thurman's grave." Roosevelt threw his head back and emptied his water bottle in one glug. "He was just a few years older than our young friend, Jordan." He tapped the empty bottle against his palm.

Johnnie blinked, turning away. "He was my oldest son's age," she offered, her voice hoarse.

Roosevelt had started to walk off when Johnnie blurted out, "Roosevelt, is your wife buried out here?" She hoped she wasn't being too forward, but she remembered how he'd said, "Got all my people buried here, so this is a bit personal."

He nodded toward a cluster of upright tombstones. "Right over there." Johnnie scrambled to her feet and followed him to a single pink granite headstone embellished with lilies and a cross. The inscription read:

Nora Odom Hill
A good wife and "mother" to many

Roosevelt's words from their first meeting circled through her mind: "That's the one thing I couldn't give her. Kids. But we fostered our share over the years until she got sick."

Johnnie noted there was no blank tombstone beside it, waiting for Roosevelt's name. She wondered if he had a lady friend. When she looked up, Roosevelt stuffed his hands in his pockets and swayed in front of a long slab of granite that stood knee high — a tombstone built for two.

"Your parents?"

He nodded and Johnnie read the names:

Henry Hill
Husband and Pappy
A Man of His Word

Hattie Dixon Hill
Wife and Mother
Home in Heaven

"These are beautiful headstones. Some of the finest here."

Roosevelt gave a slight nod and swatted at something on the back of his neck. "I made a decent living driving a truck. I wish I could afford tombstones for every grave here, but that would send me to the poorhouse."

After Roosevelt left to check on Jordan, Whit passed by, stopping to lean over and whisper, "Guess who invited me to church next Sunday?"

Johnnie's jaw dropped. "Roosevelt? When?"

Whit clapped her hands. "When you had your nose stuck in your writing book. He's picking me up at my place, too."

Johnnie grinned and pulled out her water bottle. "You know what they say about fine wine . . . ?" She tipped the bottle to her mouth, smirking as she took a hit.

"Or aged beef," Whit shot back.

Johnnie laughed and spewed water out her nose.

They giggled amongst themselves as only good friends do.

After a while Johnnie said, "Whit, seriously, he seems like a good man. Maybe he's the one."

Whit pursed her lips and studied her nails. "Oh, I'll know when he invites me over for coffee and cake. If he hauls out too many pictures of his late wife, I'll make a run for it."

Johnnie screwed the cap back on her water bottle. "Well, I didn't see a blank tombstone waiting next to his wife's, if that's any indication."

Whit grabbed her and kissed her on the cheek. "You a mess, ladybug." Gazing into the distance, she added, "Look across the road, next to the church. Which car do you think belongs to Roosevelt? The Buick LeSabre or the yellow Corvette?"

Johnnie's gaze swept past the Holy Ghost Temple of Love — an L-shaped, off-white clapboard building with a slanted metal roof — to the parking lot. "I'd say the Buick La Sabre. The church secretary's about a hundred years old. She probably drives the Vette."

They cackled like two old hens. Seeing the laughter in Whit's eyes, Johnnie blurted out, "Whit, what if you do find true love in the middle of a graveyard a few days before Halloween? That's a scary thought."

With a flourish, Whit flung her scarf over her shoulder. "Now slow down, ladybug. All bets are off if he drives that old LeSabre."

Still laughing, Johnnie turned at the sound of a dog's bark — a playful, happy sound she hadn't heard since August. Whit's cellphone rang and she excused herself to take the call.

Johnnie watched as Jordan picked up a stick and hurled it through the air, away from any visible graves. The white dog charged down the fence line after the stick, retrieved it, and ran back for more. Each time Jordan threw the stick, the dog looked up in anticipation before racing off. Surely, if the kid was rotten to the core, the dog would pick up on it.

After a while, the dog returned, dropped the stick, and lay down panting. Jordan rubbed Hal's head and sides then picked up the weed-whacker and went back to work. As she studied him, a thought crossed Johnnie's mind. *What if the kid's hateful remarks that day at the war memorial were really a cry for help? What if the flag behind the kid's truck had been the same one flapping from the flagpole in front of the uncle's place?* Regardless, the kid had learned some lessons today and none of them had rejected him for his mistakes.

Something caught her eye at the far end of the graveyard, now entirely in shadow. At first she thought it was an old campfire pit, and she found it odd that someone would build a fire inside the protected area so near to the fence. Curious, she stepped gingerly around the graves to give the site a closer inspection.

As she approached, her heart sprinted ahead in the dim light. Inhaling big gulps of cold air, she gazed at a circle of fieldstones, each one the size of a head. Her mouth dry as cotton, she tried to swallow as she began to count each stone, one by one. With the voices of the others fading behind her, she trembled when she got to seven. Huddled inside of her hoodie, she gazed at a pair of angel's wings etched on a bronze plaque at the center of the stones. In a strangled voice, she read the list of names out loud:

Priscilla, 13
Clementine, 11
Sadie and Sally, 9
Mary, 7
Martha 5,
Ruth, 4

Something brushed against the back of Johnnie's calves and she jumped, stifling a primitive cry. Hal nudged her with his nose — like Brother used to do, appearing out of nowhere. A shovel in his dark hand, Roosevelt stood next to Hal.

Johnnie's teeth chattered as she said, "Who were they, Roosevelt?"

He stabbed the shovel's blade into the earth and held onto the handle as if it were a shepherd's staff. "They were my sissies, Miss Johnnie. They were killed in a house fire in 1950. They had the sweetest voices this side of Heaven."

Johnnie shivered uncontrollably. They were the girls he was writing about in his next story, due on Glenda Hunter's desk any day. The girls Callie Ann saw at the hanging tree. The ones Johnnie had summoned that day at the dock.

Sergeant Jackson whistled from across the cemetery, getting Roosevelt's attention. "What say we call it a day, boss? Jordan will come back tomorrow. He'll check in with your secretary if you're not around."

Roosevelt flashed a broad grin and hollered back, "Sounds good, sarge. Be with y'all in a sec."

He glanced back at Johnnie, and his kind brown eyes pierced her heart. "I had the plaque made when I came back from 'Nam. Their bones are still buried under the lake."

CHAPTER 34
PORTION TELEGRAPH
SUNDAY, NOVEMBER 1, 2009

From the desk of Glenda Hunter, Editor-in-Chief:

Back in August, the paper ran an eyewitness account of a lynching that took place out by Portion Lake in 1952. Last Wednesday, President Barack Obama signed into law the "Matthew Shepard and James Byrd Jr. Hate Crimes Prevention Act." The next day, our guest columnist and his friend, an African American woman who owns a thriving gift shop on Main Street, were openly discriminated against at a popular eatery in town. It seems a member of the wait staff refused to acknowledge their presence until she took drink orders from two white women seated at the same booth, local columnist Johnnie Kitchen and her teenage daughter, a senior at Portion High.

When Ms. Kitchen and her daughter insisted that the waitress start by taking the orders of the couple seated across the table, the waitress got huffy and stormed off. The younger Miss Kitchen banged a spoon on the table and called for the manager. When the manager rushed over to their booth and learned of the situation, he personally took all of their orders, starting with the black couple. Then he comped the entire table and apologized profusely. Bravo to the youngest Miss Kitchen for her impromptu "sit-in."

Today, I'm pleased to welcome back our guest columnist from August. His story is stitched together from his earliest memories and things his parents told him before they passed. I am proud to publish his work, but I'm even prouder that he is writing under his real name.

"The Sole Survivor"
by Roosevelt Hill

My pappy worked two jobs before the lake came in. By day he worked the land around Glory as a sharecropper, and by night he spit-shined those marble floors and lavatories up at Portion City Hall. Back then, his biggest dream was to pass by those "whites only" signs and cast his vote in an election, any election — city, state, or national — it didn't matter to him. He wanted the right to vote. Mama took in ironing and raised chickens and sold eggs to help put food on the table. Back before the fire, they had a lot of mouths to feed. We'd all been to church that Easter Sunday, my sissies and me. The girls were still in their Sunday frocks that Mama made from flour sacks. I was three years old, the only boy out of eight children and the baby in the bunch.

Pappy had gone to the barn to check on our milk cow and pour himself a little drink. Mama left the oldest in charge while she took me out on the porch to rock me. I'd been running a fever ever since we got home from church. Mama and I must have dozed off because the next thing we knew, we were blown off the porch by an explosion inside the house. The whole valley seemed to shake. I was still in a daze and rolling around in the weeds, bawling like a lost calf. I remember Mama choking as she staggered toward the house. By now it was fully engulfed in flames, and she yelped like an animal getting slaughtered.

By then my pappy had torn out of the barn, his arms thrashing all over the place as he tried to get inside to grab the girls. But the smoke pushed him back.

Years later, when I went to Vietnam, every time we entered a village that had been blown up or attacked, I smelled that same god-awful stench of burnt flesh and heard the same tortured wail of the survivors.

One of the neighbors had a telephone and called the firehouse. Back in those days it was run by volunteer firemen, all of them white. My pappy told me years later that the fire chief, rumored to head up the local Klan, told the caller, "I ain't risking any of my men for a bunch of darkies in a burning shack." The neighbors did the best they could to help put out the fire, but it was too late for my sissies. All seven were gone. My pappy always wondered if some of the volunteer firemen who didn't come that day were the same boys who strung up Thurman Blue two years later.

Blacks were forbidden burial in Portion Cemetery in 1950. So they buried the girls in the cemetery in Glory. The next year, the Corp of Engineers built the dam on the Trinity River. Before they flooded the valley, most of the residents from Glory were relocated to the Pasture, an enclave of homes, a church, and a school located at the tip of Main Street on the outskirts of Portion. A white landowner donated the land for the new cemetery, renamed Mourning Glory, and an African American mortician offered to relocate the bodies. But that year we had so much rain, and the lake started filling on its own. It was too late to relocate the dead. By then, white folks were skiing in their fancy boats over the watery graves of Glory.

After we moved to town, Pappy ran a successful bait and tackle shop and continued to clean the floors at city hall. All the while he waited patiently for the chance to vote, but Jim Crow and poll taxes shut him out until after I went to war. He died shortly after I returned. At Pappy's funeral, Mama claimed he died a little bit every day, staring down at his dark reflection in the white marble of city hall. Poor Mama. Her spirit died years before her body gave out. She always blamed herself for the fire. Until her dying day, she wondered if she'd left the gas turned on in the old stove and it somehow ignited. It about killed her when I got drafted and sent to Vietnam. When I got shot, I swear I stayed alive just to thumb my nose at that old grim reaper and to come home to Mama.

I ask myself everyday why my sissies died and I lived. I've tried to honor their memories by doing right and not allowing hate to eat at my heart. Sometimes when I close my eyes, I see them in their Easter dresses. They flutter around me like butterflies.

~Roosevelt Hill is a Vietnam Veteran and a retired long-haul truck driver. To keep busy, he volunteers as the custodian for the Holy Ghost Temple of Love, where he is an active member of the congregation. In his spare time, he takes care of Mourning Glory Cemetery and enjoys reading and writing. When he was old enough to read, he turned to books as an escape from his mother's depression over losing all seven of her daughters. Mr. Hill still resides at the Pasture in the family home he and his late wife remodeled a few years before her death. You may write to him care of the *Portion Telegraph.*

Chapter 35
November 5, 2009
Breaking News

"I'm lucky if I can still play chopsticks." Mama plopped down on the bench in front of the grand piano and ran her fingers absently over the black and white keys.

A crystal vase of fresh flowers on the piano lid filled the room with a sweet scent. Johnnie took a seat in a pink and white striped slipper chair a few feet away. She'd stopped by the Dooley Mansion after class to check on Mama and found her gazing out the floor-to-ceiling window of the music room, just off the grand entryway. Before Mama spotted her and waved, Johnnie noted that faraway look in her eyes again. Growing up, Johnnie often thought of Mama as a hollow-cheeked beauty who could seem to be giving you her attention while her spirit drifted someplace else. She had the afternoon off. The last guests had checked out Monday morning, and new arrivals weren't expected until tomorrow, a

Friday and the beginning of a busy weekend.

"I bet it would all come back to you with a little practice." Johnnie paused, thinking of Mama's suicide note. She lowered her voice and fumbled for the right words to bring it up. "Mama, in your last will and testament, you mentioned that you want your old upright piano donated to charity."

Mama swiveled around, facing Johnnie. "That's right. You can get rid of it anytime you like."

Johnnie fiddled with the cream-colored fringe skirting the slipper chair. "But I'm not going to sell Granny's house until after Cade returns from Afghanistan. I don't have the energy. So there's no rush to move the piano just yet. It's safe where it is."

"Baby girl, I lost my will to play years ago. Poppy used to harp about how much money he'd spent on my piano lessons when I was growing up. 'And that piano just sitting there collecting dust and pictures,' he'd grumble to Ma."

Johnnie sat up straighter. "Grandpa was disappointed when I didn't want to take lessons."

"Yeah, well, Poppy was disappointed about a lot of things," Mama said, standing up and going to the window. She kept her back to Johnnie. “Say, I’m proud of you girls for taking a stand against that snooty waitress down at the Cottonbelt Café. I had no idea until I read about it in the paper.” She turned and batted her lashes at Johnnie.

Uh-oh. Are Mama’s feelings hurt because she wasn’t invited to join us? Johnnie pressed ahead, pretending not to notice. “Mama, that waitress is a plainclothes bigot. It was so obvious how she refused to make eye contact with Roosevelt and Whit. When I asked her to take their order first, Whit kicked me under the table. She didn’t want a scene. But it’s happened with us so many times at other restaurants, and that day I’d had enough. Callie Ann picked up on it right away, too.”

“How old was the waitress?”

“Not old enough. It’s not like she grew up in the dark ages. She’s maybe a year or two older than Callie Ann. I’d never seen her before.”

Mama nodded. “Bigots come in all ages, I’m afraid. It’s not like it’s breaking news.” Mama sat back down on the bench and crossed her feet. “I read Roosevelt’s story. I’m anxious to meet him. We’re about the same age, you know. But he would’ve gone to the all-black school and I, well. . . .” She took a deep breath and uncrossed her feet.

"You know what happened to me. I got sent off to the Denton School for Unwed Mothers. When I came back to Portion High, let's just say I kept a low profile."

The back of Johnnie's throat stung. What did that have to do with Roosevelt? Clearly, Mama had never gotten past being packed off to Denton to give birth. Johnnie scratched the back of her head. "Mama, you should see Whit and Roosevelt together. They've been inseparable since they met at the cemetery almost two weeks ago. He's been spending lots of time at the shop helping her with displays. Whit swears her business has picked up since that article ran in Sunday's paper."

Mama smiled thoughtfully. "How does Callie Ann feel now about seeing them girls at the hanging tree? Now that she's read Roosevelt's story."

Tiny chills tapped up Johnnie's spine as she considered Mama's question. "To be honest, before we were seated at our booth, she told Roosevelt it was a *privilege* — that's the word she used when they first embraced."

"And what did Roosevelt say about Callie Ann seeing them around Brother's body?"

Johnnie's entire scalp prickled as she imagined Priscilla leading her sisters in prayer and singing. Trying to keep her voice even, Johnnie began, "He said . . . he said Callie Ann must be a very special person. That she was the chosen one to carry their message."

"Their message?" Mama hugged herself. "And what's that? Besides giving all of us the heebie-jeebies."

Johnnie sighed, closing her eyes for a second. "I don't know, Mama. I think that's for each one of us to figure out."

A long silence stretched between them. The only sounds were a tree branch scraping across one of the windows and the piano bench creaking every time Mama moved.

After a moment, Johnnie said, "On Monday, some wealthy lady from Fort Worth called Roosevelt's church looking for him. She was so touched by his story that she wants to put up the money and hire an artist to create a life-sized sculpture to commemorate the sisters."

A wild look came over Mama's face. "I can see it now. Kind of like the war memorial but different. You'd have the seven girls dancing around in a circle." She bolted upright and grabbed Johnnie's hands, and the two women spun around the room. "Ring around the rosy. A pocket full of posies . . ." Mama chanted.

Johnnie joined in, singing, "Ashes! Ashes! We all fall down."

Still holding hands, they tumbled together on the plush Persian rug, laughing like schoolgirls — Roosevelt's sisters forgotten in the moment.

And then the question Johnnie had been harboring since the day Mama goofed and said something about getting her old room back — and Mr. Fred asking about her relationship with this house — overrode everything else. Johnnie looked Mama square in the eye as the words somersaulted from her mouth. "Did you used to live here? A long time ago with Miss Delthia Overby?"

Mama squeezed her eyes shut like she was in pain. Her whole face contorted into a mask Johnnie didn't recognize. She pushed herself up, breathing hard, and started in on one of her coughing jags. Covering her mouth with her fist, she rasped, "I was the daughter she never had. She was always happy to have me around. Whereas Ma and Poppy, well, I was just one big reminder of their grief. Of everything they'd lost." Backing up toward the piano, she held her right hand behind her as if she were blind and needed to feel her way to sit down. Reaching for the piano bench, she eased herself down as if every joint in her body ached.

Johnnie let out a deep sigh and fell back in the chair. Cradling her knees to her chest, she peeked up at Mama and waited for her to spill her guts about the witch lady who wore red fox stoles and drove a fancy Cadillac.

"Miss Delthia took me in when I had no place else to go. Poppy and Ma never knew. I helped with the chores and tried to stay out of her maid and butler's hair . . . and their business. If I stayed out of their business, they'd stay out of mine. That's how we worked it. Who do you think gave us the money to go on our bus trip to see your daddy before he shipped off?"

"Miss Overby?" Johnnie squeaked.

"I stayed with her off and on until she passed. Then the house went up for sale. She left me a little money. That floated me for a while after I left town for good."

Mama started hacking again, her cough worse than ever.

As Johnnie processed the news, she couldn't think of what to say except to ask Mama about her health. "Did you ever go to the doctor? It sounds like you're fixing to cough up a lung."

Mama shook her head and gasped for breath. A bowl of hard candy sat on a nearby table, and Mama plucked up a piece, unwrapped it, and stuck it in her mouth. As she sucked on the candy, the cough subsided.

From where Johnnie sat, she could see Mr. Fred strolling up the walkway toward the front veranda. He wore running togs and a portable radio strapped to an armband. "Mama, here comes Mr. Fred. It looks like he's been out running."

Mama turned expectantly as the front door opened and rubbed her hand on the polished wood of the piano bench. Johnnie shivered as a gust of cold air blew in from outside into the music room.

Mr. Fred pulled out his earbuds as he stuck his head through the archway. "Afternoon, ladies. Sorry to disturb you." He glanced at Johnnie. "Mrs. Kitchen, you've got a son in the Army, right? Isn't he deployed?"

Her heart rocketed up her throat. Why was he asking? Did he know something she didn't? Had something happened in Afghanistan and the whole world knew but her? "Yes," she swallowed, sounding small as she sat hunched over in the armless chair.

"You ladies might want to turn on the news. There's been a mass shooting at Fort Hood. They're reporting that the shooter was a soldier."

Fort Hood. Mass shooting? How could this be possible? Fort Hood was a garrison — a post — a fortress where soldiers trained before they went to war. Not a place where soldiers were supposed to get shot up. And by a fellow soldier. . . . None of it made sense.

Lost in thought, Mama turned to Mr. Fred. She sounded slow and stupid as she said, "Fort Hood is the last place where Johnnie girl saw her daddy before he went to war."

Johnnie fumbled in her purse for a tissue. Tears brimmed at the corners of her eyes.

Mr. Fred lingered in the archway between the foyer and the music room. "Oh, I'm so sorry." He stared at the earbuds in his palm as if he didn't know how else to respond. Finally, he excused himself and headed down the central hallway, mumbling about how awful the whole thing was, how at least a dozen soldiers and civilians were dead.

Mama stared out the long window, past the manicured lawn turning brown and yellow. "What kind of a madman would go on a shooting rampage on an Army post and kill our heroes? Your daddy would never believe this."

About then, Johnnie's cellphone rang. Arty's number appeared on the caller ID.

She didn't have to ask why he was calling. "Hi, Arty. Mama and I just heard. I'm here with her now at the Dooley Mansion. Are you okay?" Johnnie pressed the speaker button so Mama could hear the rest of the conversation.

"I'm fine, but poor Mae. A couple of nursing aides who came in to check on her were babbling about the news. When Mae heard the shootings took place at Fort Hood, she tried to crawl out of bed and get to a phone. She said she had to warn Francis to take cover . . ." Arty's voice trailed off.

Johnnie glanced over at Mama. She had her hands tucked between her legs and the upper half of her body rocked sideways on the piano bench like a metronome. The bench creaked with her movement. Tremors moved through Johnnie's body and her throat tightened. "I hope Mae's mind soon switched to something pleasant." Johnnie glanced at Mama, who appeared dazed. No telling what was going through her mind.

After a moment, Arty's voice cut through Johnnie's fractured thoughts. "She's resting now. Tell Victoria *hello.* I'm anxious to meet her. Oh, and tell her I don't bite," Arty chuckled.

"She's right here, Arty. I think she's worried that you're mad at her."

Mama's eyes grew almost as wide as her open mouth. She started shaking her head and giving Johnnie a dirty look.

"I hope she'll be able to join us for a little shindig that D.J. and I are putting on. I mailed the invitations today."

"Arty, is there a dress code for this art show? I don't think Dale owns a suit anymore."

"Tell Dale not to get gussied up. If any art snobs show up in tuxedoes, they'll be overdressed."

Mama held out a trembling hand and gestured for Johnnie to pass her the phone.

"Hang on, Arty. I think Mama wants to talk to you." Johnnie passed her the phone. Even though it was still on speaker, Mama cupped the phone to her ear like it was a delicate object. A slight smile creased her face as she said shyly, "Hello, Arthur. This is Victoria Grubbs. I'm real sorry I hung up on you a while back."

"Vic-tor-i-a!" Arty's deep voice sang out enthusiastically from the speaker.

Mama's whole face lit up when Arty called her name.

The invitation arrived two days later in Johnnie's mailbox:

Arthur Murphy, the father of a fallen soldier, and his great-grandson, D.J. Kitchen, the brother of a deployed soldier, request your presence at a reception and art show at the Campus Theatre located one block off Denton's historic square on Sunday, November 22, 2009 from 2:00–4:00 p.m. The show is in memory of United States Army First Lieutenant Francis Murphy, KIA in Vietnam on November 22, 1970.

Mr. Murphy holds an MFA from University of Texas and is a retired high school art teacher. Mr. Kitchen earned his BFA from the University of North Texas and is a working artist in Denton.

Chapter 36
Rainy Days and Mondays

A female announcer's smooth voice broadcast from the Suburban's speakers: "On this day in history, November 9, 1960, Senator John F. Kennedy was elected President of the United States, and twenty years ago today, the world witnessed the collapse of the Berlin Wall that divided East Germany from West Germany."

Wow, had it been twenty years? Johnnie's mind flashed to 1989 and the news reports on CNN, baby Cade cuddled in her lap in the ratty recliner as he sucked on his bottle. Parked Indian style in front of the boxy television set with rabbit ears, D.J. clapped his hands and proclaimed, "The walls are tumbling down, Mommy!" At five, he was already a news junkie.

Gray clouds hung so low, Johnnie couldn't see the airplanes taking off and landing at DFW Airport, but she could hear the drone of their engines as they flew overhead. She

The little boy had on rain boots and a slicker. He tugged on the man's pant leg and pointed up at the statue. Before she glanced away to focus on her driving, she noticed the empty bench. In her mind's eye, she would always see Mama sitting there talking to her soldier.

Approaching a red light at the intersection of Main and Merriweather, Johnnie clicked on the right blinker and thought about the hot cup of tea she would make when she got home. As she rolled to a stop, she saw a big dog in a perfect sit position on the corner in front of Farrow & Sons. *Poor pup. What is it doing out in this weather?* She strained forward, trying to get a better look as the blades on the wipers swished back and forth. The dog had a coffee-colored coat with white splotches on its face, legs, and underbelly. The white fur on its chest resembled the markings of a bird, like a dove or an eagle in flight.

With no one behind her, Johnnie turned right onto Merriweather, pulled up next to the curb, and rolled down the window. She glanced over at the funeral home then at the dog. No sign of a collar or tags. The dog gazed at Johnnie with sad eyes. Squinting through the rain, Johnnie could tell the dog was a female.

She stuck her head out the window. "Hey, Miss Beautiful. Who do you belong to? Did one of the neighbors leave their gate open?" Shifting on its haunches, the dog turned its head in Johnnie's direction.

A car came up behind Johnnie and blasted its horn. She realized she was blocking the intersection. "Crap." What should she do? She had to get home and study. The dog was somebody else's problem. Besides, she'd just spent a hundred bucks to have the Suburban professionally cleaned. No more doggie smell or dog hair. No more mud from baseball cleats, broken guitar strings, lost picks, or frayed pompoms and mismatched socks. For the first time in years, she drove a vehicle that didn't reek of animal and children.

The car honked again. Johnnie gunned the engine and blasted off down the street, glancing back at the dog in her rearview mirror. *Someone else will rescue you, girl. You're not my problem. Besides, I'm not ready for another dog. I want Brother back. His life was taken from him. He was an innocent. . . .*

That morning, before heading out to class, she leaned against the kitchen counter and stared at the back door. The house was eerily quiet as she gripped her mug with both hands. With Cade in Afghanistan and Brother gone, the house seemed so still, like it was holding its breath until one of them returned.

Then she heard it. The slightest sigh and rattle of tags. Gulping, she gazed around the room. "Brother Dog?"

She listened with her whole body, almost willing him to appear. But the only sound was a leaf-mulcher revving up somewhere down the street. Gripping her mug, she moved across the room to the back door and peeked out the window at the fence. She knew Brother's brown body was buried there, deep in the earth. She couldn't bring him back to life any more than she could bring Cade home from Afghanistan.

Sighing, she placed her mug in the sink and went to grab her purse and books. She poked her head in the laundry room. His dishes and mat were clean and stored in a cabinet over the washer. She missed the sound of Brother Dog crunching food and drinking water, licking the floor for any wayward crumbs. Brother, the cleanup crew. Brother, the buffer of family feuds.

A block from the house, she choked up at the sight of the lone evergreen Mr. Marvel planted the day he died. Johnnie was determined to keep Edwin's tree alive, regardless of what the city did with the lot.

Her mind galloped to the corner of Main and Merriweather. To the sight of that lone dog, poised there in a perfect sit, like it was waiting for its master or mistress to return. If she could help save a tree, why couldn't she help save a dog?

Barreling up the curved driveway, she screeched to a halt and dashed through the side door of the portico. Once in the house, she dropped her books on the island, grabbed Brother's red collar and leash and two old bath towels. Halfway to the door, she remembered the bag of unopened treats.

Back in the Suburban, she zoomed down the street, swerving a bit on the black asphalt slick from the rain. What if the dog got hit by a car or had been picked up by some sleazebag who was up to no good? Johnnie had heard horror stories about dogs used as bait dogs in illegal dogfights. She started to call Dale then changed her mind. What if Dale didn't want another dog? Sometimes it was easier to ask for forgiveness than permission.

By the time she returned, the dog was gone. Her heart sank as she started to turn around. But then, what was that curled up by a planter on the mortuary's big column porch? Wheeling into the parking lot, Johnnie slammed the gearshift into park and headed for the porch. She scanned the sidewalk in both directions but saw no sign of a worried pet owner looking for a lost dog.

Climbing the steps to the porch, she murmured in a soothing voice, "Hello, sweet girl. I bet you're hungry and cold." The dog lifted its head when Johnnie approached. "Will you let me dry you off?" Johnnie held out a towel for the dog to sniff. Stroking her wet fur, Johnnie began to run the towel over the dog. The dog blinked with pleasure, and Johnnie wrinkled her nose at the wet, stinky smell. "You could use a bath, that's for sure." The dog thumped its tail and panted up at Johnnie. For a stray, she had extremely white teeth. "You must not be very old. I sure wish you could talk."

Johnnie glanced back at the double doors leading into the mortuary's foyer. "You know, girl, this is a funeral home. You picked a fine place to get rescued. It's not like any of the residents are in a position to save you." Johnnie joked to keep the dark thoughts at bay. She hadn't been here since Granny died.

"You stay here," she told the dog. "Don't

run off. I'm going to ask someone if they know who you belong to." The dog whimpered when Johnnie reached for the door. "It's okay, girl. I won't leave you."

Sticking her head inside, Johnnie held the door halfway open to keep an eye on the dog.

A woman about ten years older than Johnnie looked up from a U-shaped reception desk. She took off her glasses. "Can I help you?"

Johnnie glanced around, taking in the ornate surroundings. As if upholstered chairs and sofas could ease the burden of grief. "There's a doggie outside on your porch. She's wet and cold and shaking."

The woman rose from her chair, padded around the desk, and followed Johnnie to the door. "You look familiar. Didn't your grandmother pass away a few months ago?"

Johnnie offered her hand. "Yes, hello. I'm Johnnie Kitchen. Opal Grubbs' granddaughter."

"Of course. I'm Charlotte. You're the writer." Before she poked her head outside, she looked around. In a hushed tone, she said. "It's so sad about Steven Tuttle . . . what happened to him in Iraq. He's such a nice young man. Personally, I think he should get his old job back. I don't have a problem with a disfigured person working here. I mean, really." She tittered and covered her mouth. "I've seen a whole lot worse come through the back door on a gurney."

Johnnie shuddered, but the woman didn't seem to notice as Johnnie held the door open for her to pass. Johnnie couldn't imagine having this woman's job. What was it like to work around dead people all day? One day Johnnie would work up the nerve to ask her for an interview for her column. Maybe a day-in-the-life type story.

Out on the porch, Charlotte took one look at the dog and said, "I've never seen her before. My guess is some lowlife dumped her out by the freeway and she found her way here. Poor thing. She looks sweet, though."

Johnnie cleared her throat. "She was sitting on the corner when I came by the first time. Guess I'll try and load her up and take her to the vet. See if she's been microchipped."

"I'm sorry I can't be of more help." The phone rang on the receptionist's desk. "I better answer that. Good luck."

After the woman went back inside, Johnnie opened the bag of treats and waved one in front of the dog's nose. "Brother loved these. I'm sure he won't mind if I share them with a pretty girl like you."

The dog took a polite nibble and waited for another. Johnnie rubbed her head and said, "Good girl. That's my sweet girl." She thought she saw gratitude in those honey-colored eyes. Holding out Brother's red collar, she let the dog sniff it before she placed it around her neck. Then she hooked the leash to the collar. *This dog has been trained,* Johnnie thought.

"Okay, girl. Time to go." Johnnie gathered the damp towels. The rain had stopped by the time they stepped off the porch. Out on the lawn, the dog stopped to tinkle before they headed toward the Suburban. The sun punched a hole in the gray clouds and seemed to shine a spotlight all the way to the parking lot.

When Johnnie opened the back passenger door, the dog hesitated for a second before jumping in. Johnnie threw in the towels, walked around to the driver's side, and climbed in. Backing up, she locked the doors, rolled down the passenger windows in the back, and cruised up Main toward the veterinarian's office.

In the same soothing tone she'd used with Brother, she chatted away. "We're going to take a little visit to the vet and have him check you out. See if anyone's reported you missing." The dog sat in the middle of the platform behind the two front bucket seats and stared straight ahead, just like Brother used to do. Johnnie wondered if her new friend could smell Brother's scent, even though the carpets had been shampooed a couple of months ago.

"If no one's looking for you, would you like to come home with me?" The stray placed her chin on Johnnie's right shoulder and sighed.

After Johnnie pulled into the vet, she swiveled in her seat and gazed at the white bird markings on the dog's chest.

"Call her 'Ladybird,' " Granny Opal's voice twittered as if she'd been riding shotgun in the front passenger's seat. Johnnie remembered how one time Granny had said, "Because of Lady Bird Johnson, we have wildflowers growing along Texas roadways."

An image of bluebonnets growing out of season blossomed in Johnnie's mind.

She rubbed the top of the dog's wet head. "How would you like to be named after a president's wife? She was a Texan, too."

The dog licked Johnnie's hand and wagged her tail.

Even before she got Ladybird out of the car, Johnnie vowed she would keep her.

Chapter 37
The First Time

"My guess is someone pulled up next to the curb, unhooked her collar, then let her out and drove off, knowing a good soul would come along and do the right thing," Dr. Weed said after giving Ladybird a nose-to-tail exam.

"You mean *sucker,*" Johnnie joked, stroking the dog's back in a calming manner.

Earlier, Johnnie let out a victory yelp after the technician scanned the area below the dog's neck and announced, "She's not chipped." Then Johnnie high-fived the tech again after the young lady made several calls to area shelters and the city pound. "It seems no one's reported a missing dog that fits Miss Ladybird's description."

Dr. Weed and his staff suggested Johnnie take the dog home for a few days, print out some fliers, and distribute them around the neighborhood and near the site where Johnnie found her. "If no one claims her in a few days, bring her back in for a comprehensive exam to check for heartworms and to get her up to speed on her shots." Judging by her teeth, the vet thought she was about two years old. She weighed sixty pounds, and a faint scar on her belly indicated she'd been spayed.

On the short drive home, Ladybird rested her chin on Johnnie's shoulder and let out several wheezy sighs. Johnnie figured the poor thing thought she was going to get dumped again. Before pulling into the curved driveway, Johnnie drove around the block a few times then looped down past the mortuary just in case someone was searching frantically for a lost dog. No lost-dog signs were tacked to telephone posts or stop signs. No owners were scampering up and down the sidewalk, calling for their beloved girl.

Back at the house, Johnnie stuffed the vet's paperwork into her purse, then got out and opened the back door and grabbed the leash before Ladybird could jump out. Once on the ground, Ladybird sniffed her way to the front yard then flinched and growled at the soldier scarecrow. It was the first real noise she'd made other than heavy sighs and a whimper or two. Johnnie gave a gentle tug on the leash and directed her to a spot near the white crepe myrtle where she proceeded to empty her bladder and do her business. Johnnie turned away to give her privacy.

"Well, girl, I bet you feel better." As Johnnie led her up the front porch steps to give her the grand tour of her new digs, she added, "Let's hope you're housetrained and not a digger. Dale can handle chewers and scratchers, but not diggers."

Inserting the key, Johnnie turned the knob and led the dog into the entryway. Ladybird sniffed the air and Johnnie patted her head. "You like the smell of pinto beans cooking in the Crock-Pot?" She kept her tone smooth as she flicked on some lights. Since this was the dog's first time inside the house, Johnnie kept her on the leash but loosened her grip and let Ladybird nose her way around baseboards and furniture. The sound of the dog's claws clicking on the hardwood floor sounded strangely familiar as they walked from room to room.

In the laundry room, Johnnie pulled down Brother's dishes and sat them on the mat. She filled one dish with water and the other with kibble. There was nothing ladylike about the way Ladybird attacked the kibble or lapped water. Johnnie smiled as dog sounds filled her home once again. After a quick trip out back to show Ladybird the deck and yard, Johnnie kept her on the leash as she made a mug of hot tea and settled in front of the computer. Sliding off her clogs, she opened her email and held her breath. She shouldn't be afraid of emails. Bad news wouldn't come over the Internet, would it?

Nothing from Camp Cade. She wondered if his care package had arrived with her letter. Was he out on patrol or diving for safety in a bunker with his buddies? She stuffed these thoughts down and reached for the top of the dog's head, like she'd reached for Brother all those years when she'd needed someone to lean on.

Ladybird stretched out on the hardwood floor and went to sleep at Johnnie's feet. The dog's soft snores floated through the air and settled into the empty crevices left void after the boys moved out and Brother crossed over. If the dog had been dumped, Johnnie wondered how people could be so cruel. Then she thought about Roosevelt and what his sisters had endured in their final moments. How could men who had volunteered to save lives turn their backs on seven little girls — even if it was too late to save them? The men could've still come and put out the fire.

Callie Ann called to ask about the dog and said her boss was letting her off work early.

She volunteered to round up some neighborhood kids she occasionally babysat and get them to pass out fliers.

As Johnnie gazed at the dog, sleeping so contentedly, she mulled over what Charlotte said that afternoon about Steven Tuttle losing his job after getting injured in combat. At that moment, Johnnie realized Charlotte must have read her letter to the editor two years ago — the letter that launched Johnnie's career as a columnist.

With Ladybird warming her feet, Johnnie found the clipping, smoothed it on top of the desk, and began to read aloud:

> Letter to the Editor
> Portion Telegraph
> November 2007
>
> Another boy from our community has been killed in Iraq. As I stood by the war memorial at Soldiers Park and watched his procession come up Main Street on its way from the airport to the mortuary, I couldn't help but think of a young guardsman from Portion named Steven Tuttle.
>
> Tutts, as my two sons call him, was terribly disfigured a few months ago — half his face got blown off — when his Hum-

vee crossed paths with an IED. Before he deployed, Steven worked part-time for Farrow & Sons, driving that very hearse that now carried the remains of a fellow soldier. Steven's mother, a single parent, had to quit her job so she could be with her only child as he recovers in a military hospital in San Antonio. To quote my oldest son: 'Sometimes there are worse things than death.'

Sometimes there's just death.

My dad died in Vietnam when I was six. The bomb that killed him wasn't called an IED. But a bomb's a bomb, and it blew him to bits just the same. Although I barely remember him, I can't forget him. His death was the great tragedy of my childhood. It sent my mama over the edge.

My youngest son just enlisted in the Army. He's still at basic training, but you can imagine what goes through my mind. Now Veterans Day is coming up on November 11. Everywhere I go I hear people say, 'Thank you for your *sacrifice,*' when talking about the war dead or injured. The more I hear this — especially from folks who don't have a 'dog in the fight' — I want to scream, 'Hey! I don't want my son sacrificed for anyone. Not for you. Not for the fat cats in Washington.

And darn sure not for me!

Johnnie Kitchen,
one p.o.'d mama

Ladybird stirred and Johnnie glanced up when the side door opened and Callie Ann burst in, a pink collar dangling from one hand. "Oh my God, Mom, she's adorable."

Lost in the past, Johnnie had not even heard Callie Annie pull into the driveway. She put the clipping down and swiveled in the chair. "Hi, Sis. Thanks for stopping by the pet store."

Callie Ann strode across the room, dropped to both knees, and nuzzled her face in the dog's fur. "Pee-yew, girlfriend. You need a bath." Ladybird's tail thumped against the hardwood floor and she rolled over, submissive, to let Callie Ann rub her belly. "Mom, look in that bag. I had her name engraved in cursive."

As Johnnie reached into the bag and pulled out a shiny gold tag with the name *Ladybird,* Callie Ann said, "Except for Miss Stinky here, it sure smells good in the house. What's for supper?"

"Pinto beans with diced ham. I'll heat up some cornbread muffins to go with them."

"You know what Cade would say if he were here. We'll be farting for days."

Johnnie laughed, missing her son even more. "You know what he says when I cook broccoli or Brussels sprouts?"

"Who farted?" Callie Ann bellowed and the dog started and jumped up.

"The dog tag and collar are beautiful, Sis. You think we should wait a few days in case someone claims her?"

Ignoring the question, Callie Ann scrambled to her feet and headed down the hallway. Ladybird was right behind her. "As soon as I get back from helping the kids put up fliers, let's throw her in the shower. You still have some of Brother's shampoo, right?" The bathroom door closed before Johnnie could answer.

After Callie Ann left, Johnnie let Ladybird out back while she hauled out Brother's crate from the garage and lined it with the boys' old beach towels. Ladybird could sleep in the crate the first few nights as she adjusted to her surroundings. She might need to be crated a few hours each day while Johnnie went to class.

Slipping on her fleece hoodie, she went out back to check on the dog. Halfway across the deck, she froze in her tracks. Ladybird was lying on her belly beside

Brother's grave, resting her chin on her front paws.

"Nice lookin' mutt ya got there, lady."

Johnnie whirled at the sound of Dale's voice. She hadn't heard him drive up or slip out the back door onto the deck. He tiptoed next to her and snapped a few photos on his cellphone camera. Then he wrapped his arm around her, giving her a squeeze.

"Oh, Dale, I hope we can keep her." Johnnie buried her face in his warm chest, feeling his heart beating against her cheek through his flannel shirt.

He kissed the top of her head and put his phone back in his pocket. "As far as I'm concerned, she's a gift."

Johnnie lifted her head and gazed up at Dale. "A gift?"

He gestured with his chin toward the back fence. "I think Brother sent her, and she's letting him know she made it here."

Chapter 38
Let's Face It

"Mrs. Kitchen?" The deep male voice cut through the clatter of the student union, packed with students rushing to grab lunch between classes or to hit the bookstore for supplies.

Nobody called her Mrs. Kitchen on campus. Nobody except someone who knew her outside of college.

Johnnie glanced around, steeling herself until she found him in the crowd. She'd been dreading this day. Anticipating it from the moment D.J. told her, "Tutts is moving back to Portion. Says he's going to enroll at the community college."

Bathed in natural light, Steven leaned against a wall of windows that looked out onto a courtyard. He waved his right arm back and forth in her direction. "It's Steven Tuttle," he yelled, as if she needed him to identify himself as he flagged her down.

"Steven," she gasped, weaving toward him

through a busy corridor abuzz with too many bodies and backpacks. Smells of hamburgers and tater tots mingled with Kung Pao and Orange Chicken from the nearby food court. Her stomach roiled and her mouth watered. She felt her lips twitch into a half-smile as she tried not to stare at his injuries.

The left side of his face resembled a broken clay pot that had been glued back together, each shard of skin and bone grafted into a crooked patchwork. A sickle-shaped scar swooped down from the corner of his droopy left eye — the one blinded by shrapnel. The scar cut deep into his blotchy red cheek, barely missing his nose, before it curled back around the saggy corner of his mouth where a knot of flesh protruded like a wad of chewing tobacco wedged under his bottom lip. Looping back around his lower left jaw, it ended inches below his ear.

Before Johnnie could say anything, Steven turned ever so slightly, and his intact side came into view: the smooth skin over a strong jaw line and angular features — the handsome young guardsman who could have modeled for *GQ.* His tall frame had filled out. He was not the same lanky kid in skinny jeans and long hair who played in D.J.'s aggressive metal band in high school.

Where was the monster she had expected? The Frankenstein his mother had described that day they met for coffee at the Cotton-belt Café? From the way Beth Tuttle had talked, you'd think half of Steven's skull would be missing. He looked nothing like Johnnie's nightmares. But then, he'd already been through several reconstructive surgeries.

"I know it looks like I've been bitten by a shark." He tapped a finger to his left jaw.

Wasn't that like Tutts, trying to put her at ease with his dark humor?

"Steven. . . ." She reached up to give him a hug, burdened by the weight of her book bag.

He stooped to hug her back, an awkward dance because he was so much taller and her book bag kept sliding off, taking her with it. She fumbled to regain her balance.

She found herself brushing up against his injured side. Steven didn't pull away, and she patted him profusely, knowing it was overkill. "It's so good to see you."

Why hadn't she worked up the courage to visit him before now? She'd written about him, dammit. That letter paved the way for "Roundtable." Sometimes she felt like a fraud, less brave in real life than the strong-woman image she projected in her column.

She stammered for a second, overcome with guilt for avoiding him. She'd seen pictures of him since his injury, but he was always in a bandage from one operation or another. Her mind flashed to a photograph of a bearded D.J., sketchpad tucked under his left arm, standing next to Steven's hospital bed at Brooks Army Hospital in San Antonio. Clad all in black, D.J. stood out against the white gauze of the bandages on Steven's head and left hand and the ripple of bed sheets that swallowed him.

"D.J. told me you were taking classes." She glanced around, daring anyone to take potshots at him, to stare like she had stared. The mother in her kicked in, and she wanted to drape a protective layer over him. Put up some kind of invisible shield that could ward off the curious gawkers, the insensitive strangers who had no filters.

A male student in cargo shorts and a pink polo shirt strolled by and seemed to hesitate. A *dude-bro,* as D.J. would say. *Keep on walking,* Johnnie warned him with her eyes.

But then the student pivoted, walked over to Steven, and stuck out his hand. "Hey, dude, thank you for your service. I'm sorry about your injuries, man."

Steven's mouth twisted into a crooked grin as he shook the young man's hand.

"Thanks, man. That means a lot."

After the student left, Johnnie spotted a Purple Heart emblem on Steven's camouflage backpack.

Steven followed her gaze. "If people figure out that I was injured in battle, it makes me more approachable." He shrugged. "I learned that before I ever left the hospital."

They were both in between classes. Each had a few minutes to spare. They walked outside and stood on the wide steps of the student union building. The autumn sun warmed Johnnie's skin and she was thankful she wore her long cardigan.

"Aren't you freezing?" She gestured at his athletic shorts and Texas Rangers T-shirt.

He shook his head. "Cool air feels good. I get hot and claustrophobic when I'm inside too long."

Johnnie flicked her head toward the library and science hall. "Over yonder. That's where I was when D.J. called me two years ago to tell me what happened."

Steven nodded and let out a thoughtful sigh. "Aw, yes, my *alive day.* The day I didn't die." He leaned against the metal rail and planted his feet firmly together, crossing his arms in a relaxed fashion.

She noticed his hands. His right hand was just as she remembered: long slender fingers that moved in a fluid dance, the fingers that strummed a guitar or flew over a keyboard back in high school, or turned the wheel of death on a long black hearse for Farrow & Sons.

Steven eyed her. He held out his left hand and opened and closed his fist a couple of times as if he knew she needed proof. "It just looks like it hurts. I got lucky. I have full use of it."

Somehow it was easier to talk about his hand than his face.

Johnnie scooted forward, too eager, her smile too big for the occasion of simply talking to a young college student between classes. She smiled to keep from crying, to keep from asking too many questions: Did it hurt to shave? Did the change in temperature affect his scars? Did he have a lot of pain from nerve damage? What did it feel like to have two metal plates holding his jaw together? She'd learned about the nerve damage and metal plates from D.J. How come his speech wasn't affected? What was it like to be blind in one eye?

She smiled to fend off the fear that hacked at her heart — and to refrain from babbling about Cade. Until she came face to face with Tutts, her biggest fear had been the terrifying sound of a doorbell and soldiers on her porch. But what if Cade got blown up and lived? Lived to come home with a head attached to a torso and trunk but missing all four limbs? Or his face so mangled he resembled a melon instead of a man?

She shuddered and looked away, unable to speak, and focused on a tall pine growing next to the building.

"Mrs. Kitchen, I know what you're thinking."

She glanced back at him. Oh God. Am I that transparent?

"Just because I got injured doesn't mean it will happen to Cade. He's a good soldier. Have faith in your son's ability to do his job."

She swallowed hard, her mouth dry as she fiddled with the straps of her book bag.

"Man, I'm sorry about Brother. D.J. called me right after it happened."

Her mind went blank for a minute, as if she couldn't remember how to speak. Finally, she said, "Did he tell you we got a new dog? I found her in front of Farrow and Sons. No one ever called to claim her, so she's ours now."

His right eye crinkled in a grin. "Actually, Callie Ann told me."

"Callie Ann?" Johnnie jerked her head back, surprised. "When did you talk to her?"

He scratched the right side of his head. "She didn't tell you? She's been interviewing me for her senior thesis. I'm real flattered, of course. We've met a couple of times for coffee. She's a sweet girl."

Johnnie felt her mouth open and close. She gulped, catching herself staring at his scars on the left side of his face. "I had no idea. Callie Ann's been real secretive about it." A mixture of pride and sorrow caused Johnnie to turn away, tears brimming over her bottom lashes. She recalled how her daughter told the makeup artist at the Day of the Dead Festival to leave half of her face untouched. . . . *I want the skull part to honor our friend Tutts, whose face got disfigured in Iraq.*

"You know Callie Ann worries about Cade more than she lets on," Johnnie offered, surprised by how hoarse she sounded.

Steven nodded and glanced at something on the ground. "Yeah, I know. I told her she's got to let her bro do his thing . . . or he'll end up hating himself the rest of his life."

Squeezing the mechanical pencil still in her hand from her last class, Johnnie gazed up at the clock tower next to the building. "I'd better shove off. I've got class in a few minutes. Being the old lady, I hate to walk in late."

"Guess I'll see you at the art show." He pushed away from the rail and stooped to give her a quick hug.

That's when she saw WAR-4-$$$ tattooed on the inside of Steven's right forearm. She thought back to that day, two years ago, when she and Dale spotted the name spray-painted in dark green graffiti at the base of the war memorial. At the time, they suspected D.J. as the culprit, given he was against the invasion of Iraq.

And yet. . . .

She gazed at the fractured features of this wounded warrior. At the kind young man whose looks had been defaced by war.

Their eyes met.

"Steven, did you paint the name of the band on the war memorial before you deployed?"

He scratched the tip of his nose, and the right side of his mouth contorted in a sly grin.

Chapter 39
Art Show

Dale circled Denton's square three times before he pulled the Suburban into an empty slot in front of the Confederate soldier statue on the south lawn of the historic courthouse. He rammed the gear-shift into park and turned to Johnnie. "Three's a charm. Looks like we got lucky."

She opened the passenger door and gave him a sideways glance. "Sexy man. You should dress up more often." She'd never seen him look so handsome as he did this afternoon in his white dress shirt and black tie, a silver belt buckle with the initials DK looped through a new pair of Wranglers.

Callie Ann leaned forward from behind the driver's seat and gripped Dale's broad shoulders. "Yeah, Dad, you look like a stud muffin."

"I'll second that," Mama piped up from the backseat. "My daughter knows how to pick 'em."

Flushing crimson, Dale climbed out of the Suburban and held the passenger door open for Callie Ann. "You girls quit buttering me up. My head's about to explode."

Johnnie got out of the car and went to assist Mama. "You look pretty in that gown with your hair swept up. I'm glad you wore your pearls. You remind me of Lesley Ann Warren in *Cinderella.*"

Victoria held out her arm encased in a long white glove and stepped out of the vehicle. Her sleeveless, winter-white gown with a scooped neck and empire waist swirled at her ankles. "I haven't been this fancied up since you and Dale got married." Mama ran her tongue over her teeth. "You sure I look presentable?"

You look a little thin, Johnnie wanted to say. She refrained from dispensing the same tired litany of fault-finding Granny Opal had used on her all those years, even when Johnnie's weight had leveled off to normal. Mama's color had returned and she looked healthier for the most part.

"Not many women can pull off wearing their prom dress forty-some years later." Johnnie draped a faux mink stole around her mother's shoulders and gave her a peck on the cheek. "Stop worrying. You look marvelous. Arty's going to love you."

Victoria held up a tiny embroidered evening bag. "Got my emergency stash of cough drops in case my lungs throw a fit."

"You'll be the belle of the art show, Granny V." In red platform pumps, Callie Ann traipsed around the front bumper. Her long-sleeved black dress with a mandarin collar hit just above her knees and showed off her toned calves.

Dale brushed an attentive hand over Johnnie's lower back and whispered in her ear, "You are working that dress, lady." From the moment Johnnie admired the peacock-blue gown with the plunging neckline in Whit's shop back in August, she knew she had to have it. Dale wasn't even upset at the price, especially since Whit gave her a "friend discount."

Johnnie gave him a quick kiss and marveled at the green and white neon sign of the Campus Theatre a block away on the corner of Hickory and Cedar. Even from this distance, she could read the bold letters on the marquee: "Arthur Murphy & D.J. Kitchen present FACES OF WAR: art & reception, Sunday Nov. 22, 2-4 p.m." A mixture of excitement and fear bubbled up inside of her. She had no idea what to expect. Over the phone, she'd tried to pump D.J. for information, but his response was terse: "Mom, do you read the last page of a novel first? Wait for the show." Only a few months ago she'd driven past the grand old movie house on her way to meet *the man on the square.* Today, she was going to see his art, along with her son's. Tossing her hair back, she announced, "Okay, family, let's go."

Before they headed up the sidewalk, Mama craned her neck up at the Confederate soldier stationed at the ready with his hat on and a long gun in his hands. "I read where some college students were trying to get him removed. What a waste of time. That's like burning history books. That farm boy ain't up there proclaiming whether it was right or wrong. He's just a reminder of all them boys who died fighting for a cause."

Her mouth open, Johnnie stared at her mother, who seemed to stand a little taller on the sidewalk as she snuggled in her mink stole. "Mama, maybe you should run for office." Johnnie swept her hand through the air like an airplane pulling a banner. "I can see it now: Victoria Grubbs, stateswoman from Texas."

Mama pointed her chin in the direction of the theater and motioned for Callie Ann. "Come on, sugar britches. Come help me meet your great-granddaddy Murphy."

Johnnie linked her arm through Dale's and they promenaded up the sidewalk. Right before they reached the theater box office, Johnnie heard Mama ask, "How's the new dog working out?"

Callie Ann's laughter echoed around them. "She eats toilet paper, right off the roll. And her butt wiggles when you call her name."

As Dale held open one of the glass doors at the front of the theater, a yellow Corvette rumbled by and blasted its horn. Johnnie's heart swelled when she recognized the Purple Heart license plate.

"Oh my God, D.J.'s in a tux!" Callie Ann blurted out as the family shuffled inside and glanced around the spacious lobby, beginning to fill with patrons.

Johnnie spotted her son, resplendent in a black tuxedo with a white pleated shirt and a bow tie that matched his dark eyebrows. The sight nearly took her breath away. In high school, he refused to rent a tux for prom. He and Tutts had worn secondhand suits they bought for a buck apiece from Thrift Town. The boys looked more like old time gangsters than prom goers. Their dates thought it was funny and went as flappers.

D.J. had been speaking to a cluster of young people. One young man had dreadlocks halfway down his back. A young lady next to him wore a tight sheath that showed off toned arms and calves covered in tats. Excusing himself, D.J. strode toward Johnnie and the rest of the family. He smirked as he made his way across the terrazzo floor, a pattern of turquoise, coral, and cream circles that formed a giant bull's-eye. Johnnie noticed D.J.'s stylish new dress boots. She'd never seen them and wondered if he'd spent a small fortune, as they looked well-made and expensive. It shocked her, even now, that he lived a life separate from hers. Wasn't it just yesterday that he and Cade were nine and four and ran away from home, taking refuge at the base of the war memorial? Clad in high-top sneakers and armed with his new BB gun, D.J. stood guard while Cade snuggled in a sleeping bag and sucked on a juice box until a frantic Johnnie found them and brought them home.

"Hey, kiddies." D.J. wrapped an arm around Johnnie. "Mom, you look ravishing. Your gown fits right in with the art deco design of the theater."

Swishing the hem of her gown, Johnnie smiled and noted that she and the theater were cloaked in the same blue-green, from the recessed ceilings to the frond-pattern carpet leading up the stairway to the balcony.

D.J. glanced at Dale. "Nice tie, Dad. You clean up good."

Dale reached over and slapped him on the shoulder. "Looking sharp, son. Your mom and I are proud of you."

Callie Ann poked D.J. in the navel. "Dang, big brother. What's with the tux?"

D.J. straightened the sleeves of his jacket and rolled his shoulders a couple of times. "Gotta play the part, little sis. Arthur says we're expecting some heavy hitters. College admins, professors, the mayor, the chamber folks, lots of do-gooders in town, the Arts Council." He reached into his trouser pocket and flashed his business card around. "I came prepared. Anybody need screen-printing and design, I'm da man."

He pocketed the card and nodded at his grandmother. "Hello, Victoria. You look fetching. I'm digging those long, elegant gloves."

It seemed to Johnnie that ever since Mama's latest suicide attempt, D.J. had shown more sympathy toward his grandmother. Being included in her will probably didn't hurt.

D.J. grasped Mama's outstretched hand. "Shall we go find Arthur? I believe he wants to escort you through the exhibit."

Mama's green eyes welled up. She made a face and dabbed the corner of each eye with her gloved index fingers. "Mercy me! There's nothing uglier than an old lady's tears."

D.J. gestured toward the long counter with glass corner shelves. "Help yourselves to wine and beer." He turned to go. "Oh, Dad, the terrazzo floor here in the outer lobby is original to the building. It opened in 1949."

Dale gave it an admiring once-over as Mama said, "Why, I'm a year older than the theater. We're both antiques."

With a flourish, Mama waved her hand through the air as D.J. whisked her off toward a panel of swing doors with porthole windows. The doors gave Johnnie the feeling they were on board some luxurious ocean liner and about to embark on a voyage. She wondered what awaited them on the other side of the doors where the art exhibit was in full swing.

Callie Ann squeezed Johnnie's arm and whispered, "There's Tutts. He's wearing a tuxedo, too!" She waved in his direction, keeping her voice low. "That's his new girlfriend, Melanie. They call her Mel. Isn't she cute? She's really sweet, too. I better go say hi."

"We'll be along in a second," Johnnie called after Callie Ann as she glided across the floor in her black dress and red pumps, her long, blonde hair flowing behind her like a bridal veil.

"We should lock her up," Dale sighed. "I don't want some creep getting his grimy hands on her when she goes off to college next year."

Johnnie's throat constricted. She wasn't thinking along the same lines as Dale. She gazed at Steven Tuttle in his tuxedo, how tall and distinguished he looked as he circled the room, his new girlfriend on his arm. He reminded Johnnie of the phantom in Andrew Lloyd Webber's *The Phantom of the Opera* without his mask.

Dale interrupted her thoughts. "Let's grab a drink before we head into the show."

At the counter, Dale served her a plastic cup of white wine while he took a swig from a longneck. An older lady in a pale blue suit and support hose sidled up next to them and told the older gentleman beside her, "I hear this place is haunted . . . by the original manager, a Mr. Harrison. They say he's harmless though. A benevolent ghost."

Someone tapped Johnnie on the shoulder and she jumped, sloshing wine on her hand.

Whit stood there, grinning. "You're looking spiffy, ladybug."

Johnnie dabbed her hand with a napkin. "You're not looking too shabby yourself." In wide-legged hostess pants and a flowing coral tunic with fringe, Whit was a walking festival of color. Next to Whit, Roosevelt appeared more subdued in a sleek gray suit, purple dress shirt, and paisley tie.

The men exchanged greetings. "You're some kind of storyteller," Dale told Roosevelt, pumping his hand. "You grabbed my attention right off the bat when I first read your article in the newspaper."

"Shucks, Dale. You're going to make me blush." Roosevelt's dark eyes twinkled as he toyed with a silver cufflink. He gazed at Johnnie. "Talked to my man, Sergeant Jackson, the other day. I told him our young friend, Mr. Rivers, has completed his duties to my satisfaction. Got the cemetery all shipshape. Took the kid fishing. He caught himself a big ol' bass. Going to put him to work at the church until he ships out. He's been staying with me since his uncle kicked him out. Seems the old man didn't take too kindly to Jordan associating with blacks."

Johnnie started to brag that Jordan had passed his quiz about *how we're all just made out of clay,* but she noticed how Dale's jaw clenched at the mention of the kid's name.

Dale cracked a knuckle on his left hand and took a slug of beer. His gaze drifted over to where Callie Ann stood chatting with a group of people and then back to Roosevelt. "I haven't met Rivers yet. You really think he can be redeemed?"

Roosevelt stepped up to the counter and ordered two red wines. He nodded back at Dale. "Kid got a bad start in life. Didn't have much help or hope until now. But yes, I think he can be saved. The Army might be just the ticket."

Dale scratched his nose and pressed his hand into the hollow of Johnnie's back. She could tell he was ready to move on, to go see the exhibit, to change the subject before it ruined his day.

With drinks in hand, both couples headed toward the inner lobby. At the porthole doors, D.J. breezed past, stopping long enough to greet Whit and Roosevelt. "Thanks for sending the photograph at the last minute, Roosevelt. We hope you enjoy our adaptation. The painting's yours to take home after the show."

"How 'bout that?" Johnnie heard Roosevelt tell Whit. A second later, Whit's giggles turned to oohs and aahs as the couple stood in front of the first easel on display. Johnnie peeked past Whit and saw a large painting of a young black soldier kneeling on one knee, his M16 rifle at an angle in front of him. In bold brush strokes of olive drab and brown, *A Brother in Nam* depicted a young Private Roosevelt Hill in dirty fatigues and helmet, his boyish face expressionless, as if he'd gone to sleep with his eyes open.

"I left one war for another," he whispered loud enough for Johnnie to hear. "But I came home. That's all that mattered to my mama."

Johnnie figured he referred to the cold welcome home the Vietnam vets were subjected to, along with the racism he'd been dealing with his whole life. After Whit and Roosevelt moved on to the next easel, Johnnie and Dale lingered in front of the painting.

Dale kept his voice low. "Johnnie, I've been thinking. If that Rivers kid hadn't harassed you girls back on Memorial Day, you might never have crossed paths with Roosevelt." Before she could answer, he gave her a quick kiss and left. A minute later, he was back with a wad of tissues he slipped in her hand. "I figured you might need these. Mind if I go chat with D.J. for a sec?"

She walked through the entire exhibit with

a tissue mashed to her nose. Somehow Dale understood she needed to go at her own pace, to make the first pass through the show huddled inside of herself, without someone hovering over her asking if she was okay. People seemed to give her a wide berth, as if they understood she was a woman who needed her space, a few inches of privacy — an invisible bubble — where she could stand in front of each piece in silence, to explore her feelings and emotions without having to explain or apologize for weeping.

She moved from painting to painting, stopping in front of each piece, studying, lingering, tipping her head from side to side, stepping up and stepping back, peering from different angles, before continuing on.

She circled the room and then went back to the second piece before going through the exhibit again. The large-scale painting replicated the faded photo from 1969, the photo that brought them Arty. If she could step into *A Soldier's Daughter: The Last Goodbye* and make it come to life, she would hug the lieutenant's neck one more time and tell him she loved him.

Standing in front of *An Officer and a Gentleman,* Johnnie noted how young and striking Arthur Murphy appeared — sans the goatee — with his beautiful blonde Mae at their son's graduation from West Point. Francis Murphy, a brand new second lieutenant with gold bars pinned on his uniform, flashed his devilish smile as he stood between his proud parents.

At *Victoria, Queen of the Gold Star Hearts,* Johnnie marveled at how D.J. and Arty captured Johnnie's memories of Mama seated on the bench in front of the war memorial, talking to her statue. Johnnie grinned at the tiara on Mama's head. To Johnnie's knowledge, Mama had no idea about D.J.'s special nickname for her.

Moving on, Johnnie massaged a spot over her left eye as she swayed in front of *The Candy Man,* a life-sized watercolor of a helmeted Cade doling out candy to Afghan children, his weapon strapped at his side. Beneath the grime on his face, she could make out his dimples. She longed to reach out and kiss him. If only he could be here. . . .

She felt someone brush up against her. Mama leaned her head on Johnnie's shoulder. "We got us some talented men folk, don't we, baby girl?"

Johnnie nodded, unable to speak.

"What's with the crown on my head in that painting?" Mama asked, tugging at the fingers on one of her gloves. "I'm real honored, but seems to me there's a hidden message."

Johnnie sighed, tired all of a sudden. "Guess you'll have to ask the artists." She stared straight ahead, hoping Mama wasn't offended.

After Mama meandered off, Dale took her place. He reached for Johnnie's hand and dabbed the corners of his eyes with his other thumb. "I wish Cade could see this." Dale sounded stuffed up, like he had a cold. He sniffed a couple of times and glanced over his shoulder. "What do you think of the pièce de résistance?"

Swallowing, she lifted the hem of her dress and let him lead her through the crowd. They threaded their way toward a gigantic recessed section of a curved wall in the center of the inner lobby. Earlier, when Johnnie saw the two pieces for the first time, she'd had to sit down on the padded bench that curved around the wall.

Still holding Dale's hand, she took a deep breath and forced herself to look again at the two huge black and white paintings that made up *Two Faces of War.*

"D.J. said Arty did the one that portrays the right side of Tutts' face." Dale gestured toward the two pieces. "Your son did that one — the one that portrays Tutts' damaged side."

Arty approached and touched Johnnie on the elbow. "D.J. did a fine job. He's a magnificent artist."

With tears in her eyes, she glanced sideways. For the first time all afternoon, she realized Arty wasn't wearing a tux. He had on the same white turtleneck and tan corduroy blazer from the first time they'd seen him on the square. The day he followed them into Recycled Books. She reached for his hand, gnarled and rough, but his grasp firmer than ever. "He gets it from you, Grandpa Arty."

Arty nodded and cleared his throat. "I told Victoria that her father was only doing what he thought best at the time. He was trying to protect Mae and me from more heartache. What he didn't know is that you and your mama were the very thing that could have saved us years of loneliness." Arty's voice trailed off and he reached for his hanky. "Oh, blast it to heck, I've gone and done it now." He blew his nose so loud it reminded Johnnie of a honking goose. Grandpa Grubbs used to make the same noise, and Johnnie caught herself smiling at the memory.

Nearby, Johnnie spotted a reporter from

the *Denton Chronicle* interviewing Tutts. At one point she overheard him say, "The therapy was excruciating. Morphine helped. I still suffer from facial pain due to nerve damage. What are my biggest disappointments? Veterans organizations that make big promises and then offer you only a handshake and a few tickets to a baseball game and send you on your way."

The paintings and people swirled around her. All the voices jumbled into one collective voice. She needed a break.

"Dale, I'll be right back." She headed for the nearest exit and pushed through the porthole door.

Back in the outer lobby, with no patrons in sight, she moved toward the center of the room, concentrating on the pattern inlaid in the terrazzo floor. She stopped in the middle of the bull's-eye and closed her eyes, clenching her fists at her sides. "What does it feel like to be the target of a sniper's bullet or to trip a bomb?" she asked the empty lobby. "The second your head gets split open or you turn into pink mist? What does it feel like to go to war?"

Even after viewing all the paintings, after staring into the two sides of Tutts' face, Johnnie realized this was the closest she would ever come. She was simply a bystander, waiting in the cross hairs for a messenger who might not ever come — a messenger playing Russian roulette with her heart.

"What'cha doing, honey?" Dale stood in the doorway between the outer and inner lobby. "You look like you just saw Mr. Harrison's ghost."

She caught her breath and listened to the faint sound of snare drums growing louder by the second, the snappy opening to a protest song she'd grown up with. "Do you hear it? Do you hear that song?"

Dale grabbed a handful of mixed nuts from the counter. "Yeah, it's 'War,' by Edwin Starr." He popped a few nuts into his mouth. "D.J. and Arthur timed it to come on now, after most of the guests have walked through the exhibit."

Above the snack bar, she saw a hand-painted banner she'd somehow missed when they first arrived. Her gaze swept over the message: "Faces Of War, In Memory of First Lieutenant Francis Murphy, KIA 11/22/70 Vietnam."

D.J. poked his head through the door and ambled toward her. "Hey, Mom, what are you doing there in the middle of the bull's-eye?"

Johnnie gazed into her son's inquisitive

eyes and saw her father. "I'm wondering what it feels like to go to war," she shouted over the music. "What it feels like to be your brother right now."

D.J. threw his arm around her and they swayed to and fro, as the antiwar song grew louder and louder.

"Did you know 'War' hit the *Billboard* charts the same year your dad got killed?" D.J.'s voice boomed out.

She shook her head and motioned for Dale to join them. Within seconds, others strutted through the doors, stomping their feet and clapping their hands. Through blurry eyes, she spotted Mama and Callie Ann holding hands with Arty. Tutts and his new girlfriend were right behind them, followed by Roosevelt and Whit. More and more people filed in and started dancing around the lobby, pumping their fists in the air and shouting at the top of their lungs, "War, what is it good for? Absolutely *nothing*!"

Chapter 40
The Studio

"This was our happy place," Arty explained, crossing his feet at the ankles and folding his hands in his lap. "We added on shortly after we moved in. We both needed studio space and Mae wanted a great room."

Johnnie sat opposite her grandfather in a matching low-slung retro armchair right out of the fifties. She took in the light-filled room addition with its cathedral ceiling painted marigold, chalk-colored walls adorned with paintings of every shape and size, and the back wall composed of nothing but floor-to-ceiling windows and a set of French doors leading out to a patio. "This room is magical," she gushed, noting a half-finished landscape painting propped on a nearby easel. "Your whole house is."

Arty chuckled. "Mae insisted we live like *artistes.* She thrived on artsy-fartsy without clutter." He gestured to a corner of the room where a pottery wheel sat idle. "She claimed that spot as her sanctuary. After she became a danger to herself, I donated her kiln to the senior center."

A display of multicolored vessels caught Johnnie's attention. "Are those Mae's creations? They're stunning."

Arty nodded. "Yes, that was her specialty — chalices. Some of the last pieces she worked on before her mind went. Several churches in the area use them for communion. She also marketed them as high-end wine goblets." He paused a moment then turned to Johnnie. "Say, it's a little early in the day, but would you care to have a glass of vino with me?" He winked. "I won't tell if you don't." Before she could answer, he pushed himself out of the chair and disappeared from the room.

Johnnie glanced at her watch. It was ten thirty on Monday morning, the day after the art show. Arty had invited her to come back to Denton for a little chat and to give her the grand tour of his "humble abode." The rest of the family had to work.

Earlier, when Johnnie had turned onto her grandfather's street in an older middleclass neighborhood in Denton, she half-expected to find a cramped space smelling of old people and dust. Most of the homes she passed — one-story, ranch-style houses built in the late fifties and early sixties — consisted of the same floor plan: single-car garage, three bedrooms, two baths, a living room, and a kitchen.

From the moment she'd entered the brick ranch, painted all white with black trim and shutters and a decorative beveled glass door, she knew she was in for a treat. Any misconceptions she'd had were put to rest as she glided over smooth birch floors with oversized rooms sparsely decorated with Euro-style furnishings. Walls had been knocked down to create an open floor plan. When she rounded a corner and stepped into "The Studio," she felt a positive energy in the room. This was a place where art was created, where joy and sorrow and hopes and dreams were allowed to mingle and flow up out of the heart and spirit into canvas, clay, and metal sculpture.

Arty returned with a bottle of red wine and a white cloth. He picked up two chalices, swiped the insides with the cloth, and poured wine into each cup. "To family," he said, offering one to Johnnie.

She watched her grandfather swirl the contents before taking a sip. She preferred white to red, but she wasn't about to offend him. The cabernet was richer and heavier than she was used to, but she admired the heft of the chalice. Holding the stem with both hands, she was petrified she would drop it.

She offered another toast. "To Mae and her beautiful pottery. And to you and D.J. and your successful art show."

She carefully set the chalice on a table next to her and admired a series of paintings that called to her from across the room. "Are those the paintings you told me about?"

Arty nodded and put his glass down. "Mae was a minimalist. She didn't save much from Francis' childhood. After he was killed, she donated most of his things to charity, even his trophies. But I saved a few things, and then I recreated his childhood from memory." Arty took Johnnie's hand and led her across the room. "As a good Catholic, I call this collection 'Francis, Before He Reached Sainthood.' "

Johnnie began to tremble as she moved from piece to piece. Arty stood back, giving her space. Each painting was nine by eleven and reflected her father's life from about age seven to right before his death. Except for the last painting, which depicted her father in fatigues against a jungle background, Johnnie might as well have been looking at paintings of a younger D.J. There was Francis riding a bike with training wheels, proudly holding a blue ribbon next to a Pinewood Derby car. In the next he was an altar boy in white robes. Another photo showed him in a basketball uniform, slam-dunking a ball into a net. The painting that caused her to pause, to move so close she almost brushed it with her nose, showed a gangly teenager strumming an acoustic guitar.

She glanced over her shoulder at Arty. "My father played guitar?"

Arty sighed and gave a slight nod. "He played by ear. Self-taught. Folk songs, mostly."

"Do you still have his guitar? D.J. would love to have it, I'm sure."

He shook his head. "Mae gave it to a kid down the street before we moved. You should've seen the look on his face when he realized it was a gift. All Mae told him was, 'Don't let the music die.' "

Johnnie sniffed, walked over, and sat back down in the chair. As she reached for her wine, Arty said, "There *is* something Mae and I saved that belonged to Francis." His eyes danced with a merriment she hadn't seen before. He reached behind the chair and lifted a large box wrapped in glossy white paper and tied in a big red bow. "Now

I know who to give this to."

Her hands trembled as she fumbled with the bow and paper. Removing the lid, she stared at a purple and white letter jacket with the name Francis Murphy stitched across the front. Heat surged through her body. "Oh my God. Is this my father's letter jacket from the Catholic high school? Mama told me he had it slung over his shoulder the day they met at the Palace Theater in downtown Portion."

"He lettered in football and basketball. Mae and I took turns wearing it over the years, especially on those early days when we needed to feel close to him."

As Johnnie slipped on the jacket, she asked, "What was my father like?"

Arty closed his eyes a moment as if to gather his thoughts. "He was kind. A gentle giant who was loyal as all get out."

"Was he an artist like you?"

Arty chuckled. "Poor kid could barely write his name in cursive. But he excelled in math and science."

"Those genes weren't passed on to me." Johnnie laughed, snuggling deeper into the jacket.

Arty tilted his head. "Seems to me they were passed on to your daughter. Victoria says Callie Ann's a whiz at every subject in school."

Johnnie smiled. It made her happy to know that Mama had bragged on one of her grandkids. She stared across the room at the painting of her father in fatigues. "Guess Cade got the lieutenant's soldier genes . . . if there is such a thing."

Arty cleared his throat. "I'm proud of that boy."

Was he referring to his son or to Cade? Johnnie started to ask then realized it didn't matter.

Arty picked up his chalice. "I'm proud of all my grandchildren. Such unexpected gifts." He took a sip and then turned to Johnnie. "And that goes double for you, young lady."

Cradled in the heavy warmth of a jacket that smelled faintly of worn leather and boy, Johnnie felt her father reach across time and space and wrap his arms around her.

CHAPTER 41
BIRD DOWN
TUESDAY . . .

Dry leaves scuttled the sidewalk as Johnnie and Ladybird went for a brisk walk around the block. Leash in hand, Johnnie moved at a fast clip to keep up with the dog. "You know, girl," Johnnie said as Ladybird trotted in front of her, "Thanksgiving is in two days, and this year marks the second anniversary that Mama came back. But it's also our first without Granny Opal and Brother Dog."

Every few feet, Ladybird whipped her head around and gazed up at Johnnie to make sure she was still there. "You and Grandpa Arty are double blessings to the family," Johnnie went on, "but it still won't be the same without Cade." A flock of geese — or was it a squadron? — honked overhead. Ladybird stopped, craning her neck skyward, and barked at the V-shaped formation. Then the lead bird dropped out and flew to the rear as another bird took its place at the head. "Come on, girl, let's chase them," Johnnie called out, and she and Ladybird took off running until the geese were out of sight.

After their walk, Johnnie sat at the farmhouse table and scribbled notes for a new story. She planned to write about how her son and grandfather collaborated on each painting in the art show. With no classes during Thanksgiving break, she had more time to concentrate on her column. Ladybird snored at her feet.

The side door to the portico clicked shut. Dale set his lunchbox and thermos on the island. The first thing Johnnie noticed was the somber look on Dale's face, and that he didn't remove his puffy vest — the one he wore over flannel shirts this time of year. Even on the coldest days, he preferred the vest instead of a heavy coat because it freed his arms for work.

"Come here," he said, as if he'd had the wind knocked out of him. "Let me hold you." He took a step toward her, and a floorboard creaked beneath his heavy work boots.

"Did something happen at work?" Dale was all about safety when it came to his men. Did one of them get injured on the job?

Dale pressed his chapped lips together and shook his head. "No, just let me hold you, Johnnie girl." He held out his arms, and his callused hands opened as if he needed to touch her: capable hands that knew every curve of her body. His voice, normally strong though, sounded weak. Something was wrong.

Her insides twisted and fear gripped her throat. She thought her heart might explode. Pushing away from the table, she dropped her mechanical pencil and bolted past Dale for the nearest exit. She couldn't breathe, much less swallow.

Ladybird scrambled to her feet and followed Johnnie to the door.

Something bad had happened. She had to get away. Go outside. The walls were closing in. Yanking open the door, she fled down the steps and doubled over next to Dale's truck, gasping for breath. Dusk had settled around them. Smells of neighbors cooking supper mingled with the hint of an early snow. The world swirled around her. No place felt safe.

In a tizzy, Ladybird pranced around, trying to help. Johnnie's knees wobbled and she thought she might tip over. Her gut churned and her mouth watered like she needed to retch.

Dale hovered over her, looking helpless as he ran his hands through his wavy hair. "Johnnie girl, get in the house."

Batting her hands over her ears, she stared at the concrete and stammered, "Don't tell me, Dale. I don't want to know."

She felt his strong hands grip her shoulders. In one swift move, he spun her around. "Look at me." His blue eyes searched hers and his voice grew gruffer. "I don't have anything to go on. It's just a hunch, but I've had a bad feeling all day. And then. . . ."

What did he mean, a hunch? Dale never acted on a hunch, on a feeling. He thought things through.

She pulled away from him, and a drop of saliva hung from her lip. Breathing hard, she swiped her mouth and stared at him. "Then what's wrong? Why are you acting so weird?"

He stuffed his hands in his vest and paced the length of his truck. "D.J. called me a few minutes ago, right when I pulled in the driveway." Dale rubbed his hands over his rugged face and let out a huge sigh. "A chopper went down in Afghanistan. Today."

His words sent a chill straight to her bones. She made a funny sound and started shaking. Then her mind threw a switch like the world stopped, and she glanced around, realizing Ladybird was nowhere in sight.

All the air swooshed out of her lungs at once. "Ladybird!" she called, her voice cracking. "Ladybird, where did you go?"

It was getting dark and the temperature was dropping.

Dale grabbed a flashlight from his toolbox. First he checked under the truck and then stalked around to the front of the house, shining a beam into the bushes and flowerbeds. Johnnie followed, calling, "Ladybird, Ladybird, come back!"

They heard a thump-thump coming from the front porch. Mounting the stairs, Dale aimed the flashlight by the front door and a pair of eyes glowed back. Dale knelt and spoke in soft tones. "What's wrong, girl? Did we scare you off?"

Johnnie bent and rubbed the top of Ladybird's head. "Jeez, Dale, I thought we'd lost her." Johnnie jiggled the front door, but it was locked. "Come on, girl. Let's get you inside. It's getting cold." Johnnie hooked a finger through Ladybird's pink collar and led her gently down the steps, past the soldier scarecrow where Ladybird let out a low growl, then back under the portico and up the side steps.

Once inside, the dog shook herself off and plopped down in her favorite spot on the braided rug. Johnnie and Dale fussed over the dog for a few seconds. Then Johnnie's teeth began to chatter. She gazed from Ladybird's sweet face into Dale's worried eyes. "Helicopters go down all the time in Afghanistan. At least it seems like it. Why is this one different?"

Dale shrugged and stood up. "I just have a bad feeling, that's all." He strode toward the back door and flicked on the outside lights. "You're freezing. I'm going to build us a nice fire." He held the back door halfway open but Ladybird didn't budge.

About ten minutes later, a fire blazed in the stone fireplace.

Johnnie and Dale stood in front of the hearth, holding their hands out as if the flames could lick away their fear. Ladybird circled twice and curled up next to them on the rug. She let out a heavy sigh. Just like Brother, she acted as if she carried the weight of the family on her back.

"Do you remember the first time we used the fireplace?" Dale glanced at Johnnie then back at the fire. The flames danced in front of them.

She nodded and wriggled her fingers. "Yeah. I put D.J. in his crib. Then you and I drank margaritas and made love in front of a roaring fire."

Dale sighed. "Johnnie?" Her name hung in the air.

She stared straight into the flames. "Yeah?"

"Whatever happens, we are in this together."

Her voice caught. "I know," she whispered.

They both heard the sound of a truck pull into the driveway. "Don't say anything to Callie Ann," Dale said. "Like I told you, it's just a bad feeling. It'll probably pass."

The side door opened and a cold gust of air blew in. The fire crackled as the air hit the logs, fanning the flames. "So that's what smells so good outside." Callie Ann untied her apron, draped it over the back of a kitchen chair, and called to Ladybird. "Come here, Miss Wigglebutt. Do you like the fireplace going? When my brothers were little, they used to catch bugs and throw them into the fire and watch them sizzle."

The dog snorted and licked Callie Ann's face. Callie Ann rubbed her then flopped down in Dale's leather chair, kicked off her shoes, and stretched her legs out on the ottoman. "By the way, Mom, a male cardinal landed on the windshield of Cade's pickup as I was leaving work."

Johnnie stiffened as Grandpa's words winged through her heart. "That's an angel bird, sent straight down from Heaven." Was the little bird that landed on Cade's pickup a harbinger of hope? Or a death angel? Her throat ached as she choked back her biggest fear that something had happened to Cade. Even as she clung to hope, one thought jabbed at her soul: why should her family be spared the heartache that had shattered so many others over the years?

Callie Ann nudged her in the side with her stocking foot like it was their secret about red birds.

Johnnie reached for her daughter's foot and massaged her arch and sole, kneading her fingers into the thick sock. When Callie Ann was little, she'd come to Johnnie for foot massages after dance practice. Tonight, Johnnie longed for those earlier years when her nightly worries were focused on getting the kids fed and bathed and homework done before bed.

Dale stoked the fire with an iron poker. "You girls warm enough?"

Ladybird wiggled her way in between Johnnie and Dale and gazed up at him as if she understood English.

After Callie Ann changed clothes and left to go see a movie with friends, Johnnie and Dale pulled up the news story online:

Kabul, Afghanistan, Nov. 24, 2009 (Associated Press). United States Army officials confirm that a Black Hawk UH-60 Transport carrying eight U.S. soldiers has gone down in the mountains of Afghanistan. Seven soldiers were killed and one injured. The cause of the incident remains under investigation. Names have not been released pending notification of next of kin.

Chapter 42
Blackout

Ladybird yelped out back the next morning after a car horn honked twice out front. Johnnie held the back door open, and Ladybird pranced inside, nudging her nose against Johnnie's thigh. Halfway across the den, Ladybird halted and glanced back at Johnnie as if to say, "Hurry up. We have company."

"It's only Mama," Johnnie called, her voice groggy from a night of tossing and turning. She tried to sound braver than she felt, but yesterday's news brief and Dale's hunch had kept her awake half the night. Then D.J.'s phone call at dawn had changed everything. . . . She figured that's why Mama was here. To offer support, to sit and wait, to be there if the day turned from vigil to wake.

Glancing sideways, Johnnie spotted the Blue Star Service Banner hanging over the window above the kitchen sink. Had it served to give her false hope? All this time she'd treated it like some kind of good luck talisman — as if a little blue star on white cloth could keep her family intact. But what if it turned out to be nothing more than a beacon leading a notification team straight to her door?

She shuddered and opened the door as Mama mounted the steps. She still had on her nametag from work: Victoria Grubbs, Night Manager, Dooley Mansion Bed & Breakfast. Her lipstick had faded and she looked tired from being up all night.

"I came as soon as I heard." She sounded out of breath by the time she reached the top step. "Lord sakes, baby girl. I feel like our family's been sideswiped by a tank when we were looking the wrong way." She rummaged in her purse for something.

Johnnie's heart squeezed and her stomach twisted. Dizzy, she gripped the door handle with one hand and kept a finger crooked in Ladybird's collar. "Thanks for coming, Mama. Did D.J. call you?"

Mama coughed a couple of times, unwrapped a throat lozenge, and stuck it in her mouth. "No . . . Arty." She gave Johnnie a little pat on the cheek and breezed past without making eye contact.

Johnnie's world began to spin.

No sooner had Mama crossed the threshold than Johnnie's cellphone buzzed. Roosevelt's name flashed on the caller ID. He got right to the point after she answered. "Whit filled me in. I know Dale's at work so I'm sending Jordan over there to help with your honey-do list. Spruce up the yard. Clean the house. Whatever you need done, he'll do it."

Johnnie heard Mama rooting around in the kitchen, slamming cupboard doors, and baby-talking Ladybird. "Where does she keep the tea bags? Ah, here they are."

Turning her attention back to Roosevelt, Johnnie started to protest. "But —"

"No buts about it," Roosevelt broke in. "It's the least we can do. I'm fixin' to get the prayer chain going at church. Anything special you'd like to add?"

Johnnie stood in the middle of the entryway and glared down the hallway toward Cade's bedroom. She would give anything at this moment to march down the hall, rap on Cade's door, and tell him to crank down the volume on his stereo. The lyrics to that country song about a soldier who doesn't make it back blasted in her head, despite the haunting silence that emanated from Cade's room.

"Miss Johnnie, you still there?"

The compassion in Roosevelt's voice washed over her, and she wondered how this strong but gentle man had overcome life's sorrows and indignities. Was it his faith? Without another thought she said, "Would you ask people to pray for all the soldiers over there? Not just my son."

There was a long pause, and then Roosevelt said, "You got it."

As soon as Johnnie hung up, utter terror shot through her veins when her phone rang again. It was Dale. Did he know something she didn't?

"Honey, any news?" Dale's words hung in the air like thick fog.

She ambled into the kitchen to see what Mama was doing. Callie Ann was still asleep. "No, but Roosevelt called. He's sending Jordan over here to clean up the place in case . . . in case . . . you know. . . ." *we have lots of company* she dared not say out loud.

Dale made a funny sound. "You want me to come home? I can try to get Manny to cover for me."

"No. Stay put. Mama's here with me." Her voice broke and her words came out all jagged. "I dread telling Callie Ann, though."

Dale sighed and it seemed to Johnnie that if she'd been standing outside, she could have heard his anguish all the way across town. "Well, if Rivers leaves before I get home, pay him. If he protests, tell him any man who works at my house is going to be paid for his labor."

Dale could talk about paying Jordan but not how Johnnie was going to deliver the blow to their daughter.

As Mama bustled around the kitchen, making tea and toast, Johnnie went to feed Ladybird and pour herself a mug of coffee.

Mama poked her head in the fridge then glanced back at Johnnie. "Have you eaten?"

Johnnie shook her head. "I'm not hungry, Mama." She took a sip of coffee and glanced out the kitchen window. The only vehicle out front for now was Mama's El Camino. Ladybird crunched on her kibble in the laundry room.

"Well, Lord, who is? But we need to eat to keep up our strength." Mama closed the refrigerator and hunted for a pan. "Let me poach us some eggs. They go down easy."

Poached eggs. Johnnie hadn't eaten them since she was a child. Granny Opal made them sometimes when one of them was feeling under the weather. For a second, it almost felt like Granny's spirit had swirled into the room and inhabited Mama's body.

Ladybird trotted into the den and rolled

around on the rug, wiping her mouth and snorting like Brother used to do. "Real lady-like," Callie Ann yawned, shuffling into the room. " 'Morning, Granny V. What are you doing here so early?"

Mama turned from the stove and offered a weary smile. "Making you breakfast, sugar britches."

Johnnie set her mug on the island and addressed her daughter. "Sis, I'm going to tell you straight up. A helicopter went down in Afghanistan yesterday." The words amplified in Johnnie's ears as she watched the news register on Callie Ann's face. "All we know at this point is that it's from your brother's unit."

A whimper came from the center of the room. Was it Callie Ann or Ladybird? Johnnie wasn't sure. Callie Ann stood there, rubbing one bare foot on top of the other like some kind of giant heron.

Johnnie rushed on. "Let's all try to stay hopeful, okay?" Her voice busted up even though she was determined to sound brave.

Callie Ann blinked a couple of times and twirled her finger through her hair. "How's Dad and D.J.?"

Johnnie had to strain to hear her. She picked up a dishtowel and twisted it in her hand. "They're worried, honey. D.J. called your dad around dawn after getting a text from Tutts. He found a second news brief that mentioned Cade's unit was involved. But they aren't releasing names until all the families are notified." Johnnie didn't tell her how Dale had bolted out of bed and headed straight for the computer to read the news before he flung open the back door, hung his head over the side of the deck, and retched. Then he strode down the hall to get ready for work.

Callie Ann shambled to the fridge, untwisted the lid to the orange juice, and drank straight from the carton like Cade used to do. After a couple of glugs, she wiped her mouth with the back of her hand and belched. "Yup, that's for my brother." She put the orange juice back in the fridge and slammed the door.

Mama turned back to the stove, dabbing her eyes with a paper towel.

Callie Ann leaned against the countertop and crossed her arms. "How's Grandpa Arty?"

Johnnie offered her a mug of coffee. "Why don't you call and check on him?" she suggested.

Callie Ann dumped a spoonful of sugar in her coffee and stirred it with the spoon from the sugar bowl. "This is how Cade drinks coffee." She took several loud slurps and grinned, but tears streamed down her face. "I better eat something before I call Grandpa Arty," she sniffled, sounding congested. "Cade says you can't get through life on an empty stomach."

After breakfast, Johnnie curled up on the sofa and dozed off. At some point, she woke with a start, all clammy and drenched in sweat. It took her a moment to get her bearings. She'd been dreaming that she walked into the mortuary after Charlotte the receptionist had phoned and said, "Hurry up and get here. There's not much left." Johnnie had rushed to Farrow & Sons and Tutts had met her at the door. He still had on his tuxedo from the art show. He placed Cade's beating heart in her palms, and said, "Blow onto his heart, Mrs. Kitchen." Johnnie walked through the mortuary hunched over her son's pulsing heart, trying to keep all that was left of him alive. The next thing she knew, she was back home and Cade walked in the door in jeans and flip-flops and said, "Hey, Mama, what's for supper?"

Wiping drool from her mouth, Johnnie forced herself up off the couch and went to look for her daughter. She found Callie Ann rummaging through Cade's closet. "Watcha doing, sis?"

Callie Ann yanked one of her brother's old baseball jerseys off a hanger and pulled it over her head. "I can still smell his armpits," she joked, sniffing under each arm. Her eyes glistened, and Johnnie could tell her daughter was going through the motions to stay strong, to do whatever it took to fend off the feeling of hopelessness.

The sound of country music blared from somewhere outside and Johnnie and Callie Ann swiveled toward the noise.

"It's probably Jordan Rivers."

Callie Ann's eyes narrowed. One second they were dove gray, the next they were the color of steel wool. "Jordan Rivers? What's that kid doing here?"

"Sis," Johnnie reached for her daughter, "Roosevelt sent him here to spruce things up in case —"

"In case what, Mom? Go ahead and say it. We're all thinking it." Callie Ann's words bounced off the walls of Cade's room. She whirled and stormed up the hallway toward the entryway.

Throwing open the door, she huffed out onto the porch and tapped her foot while she waited for Jordan to get out of his truck after he parked behind the El Camino.

Johnnie poked her head out the door. "Sis, that boy has no idea what we're going through. Try not to take it out on him, okay?" After Callie Ann waved her off with a flick of her wrist, Johnnie went to check on Mama. She sat on the steps of the deck, smoking a cigarette and playing fetch with Ladybird. Grabbing a quilt off the sofa, Johnnie headed out to the porch swing.

Jordan sauntered up the walkway in the same tan coveralls and grimy work boots he wore that day at the cemetery. "Hey," he offered, removing his gimme cap, "nice jersey."

Callie Ann crossed her arms and cocked her head. "Thanks. It belongs to my brother Cade. He was a pitcher for the Portion Bandits before he graduated and joined the Army."

"Yeah, I've seen his photo up at school in one of those glass displays where they showcase all the jocks."

"I heard you graduated from Portion High last May. I don't remember seeing you at school."

Jordan tugged his cap snugly on his head and pulled down the bill. "Girls like you don't notice guys like me."

Callie Ann frowned. "What's that supposed to mean?"

He peeked up from under his cap, exposing crooked rabbit teeth. "You're in the popular crowd."

She twisted her fingers through her hair. "Honestly, I don't feel like I am."

He let out a goofy laugh. "Trust me, you are."

"I'm Callie Ann, by the way."

Jordan's tanned face reddened. "I know who you are. I used to see you dance at pep rallies and stuff."

She flipped her hair over her shoulder. "I'm not on the drill team this year. Too busy."

"Oh." He cleared his throat and looked around like he didn't know what to say. "Mr. Roosevelt sent me here to help with whatever needs doing. This is a real nice place y'all got here."

"Thanks. My dad did all the restoration. He's a self-made man. He owns his own construction company. Started it from scratch."

Self-made man. Johnnie sat up straighter in the porch swing, proud of her daughter for recognizing Dale's accomplishments.

Jordan shuffled up the steps. He tipped his cap at Johnnie. "Hey, Mrs. Kitchen, I'm real sorry for your troubles."

The porch swing creaked under her weight as she swayed back and forth. "Thank you, Jordan. I guess you can start with the yard."

She gestured toward the straw-colored lawn littered with leaves. "If you want to mulch in the leaves with the mower, that'd be fine. The edges need trimming and the flower-beds need weeding, even this time of year. Callie Ann, can you show Jordan where the tools are located?"

Callie Ann started to object and Johnnie gave her *the look.* "Sure, Mom." She turned back to Jordan. "Be careful when you're mowing out back. My dog's buried out by the fence. You can't miss his headstone."

Jordan scratched at something in his eye. "Miss Callie Ann, that day you were poking along in that old Lincoln, I was late for work. I never meant for that to happen. I was trying to pass."

Johnnie listened to them banter. She breathed through her nose to keep her mouth shut and her opinions to herself. She needed to concentrate on not crying in front of them.

After Jordan went to grab something out of his truck, Callie Ann muttered out the side of her mouth, "Poor kid suffers from little man syndrome."

Little man syndrome. Now where had Callie Ann learned that? Sounded like something Grandpa Grubbs would say if he'd met the scrawny cowboy. Was it easier when Johnnie thought of Jordan Rivers as *the kid*? Before she knew his name? Before she felt sorry for him because he'd had a hardscrabble life?

Bundled in the quilt, Johnnie waited. She watched Jordan mow and trim the front yard and weed the flowerbeds. Mama brought her mug after mug of steaming tea. Only when her bladder was so full she thought it might burst would Johnnie abandon her post and rush inside to relieve herself. Then she'd take up her position back on the porch. She and the soldier scarecrow — two sad-looking sentinels on guard duty.

Arty called midmorning, but Johnnie could barely talk, especially when her grandfather got all choked up and mentioned that he still hadn't met Cade. D.J. stayed in contact with Dale and Callie Ann. Hearing the worry in her oldest son's voice was almost unbearable for Johnnie. Whit stopped by but didn't stay long. She brought a large pot of split pea soup, a box of saltines, and plastic spoons and bowls. They all gathered around the farmhouse table and ate lunch, including Jordan. Then Johnnie took to the porch, Jordan went back to his chores, and Mama and Callie Ann kept

Ladybird busy with doggie toys and nylon bones.

No one in uniform came to the door. No one called the house phone with good or bad news. Johnnie swayed to and fro on the porch swing, numbing herself by humming old hymns and lullabies. She waited for the sedan or minivan to come up her street, pull up next to the curb, and shatter her family. She waited for uniformed men to dislodge from their vehicle, file up her walkway, and recite from a script they'd memorized for such a somber occasion. If she stayed on the porch and waited for them, they would not take her by surprise. She would surprise them because she already knew. So she waited, ready to tackle the news before it tackled her. She would meet them head on, save them the trouble of having to crush her.

Finally, mid-afternoon, she went inside to use the restroom. After she washed her hands, she stared into the mirror over the basin. "How are we going to live without Cade?" she asked, but the haggard-looking woman in the mirror only blinked. She pushed away from the vanity and dragged herself out of the bathroom and down the hall to the den. The pull of gravity weighed her down, and her body felt like lead as she plodded through the house where she'd raised her three children.

In front of the fireplace, still warm from last night's fire, she stared hard at Cade's senior photo on the mantel, the athletic blond in a tuxedo who was too handsome for his own good. The way he flashed that dimpled grin, like he knew how to use it to his best advantage. "Mama, how can you resist these dimples?" his voice teased in her head, and she choked back a sob at the god-awful image of his dazzling smile melted in a heap of charred wreckage on the side of a mountain.

Her cellphone rang, and she held her breath, squinting at the caller ID. Surely they would not tell her over the phone that her son was dead. They were supposed to come to the front door. All uniformed up on her welcome mat to deliver the blow. She peeked at the number, a local one she didn't recognize. Solicitors seldom called her cell. She swallowed and hit the *talk* button. Her voice thrummed in her ears as she managed to say, "Hello."

The caller did not identify himself, but he didn't have to. Johnnie recognized Sergeant Jackson's deep rich voice. "You did not hear this from me. I'm putting my career on the line. Your son is alive. He's injured but alive.

He was on the chopper that went down in the 'Stan." *Click.*

Johnnie's mouth worked but nothing came out. *Your son is alive* washed through her body like a healing balm. Johnnie inhaled big gulps of air, filling her lungs as if she'd been holding her breath since Cade deployed. All her muscles turned to mush and her cellphone fell to the floor. Dropping to her knees on the braided rug, she collapsed as all the pent-up fear swooshed out of her at once.

Callie Ann, who had both arms wrapped around Ladybird, peeked over the top of the dog's splotchy head. "Mom, is that about Cade?" Her voice trembled.

Johnnie picked herself up off the floor, her lips pinched together. She nodded in Callie Ann's direction. "He's injured . . . but alive."

Callie Ann let out a sigh and started to cry. Ladybird bucked her head a couple of times, her ears pointed straight up. She turned her neck sideways and licked Callie Ann's face.

Johnnie looked around, but Mama was nowhere in sight. "Where's Mama?" Johnnie went to the kitchen window, but the El Camino was gone from the curb. Jordan's pickup remained out front, and a leaf blower whined from the east side of the house.

Callie Ann swiped her eyes with her sleeve and sniffed. "She left right after you dropped your phone. She said she can't take any more bad news."

Johnnie snatched her purse off the computer desk. "You and Ladybird stay here. I'll go look for her. In the meantime, call your Dad and D.J. Tell them your brother was on that chopper but he's not among the dead. That's all I know. And get ahold of Arty and Whit. Have her call Roosevelt."

"Mom, who was that on the phone? Dad and D.J. are going to ask."

"I can't tell you that." Johnnie held onto her purse. On her way out the door, she called over her shoulder, "It's someone I trust."

"Was it Tutts?" Callie Ann called back, and Johnnie choked up at the mention of their friend. She gulped back new tears. Cade was injured, but alive. Dear God in Heaven, what did that mean? The thought of him suffering or burned or half a man caused her stomach to lurch.

She stuck her head back inside. "No, sis. It wasn't Steven. But you or D.J. might give him a call. If Jordan finishes before I get back, give him those two twenties I left on the computer desk. I know we're not supposed to pay him, but this was Dad's idea." She stopped to compose herself. "And you know what a tightwad Dad is."

The El Camino was parked in front of the war memorial in the same spot where Granny's Lincoln sat the day a lonely Jordan Rivers vented his troubled soul on them. Johnnie pulled the Suburban behind it and cut the engine. Grabbing her keys, she tiptoed around the memorial and found Mama on her knees at the base of the soldier. Her head bowed, Mama sobbed into her hands and pleaded, "Please, Francis, let our grandson come home alive. It's not fair to Johnnie girl. We can't do this again."

Mama's deep mournful prayer to her dead lover and not to God or Jesus broke something inside of Johnnie. She fell on her knees next to Mama and started bawling. She barely noticed the jolt to her body when her knees hit the hard surface.

Mama started and whipped her head up, her face drenched in tears. "Oh, baby girl, I'm so sorry."

Johnnie swallowed, unable to talk for a moment. She wrapped her arms around Mama, feeling her whole body spasm with grief. Mama leaned into Johnnie, and Johnnie cradled her against her bosom.

Breathing deeply, Johnnie held the air in her lungs a second and gazed up at the bronze soldier. "Thank you," she whispered, her prayers not to the statue but to the merciful God she'd wanted to believe in since she was a little girl.

She turned back to her mother. "Mama, listen to me. Cade's alive . . . that's all we know for now."

Victoria lifted her head, her eyes brimming with hope. "He was on the helicopter that went down, wasn't he?" It sounded like she had gravel in her throat.

A reddish orange leaf fluttered by in the breeze as a set of wind chimes jangled from a nearby tree. *Whit and Roosevelt must have hung them recently,* Johnnie thought, as the music filled the air. Her throat tightened and it took her a while to respond. "There were eight soldiers on board that flight, Mama. Cade's the sole survivor."

Mama gazed up at the chimes with a faraway look in her eyes. "Listen to them bells," she sighed. "Do you hear them? They're singing seven wings to glory."

Chapter 43
Thanksgiving 2009

When Dale's cellphone rang at three a.m., he bolted out of bed and fumbled for his reading glasses on the nightstand. Johnnie's heart sprinted as she yanked off the covers and scurried around to Dale's side of the bed. As Dale flipped open his phone, she switched on a lamp.

"Some weird-looking number," he mumbled, lifting the phone to his ear. "Hello?"

"Hey, Daddy, it's me." Cade's Texas accent broadcast from the tiny speaker as Johnnie leaned against Dale to listen.

"I'm putting you on speaker so Mom can hear." Dale touched a button on the keypad and motioned for Johnnie to sit down next to him on the bed.

"Hey, Mama. Don't freak out, okay? I'm at an Army hospital in Landstuhl, Germany." His voice sounded thick, like he was doped up on painkillers.

"Germany?" She crinkled the edges of the

top sheet and leaned toward the phone, her voice shrill and foreign. "What are you doing there?"

"I'm snow-skiing in the Alps, Mama. . . ." He let out a crazy laugh. "I got blown up in a chopper. They medevacked me here. It's where they send the wounded before sending us back to the States."

She winced at his explanation. At the words *blown up.*

Dale eyed her over the top of his spectacles and massaged her shoulder with his free hand. "How are you, son?"

"My left leg's busted up pretty bad, and I took some shrapnel to the face. But other than that. . . ." He sounded drained. Not the chipper Cade who always looked on the bright side.

Shrapnel to the face? Johnnie closed her eyes against the image of Tutts' injuries, replaced now by Cade's perfect features punctured and blistered, his dimples lost among the ruins of what had been a beautiful boy. Then something stirred within her. She took a deep breath and boxed back that ancient fear, that fear that threatened to pull her into a vortex she could never climb out of. Then she realized it didn't matter anymore what Cade looked like as long as he was alive. He. Was. Alive.

Dale couldn't hold back any longer. "Son, we've been worried sick about you since Tuesday. To be honest, until you called just now, we weren't sure if you were alive."

Cade sighed, sounding irritated. "Someone from my unit was supposed to call y'all."

Johnnie longed to tell Cade about Sergeant Jackson's phone call, about how the caring recruiter put his whole career at risk to give them some sense of relief. But she stayed mum, because she didn't want to get Sergeant Jackson in trouble. And Dale, being a colonel's kid, told her how Sergeant Jackson could get court-martialed for making that phone call.

"Daddy, can you pick me up from the airport in a few days? They're sending me to Brook Army Medical Center in San Antonio to get my leg looked at. I'll fly commercial to DFW . . . maybe spend one night with y'all. Then I'll need a lift to the airport the next day."

"Sure can, hotshot." Dale masked the concern in his voice.

"I might not get to call again before I leave Germany. Y'all might not hear from me again until I land at DFW."

"Cade," Johnnie hesitated, "we've had a lot of people praying for you."

He didn't say anything for a moment. "My buddies didn't make it, Mama. One second we were flying along, the next . . ." his voice cracked and he stopped talking.

Dale's shoulders sagged. "You think it was mechanical? Or enemy fire?"

Cade blew his nose and sighed. "I have no idea, Daddy. It all happened so fast."

Johnnie picked at a loose thread on the comforter. "Did you have time to be scared?"

"Mama, I thought I died 'cuz I saw angels in the smoke. But then I realized those angels were wearing uniforms. The uniforms of the Air Force's pararescuemen — we call 'em the PJs. And that's when I knew I was still alive."

Dale cleared his throat. "I watched a special about them a while back on the Military Channel. Their motto is 'That Others May Live.' "

A long silence ensued on the other end. Then Cade mumbled, "But I don't understand why I lived —"

"Cade, listen to me." Johnnie kept her voice even. "My friend Roosevelt, he's been asking the same question since he was three years old and his sisters died in a house fire. Maybe you can talk to him when you're ready."

"Maybe one day. I got to go. Tell everybody I said *hey.* I'll see you in a few days."

"Cade?"

"Yes, Mama?"

"Arty is anxious to meet you. He's been burning an electric candle in his front window since he first learned about you."

Cade sniffed. "Tell Papa Murphy I'm coming home."

Johnnie's Journal
November 26, 2009

Dear Granny Opal,

Were you hovering by the pearly gates when those seven soldiers flew into Heaven on Tuesday? My faith has been tested by this whole ordeal. I can't stop thinking about their families and the unfairness of it all.

Please send me a sign that the grave is not the end.

I miss you,
Johnnie

Chapter 44
Home

"Are you going to miss this place?" Arty asked after they poked around her old playhouse and walked the length of the property, ending up a few feet from the bluff that overlooked the cove.

She gestured with her chin. "Looky there. The kids have already hiked down the path and hung the Christmas wreath on the dock for the last time." She sighed, filled with both excitement and a hint of melancholy. "This time next year, some other family will enjoy this view. My guess is some builder or millionaire will buy this place, tear down the house, and build some ridiculous mansion with too many turrets and fireplaces for good taste."

Arty stroked his goatee as he took in the view. "Does that make you sad?" A few sailboats dotted the lake, along with a double-decker party boat someone had rented for the day. Even from here, Johnnie could see hundreds of Christmas lights strung around the craft. An impressive sight during the day, the boat must be even more amazing when lit up at night.

"I used to dread the idea of selling this place, but not anymore. Since Mama came back and told me the whole story of the cove, how Uncle Johnny drowned saving her life, and of course mine in the process," Johnnie breathed in the cold clean air and smiled, "it's time to move on. Plus, we have you now." She looped her arm through his and they strolled to the front of the house.

Arty had gone to get something out of D.J.'s Honda when Johnnie's cellphone rang.

Mama's smoky voice came on the line, scratchy and soft all at the same time. "Are they there yet? I'm hauling buns as fast as I can."

"You mean Roosevelt and Jordan, or Dale and Cade?" Johnnie's gaze drifted to the rental truck backed up at the top of the gravel driveway, the rear doors open and the hydraulic lift lowered in place. Mama was donating her upright Steinway to the Holy Ghost Temple of Love, and Roosevelt and Jordan had come to pick it up.

"Dale and Cade," Mama snapped. "I said goodbye to that dang piano a lifetime ago."

Mama can get so cross at times, Johnnie thought, but she let it slide. "Dale and Cade just left the airport, Mama. What did the doctor say?"

"I'm not dead yet." Mama laughed. "Seriously, the X-rays don't show lung cancer. But that croupy cough of mine . . . the doctor thinks it's due to chronic bronchitis from years of smokin'. He told me to quit or else —"

"Or else what?"

"Emphysema, baby girl! Look, I'll be there as soon as I can. The last thing I need is a speeding ticket on top of my expired inspection sticker."

"Was that Victoria?" Arty propped *The Candy Man* painting against one of Granny Opal's large geranium pots and sat down next to Johnnie in the metal glider. "D.J. and I know Cade can't take his painting with him to San Antonio, but we wanted him to see it."

Johnnie stashed her phone in a pocket of her long cardigan. "Cade's going to love it. And yes, that was Mama. She's about halfway between here and Dallas."

"What did the doctor say?" Arty hiked up his pant legs and pushed off with one foot as the glider slid forward and back.

Johnnie shared the doctor's report.

"She should get one of those nicotine patches. It worked for Mae."

"I didn't know Mae smoked . . . I mean, before she got sick." Of course Johnnie didn't know Mae smoked. How could she? She'd only learned of Mae's existence three months ago. But still, a part of her felt as if she should know. Like all this knowledge she'd been denied was somehow wrapped up in her DNA, hidden in the rungs of the double helix, and her job was to untangle it and make sense of her family's history on her father's side.

Arty gazed out over the yard of Johnnie's childhood home. "Mae took up smoking after Francis died . . . the bottle, too. When I got offered a teaching job in Denton, I thought the move would give us a new start in life. Mae gave up cigarettes and booze for pottery classes and started selling her wares in some fancy gift shops around the square. Then one day I came home from mall walking and found her sitting in the middle of her studio with shards of pottery everywhere. That was the beginning of her illness. Or at least when I recognized something was wrong."

Johnnie glanced sideways at her grandfather. "I'm sorry you had to go through all that alone."

Her grandfather shrugged. "I got through it. I had to be strong for Mae. I didn't have a choice."

"You sound like Granny Opal. She told me the same thing one time when we were visiting my Uncle Johnny's grave. I asked her how she was able to go on after her only son drowned. She told me, 'I didn't have a choice. You either go on, or you die, too.' "

Arty brushed at something on his slacks. "Your granny must've been a heck of a woman. I'm sorry I never got to meet her."

At this instant, Johnnie felt an urge to fill in the blanks of their lives for Grandpa Arty, who'd been denied knowing them — not out of spite, but out of sorrow.

"Granny ran a cake baking business out of this house before the name *cottage industry* was cool. Grandpa Grubbs was an engineer at General Dynamics. He designed airplanes for the military," Johnnie rushed on, filled with a newfound pride for the grandparents who raised her.

"An engineer . . . I would've loved to pick his brain. By the looks of this place," Arthur Murphy paused and swept his hand through the air, "your grandfather was a good provider."

Arty's words floated through the air like an unexpected gift, and Johnnie reached over and gripped his hand. "Grandpa was a good man, Arty. But so are you."

Arty looked away for a moment and then stopped the glider. "Did Victoria say how much the bill was? I tried to send her some money but she wouldn't take it."

"Mama's got her pride, Arty, you should know that by now. I think the doctor cut her a deal. Guess he sees lots of patients without insurance."

Arty glanced at his watch. "Dale and Cade should be here any minute. So glad D.J. picked me up and brought me here. I wouldn't miss this day for the world."

Johnnie twisted around, hearing a cacophony of male voices huffing and puffing inside the house.

"Callie Ann, get out of the way or you're going to get run over," D.J. groused. "If you really want to help, stand over there and look pretty."

"You sound just like Dad." Callie Ann's shrill voice carried all the way out the front door. A second later she scrambled down the makeshift ramp, all legs and long hair, bringing with her the confectionary aroma of sugar, vanilla, and almond extract. The scent of *Opal's Cakery* still lingered from every room of Granny's house, even filtering out the front door. *Could such delicious smells last that long?* Johnnie wondered. Maybe she was only imagining it. Callie Ann loitered around the back of the rental truck.

Slowly, one end of the behemoth piano emerged through the front door, with D.J. and Tutts guiding it along at their end. D.J. had already removed the storm door and set it aside. Roosevelt and Jordan brought up the rear as the rest of the piano slid through the doorway on the large dolly.

"Slow it down, boys, or we're gonna have us a runaway piano," Roosevelt grunted from his end.

Arty went to push himself up from the glider. Johnnie lent him her arm, and the two of them stood on the porch as Mama's piano grumbled and groaned down the plywood plank. "My Aunt Beryl called it a buffalo one time when she and I were playing cowboys and Indians," Johnnie chuckled, nudging Arty. "She was Grandpa's spinster sister. Prickly as a cactus but with a heart of gold."

"You had an aunt who played cowboys and Indians with you?" Arty shook his head in astonishment. "Prickly or not, what a treasure."

While the guys rolled the piano onto the lift, Callie Ann hollered, "Hang on a second.

You forgot something." She charged up the ramp past Johnnie and Arty and disappeared into the house. A few seconds later, she dashed outside, carting an elegant wooden bench in both arms.

Mama's piano bench!

Tutts grinned broadly when Callie Ann offered him the bench. "Thanks, gorgeous. How 'bout a little sendoff music for this sweet old instrument going to a good home?"

As Roosevelt pressed the switch to the lift, Tutts made a sweeping gesture with his right hand like he had on coattails. Moving the imaginary tails out of the way, he sat down on the bench. Placing his long elegant fingers on the black and white keys, he began to pluck out a few notes here and there.

By now, Johnnie and Arty had joined the others gathered around the back of the rental truck. D.J. had one arm slung over Arty and the other around Callie Ann. Jordan stood off to the side, and Johnnie motioned for him to join her.

"Everyone know the words to 'Swing Low, Sweet Chariot'?" Tutts asked, glancing over his shoulder. "Sing it with me, brothers and sisters."

As the piano rose in the air, Tutts pounded

out the old Negro spiritual. The piano was out of tune, but it didn't matter. He was the showman once again.

Everyone lifted their voices and sang along:

Swing low, sweet chariot
Coming for to carry me home,
Swing low, sweet chariot,
Coming for to carry me home.

I looked over Jordan, and what did I see
Coming for to carry me home?
A band of angels coming after me,
Coming for to carry me home.

After they belted out the final verse, the blare of a horn pierced the cold air.

Johnnie's heart sprinted ahead of her. She stood frozen in place as Dale's pickup turned off Lakeside Drive and came up the long narrow driveway, kicking up gravel and dust in its wake. Dale laid on the horn a couple of times. The pickup veered off the driveway into the hay-colored grass and weeds. Before the engine cut off, the passenger door swung open and a camouflage leg appeared, attached to a combat boot that stamped the ground as if the person needed to get a good footing. Then the second boot appeared.

Arty patted her hand. "Thank God he came home alive. . . ." There was a catch in his voice as he pulled out his hanky and dabbed his eyes. "And not in a box like Francis," he added quietly, as if remembering the day he and Mae walked behind a lonely caisson in Arlington.

A cry erupted from somewhere inside of Johnnie, a cry of thanksgiving as on the day Cade was born with all ten fingers and toes, a perfect mouth and nose, two eyes and two ears. She caught her breath as both hands flew to her mouth. Forgetting everything around her, she ran on wobbly legs toward him. All she wanted to do was throw her arms around him, hug him, kiss him, and never let him go.

Cade hobbled toward her on crutches, his face bruised and swollen. "Mama, Mama!" he cried, gripping the crutch handles that propelled him forward.

She tried not to stare at the brace that encased his left leg or the lacerations on his face.

With tears blurring her vision, she threw her arms around his thick neck, breathing in his warm, familiar scent of sports deodorant and the earth itself — of grassy woods and water and sky. Rocking him gently as they embraced, she waved Arty over. "Come meet your great-grandson," she wept, forcing herself to release him and make room for Arty.

Stuffing his hanky into his back pocket, Arty held out both arms. "Cade, my boy, welcome home, son."

"Papa Murphy," Cade bellowed, leaning forward on his crutches. "You look just like my bro, only with a goatee." He reached up and stroked the white tuft of hair on his great-grandfather's chin.

Arty's dark eyes glittered. "Yeah, with about a hundred miles of wagon ruts on my face." He clapped Cade on the back. "My son would be so proud of you."

Cade buried his face in Arty's shoulder. "We've got a lot of catching up to do, Papa Murphy." After a few seconds, both men stepped back and held each other at arm's length. Johnnie observed the invisible current that passed between them, a current that bonded all the lost years and unknowns into one knowing present. As if Arthur Murphy had always known Cade Kitchen and Cade had always known his paternal great-grandfather.

With the piano loaded into the back of the truck, the others formed a circle around Cade. D.J. thrust a frosty longneck toward him and smirked, "You're probably doped up and can't drink this now, but you earned it."

Cade took the beer and studied the label. "Shiner Bock. Now I know I'm back in Texas."

Callie Ann slid her arms around Cade and wouldn't let go. "You look like you've been in a bar fight."

He half-grinned, his lips cracked and red. "I'm lucky I didn't lose any teeth."

Tutts pumped his hand and gave him a man hug. "Welcome home, brother."

"It's good to be back," Cade said, flexing his lower jaw. The friends held each other at arm's length, as if they were both remembering a time before war.

Then Roosevelt stuck out his hand. "Hello, Private. Welcome to the Purple Heart club." He glanced over at Tutts then back at Cade. "All three of us are bound by battle scars and bloodshed. Different wars. Same Army."

Tears welled up in Cade's eyes. He flicked them away like pesky gnats. "Yes, sir, roger that. I hear you and I got a lot to talk about."

Roosevelt gripped him by the shoulder. "I'm here whenever you're ready. No need to rush it."

Squaring his shoulders, Cade turned to

Jordan. He towered over the wiry recruit by several inches. "And you must be the FNG."

Jordan flinched, taken aback. "The what?"

"The *friggin' new guy,*" Cade said with a wry grin.

Johnnie cringed at the military jargon. At least Cade hadn't called him a peckerhead.

Jordan bowed his head and scratched the tip of his nose. "Yeah, guess so."

"I'm just razzing ya." Cade poked Jordan's boot with the tip of his crutch. "When you head to basic?"

Jordan let out a nervous laugh and hemmed and hawed for a second. "Sergeant Jackson and Mr. Roosevelt are dropping me off tonight at the Crown Plaza in Dallas. This time tomorrow, I take my oath, then get on a bus and head to Fort Leonard Wood."

Cade sized him up. "Those drill sergeants are gonna eat you for lunch. Don't take it personal."

Roosevelt tapped his watch and signaled Jordan that it was time to leave. "We got places to be, son."

Before he turned to go, Roosevelt gave Johnnie a quick hug. "Tell Miss Victoria we appreciate the donation. The church secretary will be in touch with a receipt if your mama wants to write it off on her taxes."

"Will do, and thanks for helping out the kid," Johnnie whispered in his ear. "You and Whit stop by the house sometime for a glass of wine."

Roosevelt winked. "I'm gonna hold you to that, Miss Johnnie."

Then the seasoned black veteran and the young white recruit said their farewells and walked back and climbed in the cab of the rental truck.

After Roosevelt fired up the engine, D.J. threw his arms around Cade and Tutts and the two brothers and their friend yelled in unison, "Keep your head down!" Jordan saluted with a big, goofy grin. The rental truck rumbled down the gravel driveway with the piano strapped inside.

Cade looked around. "Where's that new bird dog y'all got?"

Callie Ann inspected Cade's leg brace. "She's home in her crate. How bad is the break?"

Cade glanced down at his leg. "I'm hoping they don't have to amputate."

Johnnie winced and felt Dale's strong arm enfold her. Was Cade joking or serious? Sometimes she never knew with him. Gazing at his swollen face all cut up and bruised, she reminded herself that he was alive. Home more or less in one piece. D.J.

lit up a cigarette and went to lock the front door while Arty retrieved *The Candy Man* painting from the porch.

As they prepared to leave, Johnnie spotted a shadow dashing from tree to tree beside the driveway where Cade leaned on his crutches — the shadow of a big brown dog, leaping for joy. No one seemed to notice but Johnnie. Gaping at the dog, she heard Granny's voice twitter in her head, "You asked for a sign." When Johnnie blinked, Brother Dog was gone.

Then D.J. thundered from the porch, "Oh, groovy. Here comes Granny Go-Go tearing up the driveway in her El Camino."

Johnnie whirled. Even from this distance, she could see Mama through the windshield and the happiness that radiated from her ruby red smile.

Dear Friends and Family,

You are cordially invited to Johnnie Kitchen's graduation from Portion Community College on May 28, 2010. Commencement ceremonies will be held at the Portion Convention Center located at 807 Main Street, south of historic downtown Portion. Reception to follow at The Dooley Mansion, 364 North Dooley Street, Portion, Texas, hosted by Johnnie's mother, Ms. Victoria Grubbs.

In lieu of gifts, please make a donation to your local food bank or veterans organization.

In keeping with family tradition, and in memory of Johnnie's grandmother, the late Opal Grubbs, cake and spirits will be served.

ABOUT THE AUTHOR

Kathleen M. Rodgers' stories and essays have appeared in *Family Circle Magazine, Military Times,* and in anthologies published by McGraw-Hill, University of Nebraska Press/Potomac Books, Health Communications, Inc., AMG Publishers, and Press 53. In 2014, Rodgers was named a Distinguished Alumna from Tarrant County College/NE Campus. Three of her aviation poems from the book *Because I Fly* (McGraw-Hill) were featured in an exhibit at the Cradle of Aviation Museum on Long Island, NY. In 2017, the Clovis Municipal School Foundation in Clovis, NM awarded her the Purple Pride Hall of Honor Award under the "Sports and Entertainment" category.

Seven Wings to Glory is Rodgers' third novel and deals with racism and war. Her second novel, *Johnnie Come Lately,* has garnered four awards: First Place Winner for women's fiction from Texas Association of Authors 2016 Best Book Awards, 2015 Gold Medal for literary fiction from Military Writers Society of America, Bronze Medal for women's fiction from Readers' Favorite 2015 International Book Awards and 2015 Best Cover Awards from Southern Writers Magazine. The novel has been featured in *Family Magazine, Stars & Stripes, Fort Worth Star-Telegram, Southern Writers Magazine,* and on *The Author's Corner* on Public Radio. The audio edition is narrated by Grammy® Award-winning vocalist and Broadway actress Leslie Ellis.

Rodgers is also the author of the award-winning novel, *The Final Salute,* featured in *USA Today,* The Associated Press, and *Military Times.*

She and her husband, Tom, a retired USAF fighter pilot/commercial airline pilot, reside in a suburb of North Texas with their two rescue dogs, Denton and Jav. The mother of two grown sons, Thomas and J.P., she is currently working on her fourth novel.

Her future work is represented by agent Diane Nine of Nine Speakers Inc.

You can find Rodgers online at: www.kathleenmrodgers.com.

The employees of Thorndike Press hope you have enjoyed this Large Print book. All our Thorndike, Wheeler, and Kennebec Large Print titles are designed for easy reading, and all our books are made to last. Other Thorndike Press Large Print books are available at your library, through selected bookstores, or directly from us.

For information about titles, please call:
(800) 223-1244

or visit our website at:
gale.com/thorndike

To share your comments, please write:
Publisher
Thorndike Press
10 Water St., Suite 310
Waterville, ME 04901

turned off the highway and headed north on Main. Flags lined both sides of the street in preparation for Veterans Day on Wednesday.

Thunder rumbled in the distance — or was that another airplane taking off right over her head? A bolt of lightning zigzagged off to her left. Johnnie was glad she was almost home before the storm hit. Before crossing the railroad tracks by the Cottonbelt Café, she looked both ways, although the signals weren't flashing. "Don't trust those automatic arms," Grandpa Grubbs used to warn every time they approached a railroad crossing. "Always look both ways, young lady. A train could barrel down on you and you wouldn't even know it." With the coast clear, Johnnie pressed on the gas and the Suburban thumpity-thumped over the rails.

The first raindrops splattered the windshield as the radio announcer said, "Twelve soldiers and one civilian died in last week's attack when Major Hasan, an Army psychiatrist, opened fire. . . ."

"Dirt bag," Johnnie said, using Cade's Army slang as she flipped off the radio and switched on the wipers. She welcomed the sound of rain over the news reports that the shooter had yelled "God is Great" in Arabic before he mowed down unarmed men and women in uniform.

Passing by Whit's Whimsies, she spotted a late-model yellow Corvette with a Purple Heart license plate parked in front of the shop. Her mood lifted instantly, and she laughed and honked the horn twice as she rolled by. She thought she spotted Roosevelt on a stepladder in front of one of the bay windows. He had a speaking engagement on Wednesday at the Portion Rotary Club. Whit had called Johnnie last night to brag about her new beau. "With their motto of 'service above self,' Roosevelt will be perfect, especially since his speaking gig falls on Veterans Day." Then Whit giggled and said, "Girl, you know he's enjoying being a new celebrity."

"And you're his classy arm candy," Johnnie teased, smiling at the sound of Whit's laughter on the other end. Johnnie hadn't heard Whit this happy since she'd opened the shop last spring.

Johnnie cracked the window to inhale the clean scent of rain, but the water came through the slit and dampened her sleeve and shoulder. Chilled, she hit the power button to roll the window up and spotted a young man and a little boy huddled under an umbrella in front of the war memorial.